Queen of His Heart

A Crown & Heart Novel

Book 2

By

Nikki Davenport

Content Notes:

References to cancer and childhood trauma

Profanity

Explicit sexual content

Mentions and threats of sexual assault

Substance abuse

Kidnapping, physical violence, and injury (non-gory but intense)

Library of Congress Control Number: 2024921439

ISBNs

eBook: 979-8-9890545-5-8

Print: 979-8-9890545-2-7

Cover design by GetCovers.

Published by Granite Clover Publishing, LLC

www.nikkidavenport.com

First Edition: July 2024

For F—
Always.
With love.
With thanks.

Bonus Epilogue

Want more Riddick and Khara?

Unlock an exclusive bonus epilogue when you join my newsletter.

Queen of His Heart Bonus Epilogue

Chapter One

"**J**UST TELL HIM THE truth."

Khara Therin delivered the stern missive to her reflection in the ladies' room vanity mirror. She'd put off telling Riddick her true identity for such a long time that it felt ridiculous and unsavory at this point. Before anything else, she would march up to where he awaited her and spill her secret. Nothing would stop her. Not how his tuxedo hung just right on his body, not how he'd teased her with dirty talk on the way here, nothing. She wouldn't give him a chance to distract her with that sonorous voice or eyes so soulful and deep she could just fall into them.

"I am the Queen of Lytua," she whispered to her reflection, digging deep for resolve. Speaking it aloud felt strange, as she rarely had to introduce herself in this manner. Most people she met, even for the first time, already knew she was the Queen of the small island nation and addressed her by her formal ceremonial name, Queen Lillianna. *Khara* was the name for family and close friends. And sexy, unwitting architects who believed she was the Queen's assistant. Both the man and the deception tied her up in knots. She'd jumped at the opportunity to remain anonymous when Riddick mistook her for the Queen's assistant several weeks ago.

Joshua Riddick. Her maybe sorta new boyfriend? If he didn't run for the hills when he learned who she was.

He'd asked her to be exclusive just a few minutes ago. She was equal parts giddy and terrified.

What should have been a carefree fling with the hot American architect had morphed into... *what*, exactly? Would he still want to be exclusive? Maybe he'd say no big deal and they could finish what they'd started on his sofa the previous night. Her heart slammed against her ribcage remembering the feel of those big hands on her. That mouth. A sigh escaped her.

Despite the late hour, the CharityWorks ball would continue for a while longer. The need for him was so great.

She had never experienced such intense sexual frustration, and it was her own fault she was wound so tight. She indulged in imagining him unfazed by the admission of her true identity, then ripping this couture gown right off of her body and making love to her all night.

Or, leaving it on, as he'd drawled in the car, and tossing her across the console table in the hotel suite's entryway.

I want to watch you come undone for me, Khara.

The flutter in the pit of her stomach intensified. She gripped the counter's edge, recalling the ferocity in his eyes as he told her all those marvelous, naughty things.

Nope. Not backing out again. Let's get this sorted.

Khara reapplied her lip stain and was wrapping up her pep talk when the door swung open wide. It was the janitor who'd directed them to this restroom, as he was servicing the first restroom they'd tried. She gave the fresh-faced young man a bright smile. "Finishing up here. It's all y—"

"Sorry about this," the young man muttered, cutting her off.

Khara opened her mouth to question why when she saw the gun he had aimed at her. She put her hands up reflexively, flinching when he snatched her triple-strand pearl necklace off with one forceful tug. The broken clasp scratched her neck, leaving a stripe of pain behind. In a flash, he was holding her arm and unfastening her bracelet watch. She stood stunned as he stripped her of all her jewelry. Khara didn't resist. This seemed to be a simple robbery that would conclude soon enough.

He stuffed her jewelry into a zip-up bag around his waist. Then he gestured toward the door with the gun. Khara frowned. Not a simple robbery, after all? *Oh, dear.*

The Elite Guard trained her well for this type of situation. She would not be foolish. Khara remained calm, trying to memorize details. When she hesitated, the man took hold of her upper arm with a forceful grip and squeezed hard. Khara gasped at the pain. He cracked the door, peered up and down the hallway, and pulled her through. Khara's heart plummeted seeing Riddick crumpled on the hallway's carpeted floor. She drove a hard elbow strike into her assailant's ribs and pulled away when he let out a grunt and his hold slackened.

Khara dropped to her knees beside Riddick, who was unconscious and bleeding from a head wound. Hot anger burst inside her as she called his name. He didn't stir. "What have you done to him?" she demanded as she checked his breathing and pulse. She laid a gentle hand on his cheek. The handsome face she'd come to know so well and dreamed about was lifeless.

"Get up," the man said with a sneer. Gone was the amiable, helpful janitor. In his place was a calculating thug with malice in his eyes.

Khara shook her head, tugging Riddick's pocket square free. She pressed it to the oozing cut near his temple, applying pressure. "He needs medical attention." He didn't seem to be hurt otherwise that she could see.

The not-janitor cast frantic looks around the deserted hallway. This restroom was far away from the festivities in the ballroom, which must have been part of the plan. "Not happening. Time to go. Get up."

"I demand—"

Before she could think of anything to stall him, he grabbed her arm and yanked, forcing her to her feet. He reared his arm back and struck her in the face with the gun. Pain exploded in her cheek and Khara couldn't stop the cry that escaped her. The force of the blow knocked her into the wall. Further protests died away when he waved the gun at Riddick's form. Khara put her hands up again. Fearing the man would hurt Riddick again, Khara remained silent.

The man tugged her upright and gave her a violent shake, hissing warnings she'd better cooperate. He dragged her out of the elegant downtown hotel's side door and down a short flight of stairs. Khara struggled to stay upright, worried she was going to twist an ankle in her heels. Frigid late-November air stabbed at the exposed skin of her arms and back like needles. Her beautiful rust-colored gown offered little protection from the bite in the evening's wind.

A nondescript car sat idling at the curb. The man squashed her into the backseat, wedged himself in beside her, and slammed the door. The driver swiveled in his seat and barked, "Hands!"

When Khara raised her hands again, the driver yanked them together and tied them with some sort of cord. Khara curled her fingers into tight fists and pushed her wrists outward as he did, as she had been taught. Clenching the muscles and providing resistance gave her a bit of room to maneuver in her bindings she wouldn't have otherwise. They didn't tie her feet.

The driver pulled out a cell phone and aimed it at her. "Say cheese, honey." The flash was bright, blinding her for a moment.

Ransom, then. They must know who she was. The man next to her threw something over her head to obscure her vision. It might have been a pillowcase. Rough hands pushed her into a position half-lying across the back seat, presumably to prevent other drivers from growing suspicious. The material rubbed against her skin.

Khara heard rustling as the driver shifted in his seat. The car started moving. Not too fast or wild to draw attention.

"You sent it, right?" the not-janitor asked from above her. He sounded giddy.

"Yeah. I know what the plan is, asshole. You do your part and I'll do mine."

The driver's gravelly, smoker-like voice sent shivers through Khara.

She willed her thundering heartbeat to slow so she could concentrate. The side of her face was one big throbbing ache.

Whatever these two had in store for her, it would be a long night.

Chapter Two

T HIRTEEN HOURS.

His woman had been missing for thirteen hours and Joshua Riddick was ready to smash someone's face in.

The first lead they'd had since Khara went missing—the activation of the GPS trackers in her jewelry—showed her current location over 3,000 miles from DC in Nicaragua.

Every muscle in his body felt tight. Learning that the woman he'd spent so much time with these past weeks was not the Queen's assistant, but the Queen herself already blew his mind. Once she returned to him safe—and she had damn well better be safe or someone was going to *pay*—he'd look closer at all of that.

One of the Queen's—*Khara's*—Elite Guard hung up a telephone and announced, "The jet will be standing by."

Cenn, another Elite Guard, this one a tall woman with the close-cropped hair and collection of throwing knives, called the next step. She was the team's second in command. "We're wheels up in one hour. You have ten to jock up."

Everyone crowded the temporary security command center, housed in a Ritz-Carlton Hotel conference room.

The three men and women Elite Guards of Khara's personal security team conferred with the regular Lytuan Guard, who acted as support personnel. Joanne, Khara's real assistant, stood off to the side. Worry pinched the older woman's features as she glanced between the groups of FBI agents who had just arrived, and officers from the Metropolitan Police Department SWAT team.

"What connection does *Avlah* have with Nicaragua?" Cenn stared at the on-screen map.

"None that we know of." A Guard whose name Riddick thought was Wyn was shaking his head.

Riddick wracked his brain to remember what *Avlah* meant. He'd been told it was an honorific. Was it respected Queen? Maybe adored Queen? No, *exalted* Queen.

Queen, for Pete's sake.

Queen.

Good Lord, this was for real.

Just when he'd gotten his head around dating a Queen's assistant. Now this plot twist.

Cenn wasn't having it. "Why would kidnappers take her there if there's no connection? Where's the strategy in that? Has she ever even been to Nicaragua?"

Everyone turned their attention to Joanne. The petite older woman shrugged. "Not that I know of. Maybe before her election."

Then there was that, Riddick thought. An elected monarch. An entire country elected the woman he knew as Khara Therin to be their Queen and not a mere figurehead, but a true, ruling monarch. God, Riddick's head hurt. He had so many questions. The anger and worry roiling inside him didn't have an outlet right now.

"Who do we know in Central America—anyone?" Jaden Everly's deep voice was hard. The captain of the Queen's Elites was an imposing man, close to Riddick's own height of six-three. "Do we have any contacts there?"

"I do," Riddick said.

The entire room faced him. He could feel the weight of their incredulous stares. "From my Army days. I did joint operations with the military down there. I still have contacts."

"Can they help us?"

"Maybe."

Riddick retreated to the conference room's far side, pulling out his cell phone. He activated the scrambler before dialing a number from memory. He'd never write the number down anywhere. A fellow Ranger before being medically retired after a mission gone wrong, his friend had made himself indispensable to the US government with his hacking abilities. Riddick doubted he was still based in coastal Nicaragua, but he'd know anyone worth knowing in that region.

A gruff voice answered in Spanish. "*Thought you were out of the rescue game, amigo.*"

"*Special circumstances, Dade. Can you help?*"

"*You don't even have to ask, brother. What do you need?*"

"*My woman was taken. She's been missing for almost thirteen hours and her GPS tracker shows she's in Nicaragua. In a building we can't seem to find any information on.*"

The briefest of pauses hung on the line before the other man came back with, "*That's a lot to unpack, but later. What do you know so far?*"

"*Not a lot. She was taken by two assailants last night from a hotel restroom here in DC.*" Riddick gave him the short version and forced himself to stay calm as he retold what the surveillance footage revealed. Him getting tazed and knocked unconscious. A man in the uniform of a hotel janitor manhandling Khara. His stomach tightened as he remembered her concern for him as the kidnapper dragged her away from where he'd fallen in the hallway.

That asshole hitting her in the face.

The sound of keys clacking in the background filled a brief silence. "*What's your woman's name? She must be something to have you boo'd up.*"

Riddick forced himself to swallow around the lump in his throat as they continued to converse in Spanish. "*She is. Her name is Khara.*"

"*Forgive my crassness, but is Khara—pretty name, by the way—considered a high-value target to anyone? That does change things.*"

A glance at Jaden revealed he was observing with an impassive coolness. *"She's a Queen, Dade."*

"And that's a euphemism for...?"

"Not a euphemism. She's the actual Queen of a small island nation in the Caribbean named Lytua."

"Huh. Well, shit, man. Go big or go home?"

"Sort of a long story. I just found out myself. They evaded her security team, took her jewelry with the GPS trackers in it. She activated one a little while ago and it's showing her location as outside Matalejo, Nicaragua, and we're at a brick wall."

Dade whistled. *"I assume you're connected with local PD and federal law enforcement and her security team?"*

"Yeah, we're back at the hotel where she was based."

Dade's voice routed through the wireless to the room's sound system. *"Put me on with whoever's in charge."*

"This is Jaden Everly, Mr. Dade. I am the captain of the Queen's Elite Guard. My entire team is here."

Riddick nodded. Dade had made the request in Spanish. The Guard staff spoke English and their home language of Lytuan. Keys clicked in the background again. Riddick figured he was being overheard, even in another language. Odds were that at least one of the Queen's Elite Guards spoke Spanish. Khara had mentioned everyone being multi-lingual. She failed to mention that they were guarding *her*, but that was a thought for another time. After she was back.

"I'm Dade Holloway, Mr. Everly. Normally I'd want to vet you and all kinds of other shit, but if Riddick vouches for you, then we're good. I'm sure you'll be vetting me behind the scenes."

"Of course."

"Who's running the tech? One of your team?"

"I am," the lead tech spoke up. If Riddick remembered right, her name was Melanie. He'd met so many of the people tasked with keeping Khara safe in the last few hours they were blurring together.

"Jesus, how old are you? You look like you should be in a high school coding class."

"I'm thirty, jackass. Wait. What do you mean, 'look'?"

Dade's face appeared on the wall-mounted television Melanie was using as a monitor, having hacked into the conference room system. His face was as gaunt as Riddick remembered, and the same haunted eyes looked through the room. He'd lost more weight, too.

Melanie's eyes narrowed, the infiltration of her domain galling her. "This is a secure room. How did you—?"

"No time, darlin'. I'm the very best, that's all you need to know. I just sent a sharing invitation to your laptop. A courtesy, really, as I'm already through most of your security. It'll just go faster if you allow it. I'm assuming you're Melanie Goodnight, who goes by the hacker name DragonFlip. I'm familiar with some of your work. Melanie, we're going to work together on this. I hope you're up for it."

"My tech is top tier," Jaden bit out.

Ruffled some feathers there, Riddick thought.

Dade shrugged. "If you say so."

Bristling, Melanie cleared her throat. "I've accessed satellite data and encrypted communication in and out of Managua's airport."

"Good. Any flight coming from the US would be subject to extra scrutiny. What else?"

"We're getting connected with the Nicaraguan defense force now."

"We're having our jet fueled right now to get down there." Jaden gave the high sign. He raised an eyebrow at Riddick, who nodded. Hell yes, he was coming. No matter where it was.

"Uh, hold off on that. Let's see what we can uncover first. Hang on. Okay, traffic cams don't show us much beyond a two-block radius."

"How did you—? I don't even have access to that." Melanie looked impressed and irritated.

"When this is done, come meet me and I'll show you."

"Dade."

"Right. Who's Lillianna? The official Lytuan website has—"

"It's Khara's ceremonial name," Riddick said and thought again of how easily he'd fallen for her story that she, the Queen's assistant, and the Queen had gotten mixed up in the press. It was utter ridiculousness now. But then, he'd had no reason not to believe her.

"Ah, that regnal name thing, got it," Dade continued. "Whoa, you elect your monarch? That's kinda cool. Well, anyway, there's nothing official from the US into Managua today or within the last 24 hours. That's what you came to, Mel? Can I call you Mel?"

"Absolutely not."

Despite the seriousness of the situation, Riddick stifled a laugh at the affront threading her tone.

"Where exactly is the GPS pinging?"

"Sending the coordinates now. Looks like some sort of factory in the middle of nowhere right outside Matalejo."

"Send me the exact frequency."

She did, and they all watched Dade's lips move as he read them to himself.

"Hang on. Let me dig around a bit and get back to you. Don't go anywhere yet."

Riddick's heart pounded. "Dade." He had to swallow hard before he could speak the rest. *"Ella... es todo, hermano."*

"Understood, brother. I'll be back in touch." The connection dropped.

Cenn harrumphed. "Who and what was that?"

A lot of that mission and others like it remained classified. "What I can tell you is we broke up a huge human trafficking ring based there. Dade got injured, fell in love, and stayed. His wife died a few years back."

Anger flashed in Jaden's eyes. "We'll have a conversation later about how you just compromised the security of our entire operation. They must have taken her there on a private plane. Were drug smugglers involved somehow?"

Riddick's mind was everywhere at once. Had they drugged Khara? Hurt her? Incapacitated her some other way? A familiar tone rang. He pushed the answer button before registering who the sound belonged to.

"Are you on your way?" Dion Wilcox, the teen he'd been mentoring for the last two years, sounded worried.

Riddick closed his eyes. The goddamned football game. *Fuck.* "I'm sorry, Dion. I had an emergency and completely forgot. We'll have to reschedule."

"But... you never forget."

"I promise I'll get back to you soon and explain."

"It's that lady, isn't it? You dumping me to do something with *Khara*?"

Heat suffused Riddick's face. He'd never let Dion down. *Never.* The kid sounded so bewildered. "It's not like that, I swear. I'll explain everything later." The call waiting tone sounded. Riddick pulled the phone away from his ear and saw Dade was calling back. His heart lurched. "I'm sorry, I've got to go. Answers later, I promise. Soon."

He clicked over and felt the Elites looking at him with curiosity. He avoided their eyes. "Go, Dade. Talk to me."

"Well, *hermano*, I have good news and bad news."

Chapter Three

Trina Krove stifled a screech at the picture the kidnappers texted as proof they'd snatched the Queen. She was so livid she almost forgot to use the voice-altering app when she called. The phone rang only once before the goons picked up. She lit right in. "What the hell happened to her face?"

"We roughed her up a little to show her who's boss."

"You jackasses weren't supposed to hurt her!"

"It felt in character. No big deal, Boss."

Trina closed her eyes, massaging her throbbing temple. He had the nerve to sound smug. "The public won't take kindly to someone hitting her. We're trying to discredit her, not drum up more support."

There was a pause. "So, we shouldn't hit her anymore."

"No!"

"Well, you're no fun, but we got her, and you don't. Maybe we'll just do whatever we want."

Idiots. Trina forced tranquility into her voice and enunciated her words, as though speaking to a child. "I don't want her hurt. I want her humiliated. Stick with the fucking plan. And don't forget to ask her about the military!"

By the time she hung up, Trina's jaw hurt from clenching it. Good thing this chapter was coming to a close. Her nerves couldn't take much more.

She'd secluded herself in her home office, the only place secure enough for her extracurricular activities. Trina set it all up, employing the hacker skills he'd kept up since being promoted off the cybercrimes unit years ago. Ironic that she used those skills almost every day as the Deputy Chief of the Lytuan Metropolitan Police. Trina stowed the burner phone in the secret wall compartment that housed her untraceable laptop and a supply of phones.

Seething, Trina struggled to regain control of her emotions. Her senator husband was counting on her. She always came through for Corey.

That damned upstart Lillianna ruined everything, stolen what should have belonged to her family. Entering the election late in the game made a mockery of the entire process, and it made her poor Corey look foolish. He should have been the king.

And most egregious was Lillianna's refusal to consider marrying their son. He thought the world of her.

After the election, Corey grew from disliking Lillianna to reviling her. A sentiment Trina wholeheartedly shared. Trina learned how to conceal the rage she felt when she heard the woman's name.

Trina closed her eyes, running through her plan once more. This wrinkle might not be catastrophic. A battered face could make the betrayal of the public's trust that much more reprehensible.

Trina weighed a delay in moving forward with planting the embezzlement evidence against Lillianna. She'd tip off the press while everyone was feeling sorry for the Queen and grieving the death of the Elite Guard—whichever one that turned out to be. Everyone would feel especially duped.

Portraying Lillianna as orchestrating the kidnapping herself to steal the ransom money paid for her safe return? This careful scheme might be one of Trina's best. Even if Lillianna changed her mind about marrying Cyrus now, it was too late. Trina passed the point of no return.

All the pieces would come together this time. She went about her business, ensuring she covered her tracks and had an airtight alibi, just in case. Even she wasn't immune to scrutiny.

Corey bellowed it was time for them to get going. A Senate event her husband was hosting required their attendance. It was imperative that she behave normally, as though the kidnapping was a complete surprise.

No doubt she'd spend most of the night at the police station as the Lytuan Metropolitan Police offered whatever help they could provide to search for their Queen. Her boss, the Chief of Police, was the only officer on the island who outranked her.

Keeping the sheer glee from her expression over Lillianna's misfortune would challenge her in a way nothing else had. Trina couldn't wait.

Chapter Four

THE INTERMEDIARY WATCHED THINGS unfold through the rifle's reticule. Crouched on her belly on the second floor of the neighboring warehouse, her vantage point of the trio left no room for error. Their excessive noise would draw attention. She remained motionless and, for the first time in a long time, wondered how the hell she had gotten to this point.

The killing wasn't the worst part. That was what she'd trained to do, after all, and she excelled at it. This use as an enforcer pricked at her. If the Boss didn't have her by the short hairs.... The Intermediary didn't know why the Boss insisted she hire low-level criminals. Their amateurish posturing was bound to get them caught. Unless that was the plan. It didn't matter. She'd be far away from here if that happened.

The woman they'd dragged out of the car wore an evening gown. Looked to be designer. Pretty rust color, perfect for a fall event. If she hadn't spent so much time in Lytua, she wouldn't have believed the woman was the Queen. They had tied the Queen's hands and were shouting at her as they dragged her inside.

Her job was to tie up loose ends, not think too hard about what was happening. That had never stopped her before, though.

The Intermediary felt nauseated by the thought of a woman being hurt or violated as she'd been once upon a time. She'd never allow it if she could prevent it. The Boss might have money and leverage, but the Intermediary had a code. And most importantly, the Boss wasn't here. The Intermediary was a master at spinning things; she'd been doing it for years. For now, she waited for what happened next. After this job, her debt would be repaid. She didn't know what her next move would be, but that was a problem for tomorrow. She'd figure it out on a beach somewhere in the South Pacific. Some non-extradition place with first-rate hospitals.

The thick vegetation surrounding the warehouse made the air feel heavy and close inside. She stood and stepped back from her scouting position when another wave of nausea rolled over her. This morning sickness business was for the streets.

She brought *his* face to mind, and her heart squeezed, imagining his joy if she told him. How he'd hug her, spin her around, and then slap her in handcuffs. Tears stung her eyes. All these damn hormones made her weepy and introspective.

A pregnant assassin. How ridiculous could you get?

Nope, not gonna think about this now. Getting involved with a deep-cover CIA agent had been an epic mistake. Now she was paying the price.

She re-focused her mind on the task at hand. Just one last job. And she was going to do it her way. She felt ill for a moment, but it passed.

It wasn't long before the Boss's signal came and put an end to her inopportune self-reflection. The Intermediary rolled her shoulders and emptied her mind. Showtime.

Chapter Five

THE CAR RIDE HADN'T taken long, though it left Khara nauseated and disoriented. Worry for Riddick gnawed at her. The bleeding hadn't looked too bad, but head wounds were tricky.

When they'd torn the cover from her face, they were in the middle of a dingy warehouse. Her captors forced her to sit on the floor. Khara bit down on her indignation at their manhandling. Really, there was no need to shove. Regaining her composure, she let her training take over. She said nothing, offered no protest, and cataloged details, straining to make out any clues. She could smell the river and figured they were still in the city. How close was that train in the background? Or was it a plane?

Their voices echoed in the large room. Not a warehouse. Were they in an airplane hangar?

Her bound hands came away bloody when she rubbed at the dull ache in her cheek where the man struck her. The bully. As she sat shivering in the sleeveless gown, Khara thought if she'd known she was going to be abducted tonight, she would have worn a wrap. It was so preposterous that Khara had to suppress a giggle. Her shoes had come off somewhere in the fray and damn, those were her favorites. And her pretty corsage, too. That had been such a lovely surprise, a perfect complement to her dress.

A sharp longing rose in her as she thought of Riddick, but she nudged it aside for now. It was essential to stay sharp and focused. She tried to keep as much of her feet off the cold concrete floor as she could and studied her two captors. Khara was already calculating how she might play them off against one another.

The one who'd posed as a janitor babbled nervously. They seemed antsy, like they were killing time.

The second man was short and squat, with bulging eyes reminiscent of a frog. A chill went up her spine when he looked at her. He had mean eyes, gleaming with malevolence. *This* was the one she needed to worry about. His movements were quick and soundless. He was far more watchful than his companion and said little. *He's done this before.* If she had any chance to go on the offense, she'd start with him. Her only hope was to catch him off guard.

Her best guess was that they were acting on someone else's orders and waiting for instructions. Whoever was behind this gave them only the information to get the kidnapping done.

Who hated her enough to have her kidnapped? And to what end? Corey Richardson was the only person who came to mind, but the Senator was too smart to be involved in something like this. He might be a bitter political rival who'd taken losing in the election personally, but he wouldn't stoop to kidnapping. Would he?

Think, Khara, she admonished herself. How could she convince these men to give at least one of her jewelry items back? She only needed a second to activate the GPS on any of them. Perhaps she should have said yes to having them activated all the time. Jaden was going to have a field day with this.

They hadn't hurt her, not really, but at least one had no idea what he was doing. It sounded like he was reciting a bad script in a community theater production. This was a low-level American thug who yelled at her in English when he thought she didn't understand. Never mind she'd spoken English when she was asking what happened to Riddick.

Khara wondered if she should feel insulted that the mastermind behind this hadn't had the decency to hire more competent henchmen. The ridiculous thought had her smothering another inconvenient giggle.

The bigger man—swarthy, neck tattoos—had little patience for his partner. He wasn't even trying to hide his exasperation, sucking his teeth and heaving put-upon sighs. When he tired of the incessant chatter, he snapped, "Stop talking. You're giving away everything."

"She doesn't even speak English."

Khara tensed and paid careful attention to keeping her face neutral.

The man leaned down into her space. His watchful eyes narrowed as he looked for a reaction. "Hmm. So, then she won't get it when I say I'd have fucked her twice by now if I wasn't getting paid so much money not to hurt her, right?"

Not a flicker of emotion crossed her face, despite the frisson of terror at his cavalier words. She'd worked on this skill for years with a body language expert.

When she maintained her blank, lack-of-understanding expression, the man cocked his head. "See, I think she does speak English. Clever of her to pretend not to, but I don't expect her to admit it."

"That's silly. Why would she do that?"

"You might be right. Eh, nothing personal, lady."

She almost wilted with relief when he shrugged and wandered off.

This was a scenario she and the Guard had practiced many times. She should say nothing, take in as much detail as possible, and try not to let on that she spoke English, then activate her GPS. The one incompetent fool spoke freely in front of her, as though he were trying to remember the correct order of tasks. She frowned and shook her head.

Now he was using a translation app, of all things, to make nonsensical demands of her. He wanted her to order her troops to withdraw, which didn't make a lick of sense since she hadn't deployed the Lytuan Army anywhere. What was this farce?

When Khara gave no indication she understood what he was saying, the frustrated kidnapper screwed his face up in confusion. Either he wasn't speaking Lytuan or he was butchering it beyond recognition.

"You must be saying it wrong." The second man reappeared from where he'd been standing in the shadows. He eyed her again, slower this time, and treated her to a chilling little smile. A gold front tooth flashed in the dim light. He'd take glee in hurting her, that smile said. Khara fought a shiver.

The phony janitor frowned as he squinted to read what was in the app. After playing with the settings, he dictated what he wanted to say and then held the phone up in front of Khara's face. The playback was pure gibberish. This was not Lytuan.

"Here." The man threw up his hands. "*You* try speaking this shit, then."

Frogman demanded he hand over the phone. He scanned the app, then barked out a one-note laugh. After tapping the screen, and shaking his head, he held the phone up to Khara.

"Withdraw your troops and call them back home immediately," the app's vaguely British-sounding voice intoned in over-enunciated Lytuan.

"I don't know what you mean," she answered in her mother tongue.

"Hey! What did you do?"

"You had it set to Latvian, you idiot."

No recognition lit in the other man's face.

"That's one of the three Baltic State countries the former USSR occupied. She's *Lytuan*, not Latvian! It's an island in the Caribbean."

"Oh."

The second man typed into the app and held the phone up to Khara once more. *"Excuse my associate. He's appallingly stupid."*

But this gentleman was not, and that struck genuine fear into Khara's heart.

"I'm going to get some food. I'll be back in about an hour. This one's smart. Don't let her out of your sight."

As soon as the froglike man left the warehouse, Khara assessed the remaining goon. He was jittery and reedy. If she played helpless victim enough to draw him in, she could beat the crap out of him and run. She knew how to escape and evade. But without her trackers for guidance, the Elites would never locate her. She'd have to reconsider the internal tracker option.

She could cover a lot of ground in the hour until the other man returned, Khara calculated, knowing her lack of shoes would hinder her speed. How far was she from other people? City lights were twinkling in the near distance.

"I need to use the restroom."

The man looked at her, uncomprehending. Khara pointed at the phone, and he got the app opened again.

She gave him her sweetest smile when he at last understood. He was untying her hands and Khara was readying herself to attack when the froglike man's voice floated through the darkness.

"Stop!"

The skinny man froze, and they both glanced up to see the froglike man with a gun pointed at her. Did he have a military background? He moved with a sinister quiet.

Khara took one moment to ponder if she should go with her planned attack.

Even if she only got one attacker out of the mix, the odds were better. But could she outrun the heavier man when her bare feet were stinging with the cold? He'd hurt her for certain if she tried and failed. She was sure of that. He had an unmistakable air of cruelty. His very presence cast terror in her mind.

The Elites surely knew she was missing by now. They must be looking for her. There was a standard window of time they used to keep visual tabs on her. Goodness knows she'd messed it up many, many times in the beginning. Someone would have found Riddick and treated his head by now.

She tried to reposition her arms to ease the nagging discomfort of the awkward angle. Affecting boredom, she scanned for something she could use as a weapon.

The little one seemed a tad more reasonable than his accomplice. How could she use that?

He tossed desultory looks her way as he paced and chain-smoked.

After stubbing out his sixth or seventh cigarette against the sole of his shoe, the not-janitor rummaged around the bag where he'd stashed her jewelry. He whistled as he held her pearls up in the dim light. "Bet we could get a few stacks for this. They're probably real."

"This ain't no robbery."

"She looks like she can afford more."

"We put the jewelry back after the signal. Stop screwing with it before you turn it on accidentally. You know what, just gimme the damn bag."

The froglike man held out his hand until the skinny goon put the necklace back in the bag, zipped it up, and handed it over.

"You don't have to be rude, you know. You could have just said 'Lemmy, please give me the bag of expensive-ass jewelry'."

The other man froze in the act of strapping the pouch around his waist. "You just told her your name."

"Oh. Ah, Lemmy's just a nickname."

"Stop. Just stop talking."

The phone rang. It echoed loud and screechy in the cavernous space. Lemmy jumped and jostled into the other man as he clambered to answer it. The froglike man elbowed him away with a look of disgust and clicked to answer. Khara tried not to appear too interested.

"Yeah, Boss," frogman said, swatting at the other man's hand. "We left it just like you said. On the counter."

Left what? Were they talking about her purse?

Another scuffle broke out after Lemmy somehow hung up on the "Boss" while trying to grab the phone away from the other man. They both stared at it in stunned silence, then the froglike man thwacked Lemmy in the back of the head, cursing at him.

"You better not mess this deal up for me. I will fuck you up."

When the phone rang again, he sobered and put it on speakerphone this time.

A digitally distorted voice on the other end of the line berated them for their incompetence. *Disguised.* Khara couldn't even tell if the speaker was a man or woman.

"She doesn't know what we're talking about with the Army troops, Boss. Should we try to—"

"Don't worry about it. It's just a distraction."

A distraction? From what?

"We're gonna need some more money," the frogman man burst out after they'd agreed to stay put and await further instructions. Lemmy bleated a protest and tried to jerk the phone away. He got a vicious shove to the collarbone for his trouble.

An ominous silence followed from the other end of the phone. "You had a simple job, and I've paid you handsomely for it. You don't want to play this game with me." Even with the computerized distortion, the Boss's voice was impatient and laced with menace.

"We got her, and you don't. Cough up more money or we go to the cops."

Lemmy hissed at his greedy partner, trying to apologize, but the Boss had reached their limit.

"You've served your purpose and sent a message. Won't be needing both of you anymore. Consider yourself fired." The line went dead.

"You idiot!" Lemmy grumbled, staring dejectedly at the phone. "They already told us—"

"Fuck all this cloak and dagger shit." The frog man stalked toward Khara, wearing an angry sneer. She wrestled down a swell of panic. He was coming to inflict serious pain and she'd need to fight smart. "Get up!" his shout echoed off the walls. "I'm gonna—"

He reached for her, mid-threat when he stiffened. Khara heard the ping of broken glass. The frogman fell sideways, shot through the throat, and was dead before his body thudded to the floor.

Lemmy yelped and dove behind a column. Seeing her chance, Khara clambered to her feet and threw herself onto the dead man. A pool of blood spread beneath him onto the cold concrete. She stayed low and hoped whoever was shooting had meant to kill this guy and not her. She whimpered and begged, hoping to cover how she was trying to get to the man's waist bag. With her hands still tied and the frogman's dead weight, it was a Herculean task to maneuver him enough to get the bag even partially unzipped. She almost had her necklace when Lemmy grabbed her. Khara twisted and kicked out at him with merciless savagery while she kept digging in the bag to get her hands on *something*. There wouldn't be another chance. He must know what she was trying to do. Her heel connected with his groin. He folded over but didn't release her.

Khara gave a triumphant cry when her hand closed around her watch. Not a moment too soon, for Lemmy finally succeeded in hauling her up and away. He flung her aside. Khara went down hard, tangled up as she was in her gown. She jarred every bone in her body doing the best break-fall she could manage, then lay there trying to catch her breath.

Lemmy retrieved the gun from where he'd dropped it and stalked over to her. A sliver of satisfaction at him limping wedged itself into her fear. Anger contorted his face.

"You're lucky I'm not supposed to hit you," he wheezed, holding his side. Blood trickled from his nostrils and split bottom lip. She'd gotten a couple of good licks in. *Good.*

Khara ignored him, unrepentant. Blood may have covered her, and her hip and knee were throbbing from their contact with the concrete, but she'd felt the vibration sequence on the watch.

She'd activated it. Now her job was to stay safe until the cavalry arrived.

Chapter Six

"**S**PILL IT, DADE."

"Bad news: the trail is cold. The GPS is not transmitting in Nicaragua anymore. So all we have is the last known coordinates. Good news: there's nothing there."

"What are you saying?"

"It's a wide open plain, no building, no chance your Queen is physically there. I don't believe your Queen was ever in Nicaragua. I think someone tampered with your signal. Hate to break it to you, but you've been—"

"*Spoofed,*" Melanie said, her fingers already flying over her keyboard. "Of course!"

"What the hell is spoofing? Break it down for me."

Dade and Melanie both started explaining at the same time, but Dade deferred to her. "It's when someone uses fraud to convince their target that they're someone or something they trust, usually to scam them."

"Khara's GPS has been faked? Why would someone want us to think she's in Nicaragua?"

"My guess is to throw you off the trail and keep you out of the way from whatever it is they're really trying to do. What it's showing you isn't what's there. Those coordinates are to an empty field outside Matalejo, near Managua. Here's what's really at those coordinates."

A flat, open grassland plain appeared on the monitor.

"Where is she, Dade?" Riddick growled the question. "Is it possible she was there and isn't now?"

"Possible, but unlikely. The flight is five hours direct. Even if they went right away. They could have driven to another airport and flown from there. Mel, honey, you still there?"

She paused, a flicker of annoyance crossing her face at both the endearment and the shortened version of her name. But he was already correcting himself.

"Sorry, that was unprofessional. Ms. Goodnight."

"Nothing went into that airport. Nothing from the States. But if they flew somewhere else first, then went in, it wouldn't stand out."

The two techs tossed jargon back and forth as they worked, their goal to strip away the false signal piggybacking on the buried one.

"Hang on. Now run the program again and let's see what we see."

Hands shaking, Melanie did just that. The image on the wall-mounted monitor pulled back to a higher-elevation map displaying all of South, Central, and North America. The digital map shimmered, hovering for a split second as if reluctant to reveal the truth.

Riddick rubbed his eyes, shaking his head to clear it. "Come on," he hissed at the screen, his jaw aching from constant clenching, the lack of sleep catching up with him.

The room fell silent, tension quivering in the air. They all held their breath as the location pin began to move. Up, up, up. North to central Canada, then east and south, finally zooming in over the eastern seaboard to settle on a building near the Anacostia River.

She was still in the city.

"She's still here." Riddick barely trusted his voice. "Or at least her jewelry is."

Relief flooded him, easing a fraction of the tension coiled in his chest. He would have burned Nicaragua down to find her.

"So they take her jewelry, give a fake signal, to do what? Have us chasing our tails while they...?" Jaden shook his head, perching his hands on his hips. "We have the tracking info for the three pieces of jewelry, but we didn't think to look at them to see if they were live. We were waiting for them to activate. Can you figure out where this signal was generated from?"

Dade gave an emphatic nod. "Mel and I, I mean Ms. Goodnight and I will work on that."

"That's near the Community Boathouse in Southeast." One of the SWAT team pointed at the screen. "Right by the train yard."

"Saddle up, team!" Jaden called out. The tech was busy hunting up the building's schematics.

After a quick briefing with the assembled law enforcement groups to form a preliminary plan, they mobilized for a rescue mission. The warehouse wasn't far away.

As men and women got busy checking weapons and stowing gear, Riddick waited skeptically for the MPD operatives to move away. "What's the rest of your team's plan? I know you didn't tell SWAT everything."

Jaden shot him a glance but turned his attention to speaking to the other Elites in Lytuan. They were nodding and ready to kick all kinds of ass. He'd seen that familiar determination in their eyes, the focused intensity of rescuers in the zone.

When Riddick fell into step on the way to the garage, Jaden did a double-take, then shook his head and held up a hand. "Leave it with us, Mr. Riddick."

"I want in."

"I am sure you'd be a big help in a scrap, but this has to be us. Stay here."

Riddick gave Jaden a flat look. "Would you stay here if it was your woman?"

"Not a chance in hell."

"Then there you go. I've done plenty of ops just like this. Let me help."

"I get that, really, and recognize you're trained in SpecOp. But we can't risk—"

"I'll go in anyway and get her myself if I have to."

Jaden harrumphed, then swore. "You have some balls; I'll give you that."

He stopped walking and instructed the others to go ahead. A quick glance around assured him they could speak in private.

"Look, I'm sure you faced similar—husbands, fathers, brothers who want to be there to rescue their loved ones. What did you tell them when they wanted to help?"

"Goddammit. That we couldn't risk their safety or the team's and that it could endanger the rescuees."

"Exactly. No matter how well-meaning or well-trained they were, they didn't work with your unit. They didn't know all the security measures that never get written down and no one outside your team knew.

"I get it. I do, but our team doesn't know you and can't anticipate your moves the way we can with each other. That uncertainty will most likely get people hurt, if not outright killed.

"I don't care who you are to the Queen. This isn't personal. We'd tell her sister the same thing. No one outside our team knows the security measures we use. The fewer people who know, the safer she is. Of anyone, you should understand the importance of outsiders not having team intel.

"We're doing this jointly with MPD as a courtesy. We'll shove them aside if necessary. This is our Queen, and nobody is touching her. Don't fight me on this. All my energy and focus need to be on getting her back safely and keeping my team from harm."

Riddick clapped Jaden on the shoulder and nodded, a silent understanding passing between the two men. Jaden took his role as the Queen's Sentinel seriously.

"You can ride with us, but you'll need to stay by the car until this is done. We're the ones with diplomatic immunity. Let us handle this."

Standing back may have been the hardest thing Riddick had ever done, but he knew about precision teamwork and wanted this operation to run as smoothly as possible. No one in the car questioned him when Cenn handed him a bone conductor earpiece already programmed to the team channel.

If these assholes had hurt her.... The memory of Khara being struck sent a surge of anger through Riddick.

The SWAT team cleared the neighboring building and set up overwatch. The SUVs parked out of sight. Riddick watched as the Elites leapt out to get into position.

Only the discipline cultivated with the Rangers allowed Riddick to remain still, the soldier within him reawakened with a chilling clarity. Everything felt heightened. He distanced himself mentally from his emotions. For the purposes of this op, Khara wasn't a woman he cared about; he had to think of her as a mission objective.

The SWAT team sniper did recon. Her whisper-soft voice in his ear was so clear she could be standing right next to him.

"Tagging one armed hostile. Carrying a small caliber pistol. Looks like he could have another in the back waistband of his pants."

"What else?" The SWAT team commander's voice was low and steely through the earpiece, clipped and no-nonsense.

"Scanning, ma'am. There we go. I have eyes on the Queen. She is bound, but not gagged, sitting on the floor. Doesn't appear to be injured. Single Bad Guy is waving a gun around. Seems to be yelling at her. There's a second guy on the floor in a pool of blood. Looks dead. Bad Guy is grabbing the Queen."

All the muscles in Riddick's neck and face pulled taut as a voice crackled through the earpiece:

"Wait. There's some sort of commotion happening. Got some pushy-shovy."

Riddick's hands clenched into fists, the urge to protect Khara overwhelming.

"Damn, she just kneed the dude in the balls and swept him. Ooh, shit, she just delivered a wicked headbutt. That's right. Get him, honey."

"Do you have a clear shot you could take him out when we breach?"

"Negative."

A man's raised voice, angry and indistinct, echoed from inside, prompting Cenn to hurry. "This is escalating. We need to move."

Cenn's voice was firm as she called instructions. "Do not engage the Queen under any circumstances. If she doesn't recognize you, she'll fight with everything she's got."

The plan was to breach multiple entry points to overwhelm and subdue the remaining hostile. A spotter on the roof would watch for the unidentified shooter.

Riddick watched the teams fan out around the building like smoke and make ready.

Chapter Seven

Using a newer, quieter door breaching device than the traditional two-person battering ram model, the team achieved a rapid, coordinated forced entry. Even the industrial warehouse door couldn't withstand four tons of applied pressure.

A startled yelp of, "What the hell?" sounded a second before the flashbang went off, filling the space with smoke, blinding light, and disorienting noise. They overwhelmed the kidnapper. With a racing heart, Riddick tried to discern what was happening amid the scuffling, thuds, and shouted commands, sprinkled with urgent Lytuan. Subduing the suspect and clearing the room took mere seconds, though it felt like an eternity.

Riddick's stomach clenched, his fingers digging into his palms.

His heart pounded in his chest, his breath coming in short gasps as he heard Khara's voice amid the chaos. God, he wanted to be in there in the fight, but Jaden was right. It was a bad idea to introduce an unknown variable to an already-fraught situation.

The Elite Guards remained disciplined over comms, with no extraneous chatter. They limited their minimal conversation to short sentences in Lytuan.

An accented voice called out a warning. "No, don't—"

Too late. A heavy-sounding *thwack* and a grunt sounded.

"I told you not to touch her!"

Riddick glimpsed Khara's head and a flash of her rust-colored gown as they hustled her out of the building and into one of the SUVs that screeched to a halt near the warehouse's front door. It was good she was on her feet, but his heart was beating too hard. A swirl of unrecognizable emotions tumbled around inside him, crowding out reason and common sense. A restraining hand on his shoulder forestalled the urge to rush over to her. Riddick turned to see Cenn. "Where are you taking her?" It came out like a snarl.

"To the hospital."

Riddick's heart clutched. "She's hurt?"

"It's standard procedure. Link would have made sure she was safe to move first. He's our best medic and was a flight nurse before becoming an Elite."

The SUV peeled out, two MPD cruisers leading with lights and sirens activated. Walking into a hospital was always better than being wheeled in. And yet Riddick was having a difficult time controlling his breathing. "So, to the hospital, then, right?"

"No. Our orders are to wait at the hotel."

"Screw that. I'm going to—"

"That order applies to you, too, Mr. Riddick. I know you're eager to see her and make sure she's alright. We all are. You'll have to wait, though, until she gets through with this part. She knows you're here and wants to see you as soon as she debriefs."

Shut down. They must have anticipated his protest.

Cenn led Riddick over to where three others from the Lytuan team were stripping out of their body armor.

"She'll only stay if it's dire. Maybe not even then. She hates hospitals," one of the other women said. Alene, if he remembered right, which meant the remaining woman was Jonnis.

A thought occurred to Riddick. "She was Queen when she had cancer." He still couldn't get his mind around it all.

The group nodded.

"How did she know it was you if she was stunned?"

"We've trained for that, too."

"And she would have expected us."

"I knew that was why you warned SWAT not to touch her," Riddick surmised. "A coded touch of some sort to identify yourselves?"

The four Elite Guards made no reply.

They'd taken the remaining assailant alive. Riddick had gleaned that much from the comm chatter, but there was no hope of getting close enough to pummel the bastard into a bloody pulp.

"What about the kidnapper?"

Cenn's face hardened. "Jaden will deal with him."

"I hope that means he's shanking him."

Weary, relieved silence filled the drive back to the hotel. For Riddick, there would be no satisfaction until he could lay eyes on Khara and see for himself she was alright. Then they needed to have a long talk.

Riddick paced in the lobby, his thoughts a jumbled mess. He was both irritated and relieved, annoyed and confused. Vaguely insulted. *She had her reasons.* Oh, he couldn't wait to hear them. He'd been worried out of his mind. She was safe, though.

His phone rang, and he was confused when "Kingdom of Lytua" flashed on the screen. He picked up right away. "Hello?"

"Riddick. Hello, hi."

Riddick grabbed the back of the chair he was standing next to, relief punching through him at the sound of his name on Khara's lips. His heart stuttered wildly. "Khara! Fucking hell, baby. Are you alright? Where are you?"

"Still at the hospital, but I'll be back at the hotel after. I know... I know we need to talk. Will you wait for me there?"

"Yes." No hesitation. He'd never heard anything so sweet as her voice. "Of course."

A Guard was kind enough to let him know when Khara had returned from the hospital, but he wasn't able to see her right away.

Riddick continued pacing. Couldn't settle. Anytime Khara had said something about the Queen—was she talking about herself? Making it up outright? Why did she pose as her own assistant in the first place? Endless questions gnawed at him and he had not a clue what he would say.

He could feel Cenn's attention on him from where she was standing by the door. No doubt he was failing some evaluation by being antsy.

"Driscoll," she said. When Riddick stopped his pacing to turn to her, she continued, "My last name is Driscoll. You use your mother's family name as your surname, your father's as your middle. No one changes their name when they marry."

Cenn had been all hardass who wouldn't give him her last name on that first day when she escorted him up to meet with the Queen about the upcoming architecture project. She'd warmed to him a little. "So 'Therin' is Khara's mother's people?"

Cenn nodded, then cocked her head and said, "Copy." She looked at Riddick again. "She's waiting for you. Ready?"

"No, but lead the way."

Chapter Eight

THE STUN GRENADE HAD left Khara disoriented, unable to see and hear, gagging violently. She'd struggled until one Elite had given her the code they'd worked out to let her know she was safe. Apparently, she'd struck an FBI agent who hadn't heeded Cenn's warning.

As soon as the effects of the flashbang wore off, Khara insisted on calling Riddick. The last time she'd seen him, he'd been unconscious and bleeding on the floor. She was sick with worry, but Jaden refused her when she asked for his phone.

"Exam first." His flat tone brooked no argument.

It wasn't possible to stare down Jaden, the person who had ultimate charge of her safety and had known her since she was a baby, but Khara tried anyway. "This is not—"

Jaden crossed his arms, his expression mutinous. She knew that look.

"Exam first. Then call." Khara had never seen him look so unyielding.

She wasn't going to win this round. Khara's lips twisted into a grimace. "*Fine*. Right after, though."

A cold dread settled in the pit of her stomach as her anxiety for hospitals flared up. Khara fought hard to keep it in check, consciously willing her muscles to relax.

Even three years after she'd finished treatment for breast cancer, just the thought of a hospital made her skin crawl. She'd wanted to run out of there the instant they arrived. Khara reminded herself as soon as she finished getting examined, she'd call Riddick. It was just enough to ease the constriction in her chest. She used it as motivation to let the medical staff fuss over her. Her cheek was the worst of it, but the x-ray revealed no fracture, and the cut didn't require stitching.

Without a word, Jaden gave Khara his phone and retreated a little to give her some privacy. Her hands trembled so much she misdialed twice.

Hearing Riddick's voice on the phone was like a balm, but faced with his concern, words lodged in her throat. Khara kept the call brief, aware that it would be a long few hours before she saw him.

Link assured her Riddick was fine; he was knocked unconscious when he fell into the wall after being tazed. Tears welled in her eyes when she thought of him lying there on the floor.

"So he knows?"

"He knows."

"And he didn't run away?"

Link's crooked grin was full of good humor. "I'd wager running away was the last thing on his mind. He was instrumental in getting to you."

That thought allayed some of her nervousness.

The group decamped to one of the hospital's conference rooms, where Khara spoke to officials from MPD and the FBI. Even the National Park Service sent a representative, as the warehouse she'd been rescued from was on federal land.

They spent hours getting her statement and trying to figure out who was behind the kidnapping. When their hounding for details got too intense, Jaden called a halt and told everyone they could speak to her again only after she'd had a chance to rest.

Chagrined, the assembled men and women expressed their gratitude for her time, gave apologies, and departed.

Khara released a deep sigh as she sat back in her chair and thanked Jaden. He'd realized before she did that her energy was flagging.

The Lytuans returned to the hotel suite, where a flustered Joanne grabbed Khara up in a fierce hug, heedless of her injuries. She leaned back and cupped Khara's face, worry writ large in the frown pinching her brow. Then she hugged her again.

"I'm alright," Khara soothed, but her voice sounded small and fragile and her arms wound around the older woman of their own accord. Joanne Mosley was indispensable to her. Not just as an assistant, but closer to a surrogate mother. "You should see the other guy."

Joanne's breath hitched. "That's not funny. I'll get some tea." Tea was Joanne's first line of defense.

The cup and saucer rattled as Joanne poured out. "Hibiscus, your favorite."

Khara placed a hand over Joanne's wrist. "Joanne. I'm alright," she repeated. "Let me get it."

Joanne dashed away tears from under her eyes before they could fall. She sniffed, too overwrought to speak.

"Sit down, Joanne. Please. Let's take a moment."

She nodded and sat. Khara poured a fresh cup of fragrant tea and sat it in front of Joanne. She met Jaden's gaze above her head as she took a tentative sip. She nodded at the question in his raised eyebrow.

Khara squeezed her assistant's shoulder. Then retrieved a bottle of whiskey from the wet bar and added a generous dollop into Joanne's tea.

The three of them sat together, and each drank a full cup while Joanne steadied herself. Only once they'd all finished did they debrief for the official Lytuan record while everything was still fresh.

Joanne gave her a sympathetic glance and one last big hug before retiring to her bedroom.

"I've never seen her that shaken before," Khara murmured.

"It wasn't just her."

Khara looked up at her friend and her breath caught at the fierce expression on his face. "Really, I'm—"

"You scared at least a decade off my life, kid. Probably all of us."

Jaden perused her face and gauged the tension in her shoulders. "Are you sure you're up to seeing him tonight? I can put him off."

Ah, the elephant in the room she hadn't wanted to think about. But she'd run out of time. Khara felt an unpleasant flutter in her belly. "How did he respond when you told him?"

"He was confused. He put it aside because he was so worried about you. Didn't let his ego get in the way. He's going to want an explanation, though. He doesn't seem like the type to put up with bullshit. I approve."

Khara's sigh was a forlorn one. "This wasn't how I wanted him to find out. I was just getting ready to tell him. Was he angry?"

"Maybe a little. But he wanted to help and, honestly, I thought I was going to have to zip-tie him to keep him from going in with the team. Smart enough to realize he could get in the way, so he stayed out of the way."

Khara frowned, worried her lip. This sucked so bad.

"I can't help you with this, Khara."

Khara gave a small nod and sighed again, this time heavily. Of course, he couldn't. She was on her own with this.

"For what it's worth, though, it's obvious he cares for you."

Once she retreated to her bedroom, Khara was alone with her jitters and recriminations.

Hoping a hot shower would help clear her mind and buy some time to pull herself together, she washed her hair and scrubbed until she was sure every bit of the dirt and kidnapper's blood was gone. Fatigue lined the beat-up face staring back at her in the mirror. She lifted her chin and squared her shoulders anyway.

It was time to face the music. No matter what happened, she'd never regret the time she and Riddick had spent together. He might read her the riot act. If she was lucky, he'd at least hear her out. As far as secrets and betrayals went, this wasn't too bad, right?

Surprise! The lady you've been dating is the ruler of an entire country!

Maybe all was not lost. It wasn't that she was a habitual liar. She'd never done anything like this before. Part of her wanted to avoid the conversation altogether and hide out instead. Her stomach hurt. The temptation was strong to dive under the covers and forget the entire day had happened. Things had been going so well.

This wasn't how she'd wanted to do this. She wanted to tell Riddick the truth herself and put it into context for him. Too late for that now.

Did he like her enough to not care about her title, her profession, her lies to cover those up? Khara thought of Riddick's suggestive words in the limo, how he'd looked at her on the dance floor, told her some of the things he wanted to do with her—*to* her. For an all-too-brief moment, he'd been hers. And it had been grand.

No amount of procrastination was going to fix this. She might as well get it over with, come what may.

"Alright, Khara," she told her reflection. "Let's do this."

Determined to remain calm and detached, Khara told Jaden she was ready.

Riddick's face was a mask of carefully controlled emotion when he came in. Khara's heart was knocking against her ribs so hard that it wouldn't have surprised her if he could hear it. He was haggard—in need of a shave, his clothing rumpled. There were shadows under his eyes and a bandage on his forehead.

He took a step toward where she was standing, something soft and possessive flaring in his eyes. Then he crossed the room in a few quick strides and crushed her to him in a tight embrace. Khara rested her head on his shoulder, wanted to sink into him and let him hold her all night. With his fingers stroking across the nape of her neck and his breath in her hair, she'd never felt safer. Khara turned her face into his T-shirt and fought to contain her tears. So much for calm and detached.

A deep chuckle from Jaden reached her ears. "I think you two can take it from here. I'll see you in the morning, *Avlah*." He closed the suite's door behind him.

Khara's heart wouldn't listen to reason when she looked up at Riddick. Even though her eyes were blurring with unshed tears, she would not cry. She would *not*. A deep breath to steady herself helped a little.

Here goes.

Chapter Nine

RIDDICK'S HEART THUMPED HARD at the sight of Khara's bandaged cheek, cooling the temper threatening to rise.

She'd changed out of her ruined gown and now wore a soft navy blue pajama set, her hair wet. He feathered gentle fingertips over the ugly bruise forming. She was going to have one hell of a black eye. The vivid memory of that bastard hauling off and hitting her in the face just wouldn't leave his mind. "Are you alright?"

"I can explain."

"That's not what I asked."

She nodded. "Yes. Shaken up mostly. But alright."

He kissed her—quick and hard, then again, more gently and folded her back into a tight hug. "I'm glad. That just scared about ten years off my life. I'm sorry this happened." He bet she had finger-shaped bruises on her upper arm. Fury whipped through him. "I hate that those fuckers hurt you."

"I'm fine. What about you? You were tazed. And your head—are you hurt?"

He ducked her seeking hands, knowing she'd fuss over him. "No. Should you be sitting down?" Without waiting for an answer, he steered her to a nearby chair, then sat opposite her on the couch. It was the nicest couch he'd ever seen. "So, let's hear it."

Khara hesitated for a moment. "I apologize for misleading you."

She caught herself fidgeting, smoothing her hands down over her legs. As upset as he was, Riddick disliked seeing her uncertain. "Okay. Tell me why you did."

Folding her hands together in her lap seemed to help her gather herself. Her voice was a little stronger when she spoke again. "The last times I went on dates, they were... awkward."

"Most first dates are awkward."

"Ours wasn't. Let me explain and then I'll answer any questions you have. We've talked a bit about life on Lytua. Imagine photographers and the press eavesdropping on top of first date awkwardness. Disastrous. It's impossible to connect under those circumstances. It's like a fishbowl. The only time I'm off duty and able to be fully myself is within my apartment, and that's not an all-the-time thing."

"That sounds lonely."

"It is at times. This is not a poor little me gambit. I have a full life—people I love and care about, my sister, and a small group I can be off duty with. You must understand that I am under constant scrutiny and I don't want anyone I care about to face that as well. It can be exhausting and shift focus away from what I am trying to accomplish as Queen. The press, political foes—they can be brutal and unforgiving. I don't want people I care for being exploited and weaponized. So I keep them distant. And yes, it can be lonely. Trying to sort out genuine interest from opportunists became more trouble than it was worth, so I gave it up and focused on my work. Even my fiancé wasn't able to handle the attention."

"He still shouldn't have left you in the middle of a cancer battle, the asshole."

She gave him a tremulous smile. "I'm normally a very honest person. To be perfectly frank, I thought we might have a fun evening and that would be it."

"But?"

"But we connected, and I wanted to keep seeing you. It was wonderful to be myself as I am off duty, to be out and laughing and enjoying myself, kissing in the rain. Doing things I want to do." She sighed. "I wanted nothing more than to go to bed with you last night. I wanted you so very much and felt thrilled that you wanted me, too. That you liked me for just being me. But it was a line I couldn't cross without being honest with you. I wanted more time with you before telling you the truth. Of course, I knew I'd have to tell you eventually, but I wasn't ready to last night. I wasn't ready to lose it all yet. I wanted more memories to take home. And I didn't want to get you tangled up."

Riddick digested this. She was breathless and blushing, a little excited. Just how he liked her. He leaned forward, closer to where she was sitting. "You wouldn't sleep with me when you wanted to because you hadn't told me the truth yet?"

Her lips quirked up in a rueful smile. "I doubt there would have been any sleeping involved, but yes. The false pretenses wouldn't have been fair to you."

Riddick shook his head and entwined his fingers with hers. They'd been minutes from sealing the deal right there on his couch. How tempting she'd been in that sinful red dress that made him want to do wicked things to her with his tongue. "I'm already tangled up, beautiful Khara. What else?"

A flicker of surprise moved over her face. "Men I've been romantically involved with didn't seem to do well with...."

He waited and didn't jump in with his suspicions. Usually, she was never at a loss for words. It was all kinds of adorable.

"Not being first in my life." the words came out in a whisper and Riddick's heart broke a little for her. She'd been let down. By that fuckup fiancé and who knew how many others. Small wonder she'd been wary of getting involved with him.

"Being outshone, you mean."

"Yes." Her tone of wonder told him he'd put his finger right on it.

At this, Riddick gave a derisive snort. "Men who're threatened by a powerful, successful woman are small-minded asshats. I get why you'd want to avoid hoopla."

Khara's cheeks flushed, her hands still trembling slightly. "I didn't plan this. Nor did I expect it. This was not supposed to happen. You showed up early and mistook me. And you caught me off guard. You were so damned sexy. And charming. And you smelled *so* good. It would have changed things. I... you would've treated me differently. You wouldn't have flirted so outrageously with me or asked me out to dinner."

"You're probably right," Riddick conceded.

"Then you went and chose me over the project—"

"A decision I'll never regret."

That brought her up as short as the first time he'd said it all those weeks ago.

"I didn't want you to think the Queen was—I was—I kept trying to tell you and I was just enjoying you so much. I thought you'd be angry and want to end it when I told you."

He was studying her, his gaze caressing her face, lingering only for a moment on the bandage. This had been troubling her. He hated that he'd added to that. "Why?"

"I... lied to you."

After giving that declaration some thought, Riddick rejected it. "Not really. Nothing unforgivable. And you had a legit reason."

"I lost the corsage," she whispered, casting her eyes down. Her breath hitched. Her voice held a note of anxiety. "Mercy, I can't stop babbling."

"Breathe, beautiful. I'll get you another one. What else? You clearly had thoughts on this you needed to get out. We all have secrets."

"Even you?"

Past transgressions that still filled him with shame did their best to crop up. Riddick pushed those thoughts away. That didn't matter in the here and now. "We all do."

"You're making my argument for me."

"Did you mislead me about anything other than being a Queen?"

"No. Everything beyond that has been completely genuine."

"Was this what you were going to tell me before it all went to shit?"

"Yes. I was in there trying to screw up my courage."

"Let me ask you this, then. Whenever you were talking about the Queen, were you making it up or talking about yourself?"

"Everything I told you about the queen was true."

"You tried to tell me a few times, didn't you?

Khara nodded. "You were so anti-queen and convinced I was being exploited."

"I didn't let you. No wonder you were so defensive about the queen. You told me a whopper, didn't you?

"The press mix-up? Yes. It was all I could think of on the spot."

"You thought of that on the *fly*?"

"I had to come up with something. You weren't going to let it go. After that, I manipulated what you could find about the queen and talked my way out of a couple of close calls. It was quite nerve-racking at times."

"Okay, then." He plopped his palms onto his knees.

"'Okay?'" she echoed.

"I like you, Khara. A hell of a lot. You being a Queen doesn't change that. I'm not going to back off and run away in a panic. Sure, I'm a little pissed. Worried you may have put yourself in danger. Worried *I* put you in danger. Would that asshole have gotten to you if you'd had your team in place like they usually are? I seriously doubt it. Jaden's right to be pissed. Sure, I have questions. But let me tell you one thing."

"What's that?"

He leaned forward, the intensity of his gaze unwavering, his hands braced on the arms of her chair. He moved in, purposely crowding her. His gaze slid over her face like a caress. "What I said about wanting you and enjoying you and trying this long-distance thing? Everything I said when we almost had each other on my couch still stands. So does what I said in the car, at the table, on the dance floor. That is, if you want it to."

Khara licked her lips and nodded. "I do."

"Then we'll figure it out. Let's see where this thing goes, yeah?"

She threw her arms around his neck and kissed him.

Riddick guided her over to the marvelous couch and sat with her tucked into his side.

Just as she was starting to drowse, she bolted upright in his arms. "Oh, no. You missed the football game with Dion. I'm sorry."

"We'll work it out. It's not like you kidnapped yourself."

She nodded, snuggled into him again, and fell asleep almost instantly. Fresh fury welled in him at the sight of her battered face. He waited to wake her until it subsided, for he didn't want to touch her while angry. Riddick shook her shoulder gently. "Come kiss your boyfriend goodbye, Khara. It's late and you should get some rest."

Warm and sleepy, Khara snuggled closer, her warmth seeping into him. "You still want to be my boyfriend?"

"I told you, everything from before still stands. We're officially exclusive. Like I said, we'll figure it out."

They had a lazy, scorching kiss at the door. Riddick told her to get some rest and that he'd call her tomorrow. He was seeing her in a new light. That slight imperiousness he'd identified in her voice in their first conversation—he'd thought she had an air of authority, as though she were used to being in charge. Well, that made sense. She was a Queen for fuck's sake.

In the coming days, he planned to get a crash course on Lytua. He had some serious catching up to do.

Chapter Ten

RIDDICK SLOWED HIS STEPS when Jaden was waiting for him in the hotel lobby. "Figured I'd be seeing you again soon."

Jaden fell into step beside him, heading to the garage. "I'd say let's get a beer if we hadn't just been up almost 48 hours. I don't know what dimension I'm in right now, I'm so tired. Where can we get a bite? I'm ravenous all of a sudden."

"Yeah, I know a place."

"Great. Let's take a ride, Mr. Riddick."

"It's just Riddick."

Jaden raised his eyebrows. "Not Josh or Joshua?"

"Nope. Just Riddick."

Not much conversation took place during the short car ride to Ben's Chili Bowl, not until Jaden had pulled into the parking lot.

"So what's on your mind?" Riddick wasn't a beat-around-the-bush type of guy.

"I've got good instincts, but only a dumbass wouldn't at least entertain all the possibilities. And I'm not a dumbass."

"Understood. If I were in your position, I'd do the same. What are you entertaining?"

"You could be an excellent actor. You could be involved."

Riddick let out a dry chuckle. "If you really believed that you wouldn't have let me anywhere near her afterward. You wouldn't have let me near her in the first place without some sort of vetting. I'm just guessing, but I bet there's some loophole in what you do that allows for your discretion with her safety."

"Part of my job as Sentinel is to override her wishes or instructions when faced with a threat."

"Makes sense. I'm not involved."

"I didn't think so, but I had to ask. Take a look at this." Jaden pulled up a recording of Lemmy Barbenoit's interrogation in the video app on his phone. "This won't be admissible in Lytuan court, but let's see what we can find out."

The camera was trained on a slight, nervous-looking man sitting alone at a table, bouncing his leg up and down. The fake janitor. Knowing Khara was responsible for his busted-up face filled Riddick with a sense of satisfaction.

From offscreen came the strident voice of the detective conducting the interview. "Do you have any idea how much shit you're in? You kidnapped the Queen of a sovereign nation, here in the States on a diplomatic mission. And you assaulted her. She wasn't even resisting. The US government doesn't want any part in helping you. In fact, they're trying hard to avoid an international incident."

The man paled. Then he started shaking and blubbering. "I swear we didn't know who she was. You have to believe me."

"That doesn't help us, and it certainly doesn't help you. You'll be put on trial in Lytua. The extradition is already in process. You've been appointed a lawyer. She will be in contact soon. If you want a deal, you'd better tell us everything you know."

The man didn't even hesitate, he just started spilling his guts.

The burner phone he'd been provided had only connected to another burner phone. He didn't know who had killed his partner or even much about the man, whom he described as both "mean and scary." The two of them had only ever dealt with the Boss on the phone.

Lemmy stammered about the last person in the equation, the one who hired them. He couldn't give much of a description beyond it being a woman of medium height and build, who wore sunglasses and a hat the one time they'd met in person. The most distinguishing characteristic he could remember was that "she had a terrific ass."

Lemmy had been hung out to dry. He looked so forlorn Riddick almost felt sorry for him.

"One last question. Why Nicaragua?"

Lemmy's blank stare was answer enough.

At the video's conclusion, Riddick and Jaden gave identical sighs of exasperation.

Tucking his phone out of sight again, Jaden drummed his fingers on the steering wheel. "Well, he's useless."

"Useless," Riddick agreed. "Had to be ransom. It's the only thing that makes sense. Who would have paid the ransom? Your government?"

Jaden nodded. "Initially. She's covered with a robust kidnap and ransom insurance policy, of course."

Riddick was incredulous. "Kidnapping *insurance* is a thing?"

"Fairly common, from what I understand. Everything points to this being a ransom scheme, but that doesn't feel quite right."

They both fell silent, trying their best to puzzle it out.

"What will you do with him once he's extradited?"

"We're not involved in that part of the criminal justice system. He'll be handed over to the Municipal Police, then tried."

The entire situation still felt like a strange dream to Riddick. "Does us being together make your job harder?"

"In some ways it does, but it's not about me. Or you, for that matter. It's about her. Always."

"She's just as surprised by us as I am. I trust you'll tell me what I need to know to help keep her safe."

Jaden gave him an assessing look.

"We both know she's probably still in danger. There's at least one other person involved who's unaccounted for. Until we figure out who's behind whatever this is really about, she's not safe."

"Security around her will be tightened for the foreseeable future, but you don't have to do anything. That's my job."

"How open should I be about her identity? People know she's in my life, but is this hush-hush?"

"That's up to the two of you. She values her privacy, but the press doesn't. It could get messy. They respect the Queen's privacy in Lytua, but everywhere else? Word will get out; the press may pounce upon everyone you know. Talk to Khara about it in the morning."

Inside the diner, they held off further conversation until they'd chowed down a half-smoke each.

Jaden took in the retro booths and counter, the wall of signed portraits of famous visitors. "This place is amazing. Like a history book."

They talked for an hour and agreed that Lemmy wasn't smart or savvy enough to come up with this plan on his own. Was the person running things the one who'd shot the second man, or someone else entirely? Khara had an enemy somewhere. One who hired incompetent dumbasses, which suggested he or she had never done this before and had no idea what they were doing. Or perhaps it was the opposite and only designed to look that way.

Jaden explained that no one would benefit directly from Khara stepping down. No one person would automatically be in charge. There would have to be another election and the Parliament would run things until then.

"Guess that would've been too easy," Riddick said. "Who's been the biggest pain in her ass?"

"Senator Corey Richardson." There was no hesitation in the answer. "He ran against her."

"I hate him already. Tell me about him?"

A reluctant grin tugged at the corner of Jaden's lips. "He gives her a hard time in Parliament, but can't ever get a rise out of her. Been trying to get her to go out with his son for years."

"Now I really hate him."

They ended up talking for another hour. Jaden had served the previous Queen, the *Na-Avlah*. He filled Riddick in on some details Khara hadn't thought to include when telling him the truth about her life.

Jaden told him what it was like having her run and get elected, then become a novice Queen. "The citizens love her. She's a good Queen. Tough, but fair. Devoted to the people of Lytua."

"Tell me more about this Richardson asshole."

Jaden grimaced. "She crushed him in the election. Outclassed him at every turn. It was a thing of beauty. He looked like a raving lunatic. She was too young, too inexperienced, blah blah."

He huffed a quiet laugh.

"She *was* young. A little brash. Honestly, if she hadn't been my friend, I wouldn't have believed someone so young could run a country. She was only twenty-six. These last six years haven't been easy."

He leaned back in his chair.

"But she wasn't unqualified. She served in Parliament straight out of law school and her civil service was in the legislature."

Riddick snapped his fingers.

"Law school. Holy shit, that's right. She told me the Queen—*she*—went to law school. That's why she's so damn good at arguing a point."

"For a while, Richardson was the only candidate. Thought he had it on lock and was phoning it in. When Khara entered the race, he had to work. The rumor is that he damn near frothed at the mouth when he found out."

Jaden's tone cooled.

"He didn't take her seriously at first. Thought he'd coast and squash her hopes. But Khara has never been a pushover. She proved to be a formidable opponent from the outset. She ran circles around him in debates. He never forgot that. He ran against the *Na-Avlah* and lost."

A beat passed.

"Maybe he thought he was owed." Jaden shrugged. "His wife's the deputy police chief, by the way."

"Jesus. Talk about a power couple. And the son?"

"Richardson and his wife have been trying to pimp him out for years to the Queen. It's sad."

"That is pretty sad. You're protective of her. Just how far do you go back?"

"We've been friends since grade school. Our mothers were close friends."

"You knew Khara's mother?"

"Oh, yes, she was like another mother to me, especially after my parents died. Faye Therin was a great lady taken too soon."

"How hard is it to balance being her friend with being her Sentinel? The word for it was '*Zildrei*'?"

"Yes. Some days are harder than others."

"You said your team is SpecOp? Is that why Cenn looks like she knows how to use all those wicked-looking knives?"

Jaden turned wistful for a moment. "Yes, each of us is SpecOp. Cenn doesn't miss. She keeps at least one of them on her all the time, even if it's a 'no weapons' site. She saved my wife's life with those knives before we were married, so she can take them wherever the hell she wants, as far as I'm concerned."

"Shit, I bet that's a story."

"It is."

As they were nearing the hotel, Jaden said, "I needled you on purpose. Had to gauge your reaction."

"I know."

Jaden snorted. "You didn't get that Ranger tab by being stupid."

Riddick eyed him. "You know the 75th?"

"I do. Train with them every year at an international joint training. Spy School, as my wife calls it. Some of the best men and women I've ever met. Rangers lead the way."

"Rangers lead the way," Riddick echoed.

When they parked and Jaden didn't move to get out right away, Riddick's stomach tensed.

"We're aware of your past."

And here it is. Riddick said nothing at first, remained placid as a lake in winter. He'd had years of practice. "And what do you think you know about my past, Captain Everly?"

"I know that what happened wasn't your fault, and someone did a masterful job obscuring your records. Dade, I take it?"

Riddick neither confirmed nor denied but took a gamble instead. "You know I was adopted, then. And why."

"And the rest."

A long stretch of silence spun out. He'd figured, but getting the confirmation.... "Your tech, Melanie?"

"Told you she was top tier."

"Actually, you told Dade. Does Khara know?" The thought made his heart thunder in his chest, even though he kept the words light.

"Didn't affect her safety, so it's not my story to tell."

Huh. Jaden was a cool customer. Riddick wasn't sure if he wanted to thank him or act like this conversation never happened. "I'm assuming this is where you say something vaguely threatening like, You hurt her and you deal with me? Overprotective big brother mode?"

Jaden snorted and looked at him full-on. "You're okay, Riddick. You're okay. And yes."

"So what's next?"

"The courts will deal with that jackass. We'll do whatever we can to find the organizer, but I suspect that's a dead end. That person is likely in the wind."

After a few moments of companionable silence, Riddick said, "She thought I would split after finding out the truth."

Jaden nodded at this. "This part of her life hasn't been easy. As a friend who knows how great she is, that's been hard to watch."

Chapter Eleven

*A*LWAYS PRIORITIZE A SPEEDY *exit over a speedy entry*. That piece of advice from her mentor had saved her skin several times over.

The Intermediary's face remained impassive as she recalled the details of the dead kidnapper's crimes. The man was a stain on humanity with a rap sheet a mile long. Robbery, aggravated assault, attempted murder, drug charges. He'd almost beaten an elderly couple to death over $37, and attempted sexual assault. His death wouldn't trouble her conscience.

She'd been ordered to kill one of the Queen's Elite Guards, a task she'd decided right away she wouldn't complete. Even if she wasn't bailing right after, she made her own choice on who was on the receiving end of her round.

As soon as she was sure she'd eliminated her target, the Intermediary broke down her rifle and packed it away with precise, efficient movements. She made her speedy exit, using the route she'd pre-planned. She walked the several blocks to where she'd parked her nondescript rental and keyed the fob to open the doors. Dressed like any other running aficionado, she blended right in with the other dedicated folks on the trails and was on her way in a matter of seconds.

She used one of her carefully constructed identities for the rental and a different one for the hotel she now drove to. As she headed toward Dulles airport, the Intermediary removed the long ponytail wig she'd worn and shoved it into the bottom of her backpack.

She disposed of her dark clothing and the wig in a charity donation box in Tysons Corner, also scoped out in advance and jammed with holiday shoppers.

By the time she pulled into the parking lot of the Hyatt Regency Dulles, she was back in the sweater dress, bright scarf, and curly wig of dark curls she'd been wearing when she left earlier in the day. With the thick glasses and southern drawl, she was miles away from the assassin's skin she'd slipped into.

Back in her modest hotel room, Demisha activated the various firewalls and protections she'd set up to shield her location. Getting arrested now would jeopardize everything.

The Boss waited for her call. Demisha reported how things had gone sideways. With the second kidnapper in custody instead of being killed, the elaborate plan fell apart. A slow smile spread across Demisha's face as she listened to the rising panic in The Boss's voice. By the time The Boss worked out another plan or a way to salvage this one, Demisha would be long gone.

It was nearly time to expose her for the trash she was.

Demisha turned her attention to her next task. Her fingers flew across the keyboard as she opened the encrypted email program. The dossier she'd carefully assembled was ready to send to the middle-level Interpol agent she'd chosen to receive it. It contained recordings, pictures, first-hand accounts. She'd fed the Lyon, France-based Inspector actionable information before; she could trust her to keep her word. Demisha had been gathering evidence for years on The Boss and kept meticulous records. There was plenty of incriminating information, all organized and labeled with precision. This had to originate from outside Lytua, as The Boss was too powerful on her home turf. She would quash any investigation from within.

After re-reading the email draft a final time, Demisha's finger hovered over the send button. If she went through with this, it would be irreversible.

She felt a flutter in her belly after she sent the missive. This might ruin his career with the CIA. She regretted that, but this situation was always... complicated. And now even more so with this newest wrinkle.

Once she'd received a response from Inspector Reina Chinard, Demisha sighed and sat back from her untraceable laptop. The Inspector would act on the information and evidence when Demisha transmitted it at a future date. Interpol would coordinate between international law enforcement agencies and see Trina brought to justice. It might take a while, but it would happen.

Demisha had incriminated herself, providing details no one else knew to give herself credibility. She'd be a wanted woman, too, and it was a given that The Boss would send others after her. She'd never be able to return to the States or her adopted homeland of Lytua.

Only when her baby was as safe as she could make them would she turn over the evidence as promised. Her original intent had been to send it all now, then disappear. That would be harder for the foreseeable future. Moving the timeline up made little difference in the grand scheme of things, but she'd be well hidden before she outed herself. Getting settled and prepared before she got too far along was paramount.

Demisha pulled in a deep breath, placed a hand over her belly, and closed her eyes for a heartbeat.

Because she was a glutton for punishment, she called the secure voicemail she had set up for emergencies. She listened to all three messages back-to-back. It was the last one that made her want to lie down and sob.

"I hate how we left things. That can't be our last conversation. Call me so we can talk. Please. I miss you. And... I love you. I know I should have said it before, but I was being stupid. So stupid. Demisha, I love you and I'll show you if you'll let me. Please call, darling. Please."

She could almost believe he was sincere.

Her thumb hovered over the delete icon.

It always did.

Deleting it would be smarter.

It would also make it final.

She wasn't ready for that.

One day, she told herself.

Just not today.

Maybe he did love the Demisha she'd been with him the last three years. It was the closest she'd ever been to her real self in a very long time. She'd been stupid enough to give him her real first name, dazzled by his good looks like some rank amateur. And then she'd broken her own rule and fallen in love with him.

Their baby would never know him and he would never know he had a child. That thought filled her with a profound sadness she couldn't blame on pregnancy hormones.

The real Demisha Murray buried under all the false personas was in love with a deep-cover CIA agent and pregnant with his child.

For just a moment, Demisha wished she could shed her Intermediary identity forever and just—

Demisha blinked back a sudden wave of emotion. No time for mushiness or longing for what she couldn't have. She had to focus on the immediate and there was much to do before heading out the next day.

A scalding hot shower and a steak dinner from room service re-energized her. She steadfastly ignored the siren's call of the minibar. Even after so many years, every damn day was a struggle.

Just for today….

Demisha had always known who The Boss was. That woman wasn't anywhere near as clever as she thought she was.

One day I'm going to need this favor repaid and this phone will ring. Take that call, do what you're told, and then your debt is wiped clean. You'll even get a tidy sum of money for your trouble.

Trina Krove, horrible bitch that she was. A living monster.

She'd been stringing her along for just over ten years. Demisha wasn't sure it had been worth it. Yes, the men who'd hurt her were dead, and she'd made sure they experienced horrible suffering before they died. But the bargain she'd made with the detective was a gift that kept on giving.

Broken, terrified, Demisha had once been desperate to punish her offenders. Terrified of going back to the police, of having *her* life put on trial. That one call turned into many others over the years.

She hadn't always been a killer. She'd once been a shy, introverted soldier who'd planned to pursue a career in chemistry. Then one night changed everything.

Trina had facilitated this, recruited and groomed her to be her personal enforcer. By the time Demisha figured that out, her hands were too dirty to ever be washed clean.

How badly do you want to hurt the men who hurt you, stole your life? I can give that to you.

She should have asked what the price was before, but her bloodlust and outrage had been too great. Trina had taken advantage of that.

In her darker moments, Demisha wondered if Trina had orchestrated the attack that led her to where she now found herself. The thought disgusted her, but she wouldn't put it past Trina; she was just that ruthless.

She used to believe she was doing the right thing. Then the line blurred, and she found herself on the wrong side of it.

As Trina rose through the ranks of the Lytuan Metropolitan Police Department, she kept Demisha on a leash and jerked it with viciousness when she needed something. Demisha rebelled in small ways that couldn't be traced back to her. That was over now. By most accounts, Trina was a solid deputy chief, and poised to become the next chief. But she'd seen into that woman's soul, and she was up to her neck in shady dealings. And for what? Occasionally, Demisha wondered where good cop Trina had taken a turn. She'd never been able to figure out her angle.

When she'd come to her with an opportunity for justice the criminal justice system had denied her, Demisha was mad at the world, reckless and bloodthirsty. Trina had appeared like an angel.

No matter. This part of her life was over. Too many years had been devoted to it. Killing those men hadn't stopped the nightmares, hadn't undone anything. Hadn't even really made her feel better. Trina had used her, preyed upon her anguish and fear. Now she planned to fight back. A little sooner than she'd intended, but plans changed. At that thought, Demisha popped an antacid for the heartburn she felt coming. Everything seemed to upset her stomach or cause heartburn these days.

She booked a one-way ticket to Jakarta. She'd find a way to atone for her wrongdoing from there.

Chapter Twelve

RIDDICK REMAINED IN THE car after pulling into his garage, pondering sinister thoughts of getting Lemmy out of sight of surveillance cameras for a few minutes to deliver a well-deserved beatdown for daring to put his hands on Khara. How dearly Riddick would have loved to deliver it. It had been a long time since he'd resorted to solving problems with his fists. Not since those dark days on the street.

He'd had a nagging worry earlier that the Elites must know the truth about at least some of the past he'd left behind, but it hadn't mattered when he didn't know Khara was the Queen, so it shouldn't matter now.

Except it might.

Of course, the Guard knew about his past. They'd have been negligent not to check him out. Dade was going to be pissed that Melanie had gotten to the actual records. To his knowledge, this was the first time anyone had seen them since Dade worked his magic to clean things up.

I know it wasn't your fault.

Everyone had said that, the police, the judge, his adopted mother. Would Khara see it the same way?

Riddick looked down at his hands gripping the steering wheel—hands that had defended, hands that had killed, hands that had touched the sweetest softness of an undercover Queen—and closed his eyes against the tide of complicated emotions.

Once inside, he texted Dion, not wanting things to go too long before they got back on an even keel.

With the danger passed, exhaustion washed over Riddick, his limbs heavy, his eyelids drooping.

Just one last thing.

Dade picked up his call on the second ring. He had been his platoon sergeant in the Rangers and his voice still carried the jocular, yet no-nonsense tone of a good NCO. Riddick thanked him for the assist earlier.

"I get that a monarch's team of security specialists is way different from your average Joe, but can you check my juvenile records? Are they still holding up under moderate scrutiny? The Elite Guard knows about my past."

"Nobody's seen anything, Riddick. But it has been a while since I looked. Hang on."

Lack of sleep left Riddick's eyes gritty, exhaustion weighing down every muscle.

Riddick forced down headache tablets and sat at the kitchen counter. He yawned and waited patiently while the keyboard clicked in the background. Dade was going to be annoyed as hell with what he found.

"Wait." Dade's disbelieving tone was almost enough to make Riddick smile. "How the—"

The clacking of keys intensified, Dade uttering curses as he went.

"What did you find?" Riddick managed to keep the amusement out of his voice. Nobody bested Dade Holloway, and it was a good bet he wasn't going to take it well.

Silence stretched over the line, punctuated by Dade's sharp intake of breath. "Someone... holy crap. Melanie Goodnight got through."

"How about that."

"And she got through *months* ago. Riddick, she got through to the real shit. Her hacker trademark is here, but there's no other trace of her. She wanted me to know she'd gotten through. Showing off. Son of a bitch."

Poor guy, his ego's going to take a big hit, Riddick thought. Bet he didn't think today would be the day he got hit with an existential crisis. Nothing to do but give him a hard time about it. "You must be slipping."

"Bite me. That was some of my best work. I've got to meet this woman," Dade muttered under his breath, prompting a snicker from Riddick. "Everything's intact otherwise."

"Tell me again why it was a bad idea to just remove all traces of me?"

"Falsified is better than disappeared here. It would look weird and *sospechoso* if there was *no* record at all. Long shot that anyone would be looking for it, but a complete absence of records? That might raise red flags and lead to unwanted scrutiny. That could also throw suspicion on the people connected to your case."

Riddick huffed out a breath. "That's right, and I'm not doing that. This is old news."

"You might just want to tell Khara, you know. Then you won't have to worry about any subterfuge."

"No need."

"Up to you. While we're at it, lemme check if anyone's been poking at that exemplary military service record of yours. All those citations and shiny medals and such."

"Like you don't have just as many, if not more."

Dade grunted noncommittally in response. "Well, DragonFlip strikes again. She got a good gander, but there's nothing buried here. I still can't believe she did this."

"Can you look into a guy that's been giving Khara trouble? There's a senator named Corey Richardson she spanked in the election. Look at him hard, Dade. He's the only one who seems to have a bone to pick with her."

"You don't think her security would have?"

"I think they're not you and looking at it from the outside, you might see something they've overlooked."

Dade promised to get on it. He called back an hour later, pulling Riddick from the exhausted doze he'd slipped into. The man worked fast.

"Far as I can tell, Corey Richardson's just a whiny asshole malcontent. His beef with your Queen—who's a total babe, by the way, I gotta say. Reminds me of Jessica Rabbit or one of those pinup girls from the forties with all those—"

"Dade."

"Right-o. Whiny asshole malcontent's beef with your pin-up-worthy lady goes back years, all the way to the election. She spanked him, alright. Nothing suspicious in his financial dealings. He's a nut sack, but he's on the up-and-up. I dug into his wife and son. Nothing untoward on her, but their kid has been in some scrapes involving assault, domestic violence, and attempted sexual assault. No convictions, alleged victims recanted. Looks like he's had some emotional and mental health challenges and done some in-patient care, but nothing recent."

Riddick frowned, the idea of Khara's number one enemy trying to fix her up with his anger-issues spawn troubled him. "If Richardson's behind this, why would he wait so long to move against her?"

"Well, are we sure this is about her and not you?"

The question made Riddick's blood run cold. "She's the logical target, but I won't completely discount that thought. But who might be capable of something like this? Just hypothetically. We pissed off a lot of people with the rescue work we did."

"Offhand, I can't think of anyone having the resources to pull this off, but I'll do some digging. Give me a bit."

Dade didn't reach out again until midnight had come and gone.

"Remember that last mission? Several of the Nicaraguan team involved in that died under mysterious circumstances, but nothing recent. And none of that could be definitively connected to the cartel. They don't typically have the resources to come after the American teams. But why would they wait all this time?"

Cradling the phone to his ear, Riddick pinched the bridge of his nose. "Jailed leadership of a cartel has nothing but time and bitterness. And zero desire to take responsibility for their own actions. But didn't most of them die in prison? This feels like a stretch."

"What about Sergio Blandon?"

Riddick's breath hitched. "From *Guacamaya Roja?*"

"That's the one. He's out, and the government lost track of him three weeks ago."

Sergio Blandon was ruthless, persistent, sadistic. A true villain. The Barlomba region sighed in relief when he and the cartel were toppled with critical assistance from their Ranger team.

"Anyhoo, forget that piece of shit for a moment. Can we just pause for a sec here to appreciate that your fine-ass Jessica Rabbit girlfriend is a sitting Queen? I knew you had game, but damn, brother. Respect! Send some of that juju my way."

Riddick's brain refused to shut off.

Every time his eyes closed, Khara kneeled at his side, her face bloodied, or that jackass was touching her. Seeing her manhandled incensed him.

He wanted to destroy something.

The art kit started calling to him. He didn't resist, just retrieved it, set the materials out, and let inspiration flow through him without overthinking. He'd learned years ago to let the talent do the guiding. Riddick locked that gift away for many years, until recently, when he felt compelled to draw again after an early date with Khara.

He let his jumbled thoughts untangle and unfold as he poured them onto the paper.

Even in his early teens, Riddick was big for his age, a fact that deterred most people from messing with him during the year he spent on the streets. Having abusive drug addicts for parents was its own brand of hell no child should ever know, but so was foster care. Well, most of it, anyway.

He'd freaked out and run away when the woman he thought of as his mother told him she wanted to adopt him.

Given the chaotic nature of his childhood, Riddick learned how to take care of himself from an early age. Living on the street still wasn't as bad as some of the precarious living situations his parents had dragged him into. In a way, he'd been relieved to be removed from their care after a scam gone wrong.

The man he'd killed on that humid summer night had a reputation in the community of homeless. Whispers of his unpredictable violent streak and temper circulated among those who lived on the streets. Riddick had run into him once before, when the man falsely accused him of theft and lunged at him, spewing profanities. It took two others to subdue him. The unprovoked attack had left Riddick so shaken that he made himself scarce whenever rumors of the man's presence surfaced.

Toxicology revealed the man had been high as a kite on a dangerous cocktail of drugs that fateful night. Riddick had left the soup kitchen at a homeless shelter on the outskirts of downtown, heading around the building to where he had stowed his sleeping bag. He was arranging it for the night when a vicious kick caught him in the thigh. Before he could react, the man had him on the ground and was kicking and stomping him, screaming obscenities. It didn't occur to Riddick to call for help. He fought back blindly, panic surging through him as the man drew a long, wicked-looking knife.

Even years after, Riddick wasn't entirely sure how it happened. He'd been told he flailed wildly, kicking and shoving in desperation until he threw the man off. The attacker stumbled over a pile of broken parking bumper blocks, lost his balance, and toppled backward, whacking his head on the nearby jersey barrier. He crumpled to the ground and didn't get up. Lightheaded with hunger and fear, Riddick had crawled over to him and saw the unnatural angle of his neck. Then Riddick started yelling for help.

Freak accident.

Bad luck.

Just desserts.

They'd called it all those things.

The man—Tom, as Riddick later learned—went down at just the right angle to snap his neck.

His death had been instantaneous, an accident and a consequence of his own aggression. Riddick wasn't even charged. The knife was recovered at the scene and witnesses described it as an obvious case of self-defense. As he'd been a minor, the records were sealed, leaving him a clean slate. But the incident haunted him. He'd joined the Army the first chance he got. That discipline had helped him get his head on straight.

When he sat back to check out his work, Riddick was only marginally surprised to see he'd drawn Khara's face again. Not as he'd seen her after the kidnapping, but earlier in the evening on the dance floor, right before he asked to be exclusive. With the mischief in her eyes and that blush that told him he'd pleased her with his flirtatious talk.

His Khara was Queen Lillianna. What would that mean for them? This was weird.

Beautiful, brave Khara. Sweet. Sexy. Vulnerable. She'd nearly brought him to his knees with her vivacious spirit. What the hell was he going to do? This was still the woman who'd watched him with boldness as he brought her to climax on Thanksgiving night.

Don't overcomplicate it. It being that his girlfriend was the queen of a freakin' nation.

Riddick pulled up Khara's official state portrait and gazed upon the face he'd admired over candlelight. The bearing of authority was unmistakable. Just as he'd detected in her voice the first time they spoke, when he'd been rude and hung up on her, believing her to be part of a prank Dion had played on him.

A wave of guilt washed over him. He'd have to ask her about this portrait, about the secrets it held. But there was one secret he would never share. The memory of Tom, the man he'd killed, was a burden he would bear alone.

Chapter Thirteen

I N THE SUITE'S LIVING area, Khara was startled to find Riddick waiting for her first thing in the morning. With coffee. Her breath caught in her throat, a flutter of excitement rising in her chest.

"Is that what I think it is?" She waved to indicate the bakery bag he held.

"If you think it's a chocolate pumpkin muffin from Lot 38, then yes. You said you love decadent American breakfast pastries. Doesn't get more decadent than this."

"Thank you. I haven't been able to stop thinking about that place since our breakfast there."

He gave her a warm smile, then kissed her in greeting. "At least I didn't make you burn yourself like when we first met." He cupped her cheek, his gaze roaming her face. "You didn't sleep well, did you?"

"Not really. Nightmares. How did you get in here?"

"Your boyfriend can be quite charming, you know." He waited until she'd had a few fortifying sips of her coffee before saying anything else. "I want to apologize. I was harsh last night and didn't mean to be. Everything just caught me by surprise is all. How are you feeling?"

Khara scowled. "Like I'm going to need all the pain meds and skillfully applied makeup to get through this day."

"Can you stay in and just take the day off? You're injured. No one should be expecting you to be at a hundred percent for a few days, at least."

"I can't just—"

"Take a sick day? What would you tell Cenn if this had happened to her?"

"I'd tell her she better not come back to work before—"

"Exactly. Joanne says she cleared your calendar for the next three days. The only thing expected of you right now is to binge-watch TV and indulge in room service. They'll be here in a bit with more decadent American pastries and a full spread. When's the last time you took an actual sick day—four years?"

That was about right, Khara realized. She'd worked through the flu, a broken ankle, and most of her breast cancer treatment. But still. "I can't just play hooky!"

"Sick leave. That's different. And *I'm* playing hooky this morning to keep you company. So I'll have breakfast with you, watch a movie so bad it's good, then leave you to take a nap."

It seemed he'd outmaneuvered her. "Fine. I'm staying in my pajamas, though. What's for breakfast?"

The Elites had given Riddick strict orders to leave plenty of time for Khara to rest. He knew the trainer would be by later to take her through some light stretching to alleviate the stiffness.

Over omelets and fruit-studded Belgian waffles, they chatted about next steps with the kidnapping case. There would be a criminal trial after the extradition. Khara told Riddick he might be called upon to testify. He'd given his statement to MPD, but it would be a whole new procedure in Lytua.

"So, Jaden tells me you trounced this Richardson guy in the election. What was that like?"

Khara's version was more understated than Jaden's. She didn't think she'd done anything spectacular. Simply stood up against someone she thought was a poor choice, in reality just expecting to force Richardson into becoming better, thinking more broadly. He'd been a very sore loser. Then she did her best every day on the job. "He was gunning for me even before I started. Go down swinging, though, right?"

Riddick shook his head. "Swing hard enough to keep from going down in the first place."

"Ooh. I like that a lot."

"Why are you Queen Lillianna and not Queen Khara?"

"Being Queen is a profession, a job. It's not who I am. When you ascend the throne, you honor an ancestor by choosing their name. It's a tradition to keep you grounded in your service."

"So who's Lillianna?"

"My great-grandmother."

"Why did you choose to honor her?"

"She was gone before I was born, but I've heard stories of her my whole life. Lillianna was an accountant, widowed young, with three small children. She had no family to turn to on either her side or her late husband's. With the help of friends, she worked very hard to open her own firm and eventually a bank that specialized in affordable loans to women who found themselves in similar situations. A larger company tried to force her to sell her business, but she refused and fought back. She was a champion for single mothers and fearless by all accounts. I hope I'm making her proud."

"Of course, you are."

They'd just finished eating when Khara said, "It's not my favorite topic, but we should talk about the media. I'm sure the kidnapping was on the news."

"It was. You've got press staked out around the hotel."

A cascade of emotions flowed over her face. "We won't be able to spend as much time together anymore. If we go out, that is."

Instead of responding right away, Riddick watched how she twisted her napkin between her fingers in her lap. Abrasions encircled her wrists from being bound. *Dammit.* How had he not noticed that the night before? "I can handle the media, but I don't want you to stress about it. A better question may be, what do *you* want to do?"

"I don't want your life to become a circus. You'll have to tell me how much you are comfortable with. With the media attention at present—we'll be hounded if we go anywhere beyond the hotel. There will be wild speculation and inconvenience to your day-to-day. And goodness, your assistant will be bombarded."

At this, Riddick grunted. "Lena can definitely handle the media. That's what you don't want. What *do* you want?"

"I... I want to protect this. Us." She pointed a finger between the two of them.

"Okay, how can we best do that?"

"The press interest will die down, I am sure. They haven't connected you to me, so for now at least, your privacy is preserved. By the time you get back from your conference, they'll have moved on to the next juicy story. I'm not terribly exciting."

"Hmm. You are wrong about that."

She blushed, taking his meaning.

Truth be told, he hadn't given the sustainable architecture conference in New Mexico any thought this morning, although he was supposed to leave in two days. Khara picked up on his hesitation and urged him to go, reminding him they were both working professionals with prior obligations to be honored. She herself would be presenting at a symposium on global justice in Istanbul the following week.

"You mentioned last night that you have much more freedom overseas. Should I not tell people who you are?"

She shook her head, but it was cautiously. "We're not a secret or anything. I do regret that I misled the Sloanes at Thanksgiving. Your partner's family was the sweetest. Please apologize to them for me. And to Dion."

Riddick was about to quip that he didn't think they'd hold a grudge, but a hint of uncertainty flashed in her eyes, piquing his interest. "So, what's really on your mind?"

Conflicting emotions flitted across her expression, as though she were cycling through potential word choices. "I've put off my return home, but it's time for me to go. I confess part of me doesn't wish to. This time with you has felt very charmed. Except for the kidnapping, of course. I don't know what will happen when we're apart."

"Hey, we'll figure it out. This is a busy time of year for both of us and you're heading right out again to the symposium, right?"

"Yes. You're, ah... welcome to join me there. If you wish. And if you aren't already committed, of course." Her words spilled out in a breathless rush while she fidgeted with the cuff of her pajama sleeve.

The thickening of her island accent betrayed her nervousness. Her fingers played with a loose thread on her pajamas, and he suspected this asking him to share in her life was as foreign to her as how much wanting to be a part of it was to him. It was unfamiliar territory for them both.

Riddick watched as a faint blush spread across her face and chest. He used a finger under her chin to tilt her face up to his. God, those eyes got him every time. "Would you *like* me to join you there, beautiful Khara?"

"It would make for a lot of travel and jet lag, but I present on the first day and then we could—"

"Khara," he interrupted, and she fell silent, something near panic skittering across her face. "Do you want me to come?"

Her blush deepened, prettily, but she held his gaze. "Yes, I do."

"Then I'll come."

"You will?"

"Yes, I will. I'd love to check out Turkey with you. I'll talk to Lena. As long as I'm back the day before the holiday party."

She pulled in a deep breath, her shoulders relaxing. The relief in her eyes was heartbreaking. This must be the vulnerable point where others had let her down. The joy she derived from even the smallest things made him want to please her all the time, just so she would aim that killer smile at him. He stroked her cheek and dropped a light kiss on her lips.

She jumped when her phone gave a distinctive, happy-sounding chirp. She lunged for it, then winced when her bruised body protested. After reading the text she'd received, she gave a delighted squeal. "Oh, yay, little Gabriel's here! My best friend had her baby! Look at my godson! He's beautiful."

She dialed and had a brief, excited conversation in Lytuan, then switched to French, presumably to speak to her friend's husband. The Cadieux family lived outside Paris and this was their first child. Riddick couldn't make out much of the conversation, but the joy was unmistakable.

As they piled the breakfast dishes back onto the room service cart, Khara asked, "Were you able to connect with Dion?"

"Not yet. He won't talk to me."

"I know how important his trust is to you. Perhaps if I talked to him?"

"I think that might actually make things worse."

"I hate that you had to—"

"Nope. Don't do that. This isn't your fault. I'm not upset with you and I'll sort it out with him at our study session later."

Despite the morning's excitement, Khara's eyelids drooped before the zombie alligators movie hit the halfway point. Riddick draped the striped throw blanket over her, then paused to tuck a coil of hair behind the perfect shell of her ear before pressing a kiss to her forehead. With a soft click of the remote, he turned the television off, and then slipped out, taking care to close the door quietly behind him.

Chapter Fourteen

RIDDICK SCOWLED AT HIS cell phone when Dion didn't pick up.

The kid hadn't returned his texts or his calls. He didn't bother leaving a message. Now that Khara was safe, he wanted to turn his attention to fixing things with Dion. But he couldn't do that if he couldn't get him on the line. Was he pouting?

To hell with this.

Riddick checked the time. Fine, they'd work it out when Dion came to his office to work on schoolwork.

But Dion didn't show at his expected time. Where the hell was this kid? Riddick was pondering what to do when Dion's foster dad called. Dion had ditched school that day. He was home now, locked in his room and not answering.

"I'll be right there."

Emotion choked Riddick's throat on the drive over. After a brief discussion with the foster parents, he climbed the stairs and rapped his knuckles firmly on Dion's bedroom door. "Dion, it's Riddick. Open up so we can talk."

The response was a muffled, "Go away. I don't want to talk to you."

The words struck Riddick like a well-aimed arrow. "Dion—" He bit back a harsh retort and took a deep breath, forcing himself to relax his shoulders and soften his tone. "Dion, you're entitled to an explanation."

Bracing his hands on the doorway, Riddick shook his head to clear it before old hurts could resurface. "You don't have to say anything, just listen." The words dried up. He would never be able to undo the disappointment, and that cut deep. "It did involve Khara, but not the way you think. I didn't choose her over you. There was an emergency."

"You promised me you'd never miss our meetups."

"Yes. I did, and I didn't intend to miss this one."

"So what, you're pussy-whipped now? Figures!"

Riddick fought the urge to lash out, reminding himself that this wasn't about him. Dion was hurting, and his lashing out was a cry for attention. Forcing calm into his own voice, Riddick told him, "You have every right to be mad at me and tell me off, but you won't be disrespecting Khara while you do it."

There was a pause, as though Dion was thinking about it. "Whatever, man."

"Open the door and we can talk man-to-man."

He wasn't prepared for what happened next. The door flew open, and Dion launched himself at Riddick, a wild hook catching him on the chin. Stars exploded in his vision as the kid rained blows upon him, screaming for him to shut up. Riddick warded off the blows and angry words. Dion's face was a mask of fury and indignation. Riddick didn't try to stop him as he shouted his disappointment at him.

"You promised! I trusted you! I hate you!"

Dion's narrow chest heaved with the great sobs that tore from him, gutting Riddick. He knew what it was like to be let down by someone you trusted. Dion's anger was about so much more than a missed football game. Riddick was bearing the brunt of all the broken promises, all the heartache the kid had endured.

It wasn't until Dion's blows weakened and his rage dissolved into uncontrollable sobs that Riddick reached out. Dion struggled at first, but Riddick held on. And then he broke down into sobs that destroyed Riddick.

Grief split Dion open, and he railed at him, cursing and crying. Faced with this rage and pain, Riddick held on, tucked Dion into his body and did the only thing he could think of—he rocked the kid who was almost as tall as he was, but who was still just a scared kid inside.

Riddick rocked, his cheek resting on Dion's head, swaying gently as if comforting a baby. He offered no explanations, no admonishments to quiet down—just a steady, unwavering embrace. He rocked until Dion's sobs gradually subsided into occasional sniffles. Riddick had never witnessed such raw, unfiltered grief. He rubbed Dion's back in soothing circles, offering what comfort he could.

The time wasn't right to tell him the truth of Khara's identity, but he had to give the kid something, some reassurance, or he'd never trust him again. "I'm sorry. Only life or death would stop me from keeping my promise to you. And that's what it was."

Dion said nothing, his face buried into Riddick's chest.

"Let me tell you what happened and then you can decide what you want to do. I've always told you to get all the facts before making a decision. Khara was kidnapped last night. I know it sounds farfetched. You know she... has a high-profile job. Bad men took her from the event we went to. I spent all night with her team, working to find her."

There was a stunned silence when Riddick finished recounting the abbreviated version of the kidnapping. "Is she okay?"

"They hurt her some." Riddick couldn't keep the snarl from his voice. "But she is okay." He would explain further about Khara another time. Now needed to be about making amends.

Dion sniffed. "She's nice."

"She is."

"Don't fu-mess it up." Sniff. "I don't really hate you."

"I know. Skipping school is not an option, though."

"I know. I'm sorry."

Riddick drove them to his favorite taqueria. He didn't force any conversation, allowing Dion space to process his emotions. Their stilted exchanges were about inconsequential things. By the time Riddick dropped him off, a fragile truce settled between them. Riddick folded Dion into a tight hug before saying goodnight and reminding him they'd set up a make-up study session for the next day. It was a start.

Chapter Fifteen

A STATE DINNER IN her honor.

That was what the formal event Khara "couldn't get out of" turned out to be.

When she asked if he had another tuxedo, Riddick had questions. She'd shrugged and warned him, "I suspect it will be a complete bore, though, and we won't get to spend much time together. Want to come with me and liven it up via text?"

Khara had a way of downplaying *everything*, even a State Dinner. Perhaps she was just so used to seeing her role as that of a public servant that even such a grand occasion seemed mundane to her.

Sure, he'd agreed. He had another tuxedo. He'd trashed the one he'd been wearing the night of the kidnapping, even though the dirt and blood-stains might have come out. That was a reminder he could do without.

Only a few die-hard paparazzi camped out in front of the hotel. They weren't interested in him, although they would have pounced if they'd realized he was visiting the Queen who'd been kidnapped and saved during a dramatic rescue.

Even days later, Riddick was still trying to wrap his mind around Khara being the Queen of Lytua. It was almost as though he had to re-learn her and get to know her all over again with this added dimension. He'd told no one in his circle the truth of Khara's identity. Everyone would have questions he didn't have answers to, so he'd hold on to the knowledge for a little longer. Reactions should be entertaining. He looked forward to that part. How often did a kid who'd started off in foster care go *anywhere* with royalty?

Over dinner the night before his departure for Santa Fe, Riddick expressed some trepidation about leaving Khara, especially with the threat of danger still lingering.

She smiled at his concern. "The Elites are back on duty. They'll keep me safe."

"I forget you have a cadre of special forces protectors. You don't need me."

"Not to protect me, no."

When Melanie, the feisty Guard tech, arrived to upgrade his laptop and cell phone to secure lines, Riddick thanked her for her instrumental role in Khara's rescue. She seemed amused that Dade had been equal parts impressed and irritated with her skill.

"Serves that cocky *jozelin* right," she muttered with a smirk, adjusting her smart-girl glasses. "Perhaps he won't be so quick to dismiss someone based on their appearance next time. This may be my first big assignment, but I'm not fresh out of a high school coding class."

"I think it was more surprise. He's not used to someone being able to keep up with him. He asked about you when we talked."

Melanie's hands paused for a split second over the disassembled laptop. She gave a noncommittal hum that made him smile before returning to her work.

Maybe he could persuade Dade to visit Lytua and arrange for a casual run-in. The two of them might hit it off. Riddick shook his head at himself and a chuckle escaped his lips. He was as bad as his mother and her friends at the senior living facility.

Riddick made a mental note to email his mother. The kidnapping might have made international news, and he wanted to tell her about it before she saw it in the press. Now, he couldn't remember where she was in her whirlwind around-the-world cruise.

A woman he knew from a West Coast firm sidled up to him at the conference's opening reception, surprising him with a hug that felt a little too intimate, lingered a touch too long. She'd been waiting for him, she purred, pressing her voluptuous body against his. She'd made it clear at last year's conference that she was interested in being more than professional acquaintances. Riddick belatedly recalled the email she'd sent a few weeks ago, saying how much she was looking forward to seeing him again in the desert. He'd been distracted by getting ready for a date with Khara and hadn't responded.

The flowery perfume his fellow architect doused herself in was overwhelming. She remained plastered to his side, batting fan-like eyelashes and pressing her breasts into his arm. "Hi, Jeannie."

He subtly tried to extricate himself from her grip, but she didn't take the hint.

"Hoping you'll find me sooner rather than later to do that thing with your tongue you mentioned last time."

Riddick sputtered his Old Fashioned, his cheeks growing hot. *Aw, hell.* "Jeannie—"

"My room has a spectacular view of Old Town."

Riddick cleared his throat. "I won't be doing that."

"Oh, maybe the *other* thing you mentioned?"

Jesus Christ, he'd never thought of himself as a manwhore, but Riddick gave the title serious consideration now. They'd engaged in some serious flirtation at past conferences, but he'd never intended for it to go this far. What had once seemed playful and alluring was now coming across as brazen and inappropriate.

"I have a girlfriend now, Jeannie."

"Oh?" Her pretty face fell. "Oh. Of course, you do. Yay for her, but sucks for me."

"I would have totally gone for it if I didn't, though." Riddick wasn't sure that was true, but he was willing to give her a graceful exit.

"You're sweet, trying to make me feel better. Well, I knew it was a lot to hope for that you'd be single forever." As quickly as she'd turned it on, she straightened, dropping the sultry act.

Single. Huh. Was that what he'd been? He would have described it as... incomplete.

"Can't blame a girl for trying. No hard feelings." Jeannie raised her wineglass in salute. "To her good health, then. May she be enthusiastic and giving."

Riddick frowned at her retreating back.

Eric Sloane, his longtime business partner, approached from the bar, shoulders shaking with laughter.

"You could have saved me from that anytime, you know."

"Oh, I know, but that was far too entertaining to cut short. I should've filmed it."

Riddick shot him a glare, then sighed and drained half his drink. "She was... sort of obvious, wasn't she? No subtlety at all."

"She's no Khara, that's for sure. Hope you know you hit the jackpot with that woman." Eric slapped him on the shoulder. "C'mon. Let's grab a seat."

Back home in Virginia after the conference, Riddick donned his second tuxedo with care for Khara's event. He handed off his Audi to the Ritz-Carlton's valet upon his arrival.

When Khara came sashaying into the living area of the suite, resplendent in a cerulean, floor-length gown that managed to hug her curves and exude an air of regal modesty, Riddick had to unglue his tongue from the roof of his mouth.

Once again, as he had on the night of the kidnapping, he found himself utterly captivated by her beauty. This was his first time seeing her dressed in formal vestments of office. The swoops and whorls in the Kitenge skirt reminded him of peacock feathers.

She was luminous. Like a fairy-tale princess.

Jaden trailed her, the two bickering like siblings as they went over the evening's safety protocols. Security had been tightened considerably since the kidnapping, and Riddick listened attentively to Khara's instructions, committing them to memory. The men greeted each other with chin lifts when Jaden finished.

Khara lit up with joy when Riddick presented her with a replacement corsage. His knuckles brushed the sensitive skin at the curve of her breast as he fastened it with the magnet. His florist was adamant that no formal wear be harmed with her otherworldly creations. "Joanne helped me with the color. Is there anything she can't do?"

"Not much that I've seen. This is lovely. Thank you."

Riddick couldn't help but tease her a little. "What, no crown?"

Her eyes were sparkling, but nerves tinged the edges of her smile. "Yes, actually, but not until we leave. It's heavy."

"The head that wears the crown?" he quipped.

"No, the actual crown, Mr. Smartypants."

Riddick shook his head in disbelief, a smile still tugging at his lips. "Surreal."

"What?"

"Trying to get my head around the fact that my girlfriend is a Queen. You're ravishing."

"My stylist Maxine's go-to is jewel tones." Her smile widened with the pretty blush that warmed her cheeks, then faltered. "And you're sure you're alright with not sitting together?"

"Yes, really." Riddick didn't care one bit about potential media coverage, but since it worried her, he was willing to jump through a few hoops. "There probably won't be much time for actual talking, anyway."

"I'll understand if you get bored and wish to leave."

"With you looking this delicious? I'm not going anywhere."

Khara sat when Joanne came in, carrying a black case. Riddick stepped back to observe. Khara closed her eyes, still and serene as her assistant fitted the crown onto her head. It was a show-stopping piece of jewelry, he had to admit.

When she opened her eyes and stood, a subtle transformation had occurred. The Khara he knew was still there, but a new facet of her personality had emerged. The slight nervousness she'd exhibited earlier disappeared when she stepped into her role as Queen.

If he hadn't seen it happen, Riddick might not have believed it possible.

Even her voice sounded with an almost imperceptible shift when she asked, "Shall we?"

The last time Riddick had been to the White House, it hadn't been for anything near this fancy. This level of political theater was an entirely new experience for Riddick. Seeing Khara in this new light—he was having a challenging time reconciling what he knew of her—passionate, sweet, and hot—to the poised, controlled, and no-nonsense.

Lillianna was all confidence and polish.

In the limo, Khara explained the no-touching rule and that he would have to keep his hands to himself for the duration of the event. When he leaned close and promised he'd just have to put his hands on her afterward, he relished her telltale blush.

President Thomas and her wife welcomed Khara with formal Lytuan greetings when she alighted at the foot of the Grand Staircase. Riddick, after a brief detour around the block, disembarked from the limo and was escorted to the State Dining Room by a military social aide.

He caught sight of Khara as he made his way to his assigned seat near the head table. The luxury on display almost had Riddick gawping like a yokel. The architectural nerd in him wanted to examine the detail on the fireplace beneath the famous portrait of Lincoln. With those dramatic centerpieces and candlelight glinting on the crystal at the place settings, the room was striking in its decadence.

He was amazed at just how charming Khara was. It was a masterclass in diplomacy.

Watching her and the world she moved in was a fascinating experience. The receiving line moved at a brisk pace, with several of the Elite Guard stationed strategically throughout the room. From his seat, Riddick watched Khara flash that megawatt smile of hers and posing for pictures. She exuded warmth and friendliness, even as she refrained from touching anyone. The guests must have been briefed, for no one even attempted to touch her.

He'd thought people might be curious about his presence, but he wasn't out of place. It was like any other upscale social event in the city, filled with polite small talk and superficial conversations. While not his favorite activity, he managed to make pleasant conversation with his table companions. Plus, he had a view to the prettiest woman in the room, even if no one knew they were together.

This had to be one of the most secure rooms on the planet, yet a nagging sense of unease lingered. Khara's kidnapping had taken place a mere week ago. What was to stop the missing third person from trying again?

Chapter Sixteen

J UST WHEN SHE THOUGHT she'd finished, Khara spotted the Speaker of the House heading her way with a tall, good-looking man in tow. So, this must be the eligible bachelor son she kept talking up. Supposing it was only a matter of time, Khara summoned a welcoming smile. They'd waited to be the last in the receiving line to get more face time with her. Clever. *Well played, but not today.* Perhaps she could nip this in the bud for good.

The Speaker gushed her relief at seeing Khara safe after her harrowing experience.

"Thank you, Speaker Crosby. How lovely to see you." *Liar.* It was anything but lovely to see her. In an egregious lapse of protocol, the Speaker neglected the formal greeting.

The Speaker waved it away with, "We're such good friends we don't need that stuffy, formal greeting, now do we?"

Without waiting for an answer, the Speaker thrust her son forward and introduced him. "He doesn't need it either, right? Wonderful!"

It was, in fact, a terrible insult, but Khara kept her hands folded in front of her as they made forced small talk.

He was handsome. She'd give him that. He was nattering on about asset allocation. Rufus Crosby was the essence of photogenic, with those dimples and big, piano key-like teeth gleaming so white they all but seared her corneas. But he was giving off sleazy vibes, especially with the way his shrewd, calculating gaze raked over her body. The nerve.

She knew his kind—far too accustomed to women falling all over themselves for his attention. He'd be more interested in himself than anything she'd have to say. Her role would be a silent one and he'd expect her to behave like a mindless trophy, sheer decoration. He'd never accept her having the spotlight. His ego was too fragile. Which was incongruous with his mother being such a powerful woman. How had that happened? He leaned in to put his lips next to her ear to say something, but Jaden was faster.

The Speaker's son gave a high-pitched yelp when Jaden squeezed his arm just above the elbow. "Stand back from the Queen, please, sir, or you'll be escorted out."

Rufus retreated out of Khara's space, anger flaring in his eyes. Jaden let him go, but stayed close. "I was just going to tell her how exquisite she looked." His voice was petulant, grating on Khara's nerves.

"That's exactly what her date said earlier. Kindly move along."

Khara laugh-coughed into her fist at Jaden's barb. Rufus grabbed at the tattered remains of his dignity, said he'd see her soon, and slunk off. *Irritating little twerp.* The whole encounter left a sour taste in Khara's mouth, although she was far too disciplined to let it show.

The Elites had been uneasy preparing for this event, and she didn't underestimate their concern. Rufus Crosby couldn't have chosen a worse time to try to cozy up to her.

As a few dignitaries were within earshot, Khara switched from English to Lytuan and said, "*Well, then, time for the festivities to begin.*"

Jaden gave a low chuckle. "*Cenn says he's seated next to you.*"

"*How wonderful.*"

"*He thinks so. Try not to hurt him too bad.*"

"*I can't make any promises. Feel free to tranq him if he gets too close again.*"

The Speaker must have pulled some strings to make that seating arrangement happen. That woman was relentless. Khara could imagine the scandalized expression on her face if she climbed into Riddick's lap and kissed him right there in front of everyone. Hell, even that might not be enough to halt her efforts. She'd probably tell Rufus to share her if it meant getting a piece of the Lytuan throne. Khara already explained that if she married while in office, her husband would be Consort, never King, even if she predeceased him.

Riddick caught her eye as she approached the head table. When *he* looked her up and down, it was like he caressed her with his gaze, not sizing her up as a potential ally. He was yummy in that tux, somehow even better than the last time. He looked so hot she'd wanted to blow this whole thing off so they could make out. Blow off a State Dinner. Khara almost giggled. Only her training kept her features still.

Her phone vibrated.

Riddick: What was that about?

Khara: Determined matchmakers. Again.

The corner of his mouth quirked up in that saucy grin she so enjoyed.

Riddick: He probably just wants to see that pretty blush on your face.

His flirting prompted a chuckle from her, along with a playful urge.

Khara: But I only blush for you.

When their gazes met this time, the heat in his promised he'd most definitely have her blushing later. She couldn't wait.

Chapter Seventeen

O*H, HELL.* N*OW* *ALL* Riddick could think about was how many ways he could make Khara blush for him. Thank goodness he could hide his hard-on under the table.

Khara's body language changed as she finished the receiving line, alerting Riddick that something was amiss. He wasn't the only one to notice. He tensed when Jaden stepped forward to hurry a man and a woman—the Speaker of the House, if he wasn't mistaken—on. The Elites were attuned to Khara. They read the slightest change in her posture. Then again, they'd been a close team for almost seven years. And they were still overprotective after the kidnapping.

When President Thomas introduced Khara, she spoke of how dedicated Lytua was to advancing medical research and how much she was looking forward to their research partnership the following year. The two women hugged before Khara took the podium. She delivered a brief speech and was a brilliant public speaker, even in her second language of English.

Riddick considered himself a hard man to impress, but she wore her authority so lightly.

He spent most of the dinner fending off the surprisingly direct propositions of the woman seated on his side. What she'd written on the note she passed him during the soup course was enough to make *him* blush. What she'd suggested would require a great deal of stretching beforehand, some electrolytes, and a contract negotiation. Riddick gave her what he hoped was a polite but discouraging smile. She was older, and still a looker with a bangin' body. And unaccustomed to getting the brushoff. Riddick got the feeling she would eat him alive. Another time, another place, he might have been all about it.

Riddick would have to watch his six when he visited the men's room. She seemed like just the type to follow him in and start trouble.

He unlocked his phone when it buzzed with an alert.

Khara: I think your lady-friend is already planning what to make you for breakfast.

Riddick found the would-be seductress watching him with interest. She winked and showed him she'd tied a cherry stem into a knot with her tongue. *Uh-oh*. He turned his attention back to Khara, who was engaged in a deep discussion with the First Lady.

On her other side, the man Jaden had hurried along in the receiving line was eyeing Khara like he was trying to figure her out. His gaze roved over her body when she wasn't looking. He caught Riddick's eye and gave a little shrug and smirk at being busted, as if to say—what are ya gonna do?

I'll fucking kill you if you even try, Riddick thought amiably and gave the man a mirthless smile that told him so. Maybe the man would stop ogling his girlfriend. The Queen. His girlfriend was the Queen. Still surreal. He wanted to bury his nose in the soft skin of her neck and inhale her.

Not normally given to jealousy, he did envy those around her, getting to bask in her attention.

Chatting with the others at his table passed the time, but his gaze stayed on Khara. An older gentleman noticed and warned him he wasn't being as discreet as he should be.

"You should ask her to dance. She is lovely."

She was, but Riddick wasn't sure his acting skills were good enough to pull off pretending to newly make her acquaintance. Not when he knew how delicious she tasted.

With a secret smile, Riddick knocked back the rest of his drink and signaled for another. He intended to have his girl screaming in pleasure before the night was over.

Chapter Eighteen

WITH ASSISTANCE FROM THE Elites, Riddick slipped out at the end of the dinner a little ahead of Khara so that he could wait for her in the limo. Delight lit up her face when she caught sight of him as she climbed into the back seat. The door barely closed behind her before Khara grabbed Riddick by the lapels and pulled him into a long kiss. Just when it was getting good and steamy, she pulled back and smoothed his shirt and jacket. "My apologies."

"For what?" Riddick asked, nuzzling her ear, sending shivers through her.

"I'm wrinkling your tuxedo, in addition to treating you like a piece of meat."

"No complaints here. I found it extremely hard to not touch you at all tonight. I've gotten used to feeling how soft your skin is anytime I want."

"Will this be a problem?"

"No, that's not what I meant. I meant every time I looked at you, I wanted to touch you, and I don't mean politely. It gave me a chance to... marinate." He slid his palm up her ankle and calf, beneath the full skirt of her gown. "This blue is gorgeous on you. I couldn't take my eyes off you all night. If I get started touching you in this car, I don't know if I'll be able to stop until you come. I do like the mental picture of me giving you a toe-curling orgasm while fully dressed, though. Could you be quiet if you needed to be?" The smile he flashed her was mischievous.

Khara gulped and pushed herself into a sitting position, her face flushed. She pointed to the far side of the back seat. "Go sit over there before you make me forget myself entirely."

Instead of moving away, Riddick chuckled and moved in closer. "I want to watch you come again. I want you to ride my fingers again, Khara. Better yet, my face and tongue."

She let her eyes drift closed, perhaps to imagine that.

He pushed her knees apart and nestled himself between them. He took one of her ankles and draped it over his shoulder, sending her dress tumbling back to her hips. It gave him a clear view of heaven. "All this glorious skin. So soft. So kissable." He skimmed the pads of his fingers up the outside of her thighs. "There's that blush. *My* blush."

"We can't," she gasped, but he was already placing open-mouthed kisses over the tender spots on the inside of her ankle, calf, and knee. She fought not to moan.

"We can. We will." Her skin was hot and satiny soft beneath his hands as he glided them up her thighs and hips. "*You* will, anyway. And I get to watch." He didn't take his gaze from hers as he teased her swollen clit through her lacy blue panties. They were soaked.

The way she sighed his name and bit her lip made his hard dick throb.

"Hmm. You're all wet for me again, aren't you?" With careful precision, he stretched the tiny thong's crotch down a little so he could move it to expose her treasure to him. He wanted to rip the scrap of lace off and plunge his cock inside her more than he wanted his next breath. He wanted to take her hard, fast, still dressed. With her legs thrown up on his shoulders or bent over the seat with her dress rucked up to her waist. There was so much pent-up lust churning inside he wanted to expend. He wanted to expend it on her and he wanted her moaning his name while he did it. He'd wanted it all night. Hell, it felt like he'd wanted it his whole damn life.

Steady, Riddick reminded himself. He wasn't going to fuck Khara in the back seat of a limo like they were a couple of low-rent college students. No matter how tempting.

Riddick took a good, long look at the masterpiece that lay beneath him. Khara's pretty, perfect pussy was open and wet for him again, for fuck's sake. How readily she creamed for him. The alluring sight made him want to dive in, to lick and suck and get his fill of her sweetness—if that was even possible. He pushed her legs wider and leaned in, overjoyed to get his mouth on her at last. No doubt he was going to be addicted to her.

"Oh, God, I'm not ready for that."

Riddick's mouth watered for the taste of her. He felt the tiniest sliver of frustration that he wouldn't get to.

"Your mouth will be too much for me, I know it."

He flashed her a wolfish smile and continued to stroke her heated flesh. But she was breathing too fast. She'd tensed a little, and her pulse hammered in her throat. He never wanted her in doubt. "Just my hand, then, this time, beautiful Khara."

And he got to work.

He brought her that toe-curling orgasm with her gown pooled at her hips. Not a hair out of place, just her juices in his hand. "I told you last week I was going to touch you like this, didn't I? Everything still on, remember?"

"*Yes, yes,*" she gasped in Lytuan.

Tracing his other thumb over the inside of her knee, Riddick let out a soft groan. "I love how responsive you are. I stroked my cock and thought of you last night, Khara. Thought about how I wanted to bend you over in that red dress so I could watch this sweet pussy swallow my cock. I said your name when I came."

She tightened around his churning fingers with a quiet whimper. "Oh, God, *Riddick—*"

"That's it," he coaxed, staying with her as she writhed. "Don't try to hold it back, Khara. You can't. You're going to come for me right here."

It didn't take long for her to come. She was primed and started to shudder and clench around him, her breathing ragged. She might not have been ready for oral, but she sure as hell was turned on. A muffled yelp escaped her as she went over the edge; she bit her hand to stifle it.

Riddick closed his eyes to savor the sound of her accelerated breathing in the car's quiet interior and tried to will his now-painful erection away.

She wasn't ready, he reminded himself sternly. He needed to remember that and stop pushing her. This was not the time, with them both so turned on their judgment was straying into questionable-at-best territory.

Riddick straightened the skirt of her dress and settled back to enjoy the ride, planning on touching her at least once more before they arrived. He wanted to demonstrate that her pleasure would never be perfunctory. They had a good half-hour car ride back to the hotel ahead of them.

His eyes flew open when she unzipped him and slid her hand inside his pants to rub over the hard ridge of his erection. *Shit*. He grabbed for her, but she wasn't having it. She pushed his hand away and pulled his cock out into the open and stroked. She smiled at the sight of him, causing him to twitch in her hand. Riddick could only watch fascinated as she reached beneath her dress. He thought it was to touch herself, which would have been hot as hell, but she did something even hotter. Khara gathered some of her own wetness to lubricate his cock as she stroked him. Oh, *hell*. This woman.

Khara slid onto the limo floor between his legs, all honeyed skin and puddled, satiny material.

Riddick noticed everything—how her dark nail polish matched her lipstick. Seeing that splash of color next to his skin did something to him. How her other hand felt squeezing the inside of his thigh. He tugged her hair in a panic when she made to suck him into her mouth. He couldn't take that. Not tonight. He almost lost it when she licked her coral-painted lips and looked up at him through her lashes. With a multi-million-dollar crown sparkling on her head. Jesus.

"You're coming for me tonight, Riddick. Just like when you touched me the first time. There's no stopping it."

He watched her, enthralled. Her grasp on his cock was everything he'd imagined. Confident. Perfect. She brought him up so quickly it might have been embarrassing if she hadn't done it on purpose. "Shit. Sweetheart, I'm about to—" He managed to grab a handful of napkins from the wet bar and get the head of his cock covered just as he exploded, his hips jerking. It was a struggle to stay quiet.

He lay there on the seat, panting after he cleaned up and tucked himself away. She'd turned the tables on him right proper. Her mouth would have done him in. She looked a little pleased with herself as she took the seat next to him and re-arranged the gown's skirt around her. As well she should.

A slow smile curved her full, sensuous lips. "I still control the timing?"

"For our first time, yes. That hasn't changed. After that, all bets are off. I'm going to be seducing the hell out of you at every turn. Fair warning." He cupped her face and brushed her lips with his. "When we have each other, it's going to be an event. You know that, right?"

Khara smoothed trembling hands over her thighs before meeting his gaze. "I have no doubt."

Everything in his entire being pulsed, and Riddick wondered at it.

Chapter Nineteen

I N A STROKE OF serendipity, a lurid sex scandal involving two of the Supreme Court Justices broke out. The media nearly stampeded in their haste to decamp from the hotel to cover the story 24/7. Khara ventured out twice to test the waters, but no one bothered her. Either the obvious security personnel deterred them or they had all moved on.

The Elites remained on heightened alert and had stepped up her already rigorous sparring and self-defense practice. Khara refused to let the kidnapping dictate everything and carried on as though it wasn't paramount in everyone's minds.

Istanbul proved more eventful than anticipated, but the press coverage had been minimal.

Only after meticulous planning did she and Riddick attempt their first public outing together. It was a simple, low-risk trial run, but her knees were all but knocking when she and Riddick were walking along the riverfront in the Navy Yard after dinner.

The Elites were stationed around them, closer than usual. Their proximity felt like an invasion of her privacy. But it was the only way Jaden and Cenn would allow it. Everyone was still a little on edge.

Keeping her voice low so that her protectors wouldn't overhear, Khara told Riddick she had an idea and invited him to her home to celebrate New Year's. "This is our big holiday. Think of it as the Lytuan equivalent of Thanksgiving. You shared yours with me, and I'd like to share mine with you."

"You didn't have to do that. I know you had other plans."

Khara slipped her hand into his and wondered if she'd miscalculated. "What good is having a boyfriend if you can't do the good stuff with them? I'll make the dishes and we'll do all the things. Then we can celebrate your birthday the next day."

"I'd love to," Riddick gave her a hearty kiss and thanked her. "Plus, a Caribbean island during a DC winter? Not a hard sell."

Khara blew out a shallow sigh of relief, a tentative smile twisting her lips.

He brushed a knuckle over her cheek. "You keep sounding surprised that I want to do things with you."

"Oh, I...." She didn't know how to finish that sentence. She cleared her throat. "I want to be careful and not oversell it. I'll be off island for a few days right before the holiday, so you'll have a chance to play tourist without me. There's a guest room, plenty of space. It will be very different than here, but you can see my home and...."

"See if I can handle the fishbowl?"

"Yes. It's a lot to ask anyone."

"You're worth it, you know."

She took a breath, her eyes going wide. Her hand went to her chest, trying to soothe the sudden tightness there upon hearing such miraculous words. "I don't know how to do this."

"Be adored? You don't have to do anything. Keep being your wonderful self."

Khara melted into his kiss.

While they were sitting together on a bench along the river walk, Riddick asked a burning question he'd had since learning the truth of her identity: what had gone down with the fiancé? He was seeing him leaving her during the chemo in a new light.

Khara explained that the engagement hadn't been public knowledge yet and got pushed aside when she received the cancer diagnosis. They'd met at university.

"There's no kind way to ask this, so I'll just spit it out. Why were you going to marry this yahoo?"

She was quiet for a long moment, gazing upwards at the night sky. "Two years into my service, we reconnected and started dating. I seem to remember him being a lot more interesting at university, to be perfectly honest. But he was steady and dependable. He proposed. I accepted."

It was adorable that she referred to being a Queen as her service. It said a lot about what she believed her role to be.

"Well, he was getting the better end of that bargain for sure. Yet he cut and ran at the first sign of trouble, the dick." Riddick still found it hard to believe. "You deserve so much more than 'steady and dependable', Khara." He cupped her cheek so he could look her in the eye. "You deserve the world."

Khara covered his hand with her own. "Thank y—"

They both glanced up at the nearby sounds of a scuffle. In a blink, three of the Elites had swarmed the bench, weapons drawn.

"Get off me! I'm a member of the press!" A woman's raised and indignant voice sounded. "Dammit, you broke my camera!"

"I'll break more than that if you don't stop squirming." Cenn had a disgruntled journalist face down on the pavement with a knee in the small of her back. "Found her lurking. Do you have any weapons on you?"

"No, I don't! You didn't have to tackle me. Jesus."

Khara stood, already wearing Lillianna's coolness. "Let her up, please."

The woman bitched about a potential lawsuit as Cenn pulled her to her feet. One of the other Elites gathered up the broken camera equipment that had scattered. The journalist snatched it and tutted over the pieces.

"My apologies." Khara gestured to the seat next to Riddick. "Please, won't you sit? We should chat."

The journalist's suspicious gaze darted between them. Satisfied that it wasn't a trick, she perched herself on the bench's edge and crossed her arms in defiance.

Press credentials in her wallet verified her identity. Weapons holstered, the Elites faded back. Now this was a bit of theater Riddick wouldn't have missed for the world.

Still standing, Khara studied the other woman. "Why are you not covering the sex scandal like the others?"

"I figured you'd be relieved to have them move off and let your guard down, eventually."

"That's smart thinking. What is it you want?"

The woman straightened her shoulders and lifted her chin. "An exclusive."

Ballsy.

Riddick's respect for Khara deepened as she negotiated an arrangement with the journalist. To her credit, the journalist wasn't a pushover. She balked at Khara's condition that she published nothing until after she left the area.

"I leave in two days. I will give you enough that it will be worth your time and earn you professional accolades."

The journalist forfeited the deal if she reported on anything that took place before the official interview.

"Think it over. Call my assistant when you've decided. We'll replace your camera either way, of course. That was an accident. We've all been on edge."

"That's a very clever way of shielding him."

Khara smiled at the accusation. "As much as I can for as long as I can."

Riddick stared at her in awe once the journalist departed, clutching Joanne's card in her fist. "I see what you did there. Clever, indeed."

"There was bound to be an ambush sometime. If she's smart, she'll leverage this opportunity. Now, where were we?"

When it was time to say farewell, they lingered in Khara's suite, kissing and laughing and talking.

"Here's a thought," Riddick said. "What if after New Year's we avoid the fishbowl altogether and go someplace different, where we can just hang out? Is that possible?"

"That is a splendid idea. I have a couple of things at home to see to post-holiday, but I'd planned to take some time off after."

"Can you think of someplace Lytua-like where we can play out of the spotlight?"

They settled on Nevis.

Riddick sent Khara home with lips swollen by goodbye kisses, with a promise to see her at the new year.

Khara had preexisting plans to spend Christmas with Yvanda and her newly expanded family in France. Riddick had already promised Dion he would be around for the winter school break and didn't want to break his word again.

Dion was confused when Riddick told him he bought tickets for a Christmas Eve Commanders game.

"You didn't want to spend Christmas with Khara?"

"She invited me, but you and I already had plans."

"And she was okay with that?"

"Why wouldn't she be?"

His pronouncement to Dion that Khara was a Queen had been met with disbelief. Dion was positive Riddick was paying him back for the Nigerian prince prank he'd played on him. The kid refused to believe until he spoke to Khara directly. Then he was agog and full of questions. Khara didn't seem to mind and had answered every one of his rapid-fire inquiries and invited him to visit.

Riddick and Dion had healed much of the rift in their relationship. It wasn't starting back at zero, but they'd lost some ground. Riddick was determined to gain it back.

Chapter Twenty

Christmas in Paris.

Was there anything more beautiful?

Khara was thrilled to holiday with Yvanda, Jamal, and meet her godson, Gabriel. Their connection was instant, a mutual adoration that warmed her soul. Khara loved seeing her best friend with her sweetheart of a husband in the home they'd created together. They'd blossomed even further in love with their little cherub's arrival.

The Cadieuxs surprised her by meeting her at DeGaulle. A cry of pure delight escaped Khara as she sprinted into her friend's arms. She and Yvanda had been besties since grade eight. They'd last seen each other six months prior during a girls' weekend after Khara's well-attended guest lecture at Assas Université.

As usual, they embarked on a culinary adventure through the city, hitting up new-to-them hot spots as well as old haunts. At Café Pavane, Yvanda's favorite tea salon for hot chocolate, they caught up while they savored steaming cups of rich flavor. The seasonal pastries at Butterfly Pâtisserie were otherworldly, including the decadent bûche de Noël that was worth the trip alone. Khara shipped some to Eric for his daughter and pregnant wife.

Yvanda and Khara spent a day meandering through the Christmas market at Tuileries Gardens, gorging themselves on artisanal treats, and watching glassblowers and woodworkers create their masterpieces. Yvanda caught her daydreaming as they explored and broke into her fanciful thoughts. "You're a million miles away."

"Oh. I was just wondering if this was something Riddick would enjoy."

"One way to find out."

As evening fell, the pair wandered along the Champs-Élysées, admiring the dazzling window displays of the shops. The live music and fireworks were a perfect finish before heading home.

After Yvanda nursed the baby and handed him to Jamal, the two friends settled in front of a roaring fire in their pajamas, cradling hefty mugs of spiked hot chocolate. Khara swirled her candy cane spoon through the froth and sipped. She and Riddick had spoken earlier in the evening before he and Dion headed out to the stadium for tailgating fun ahead of the football game. Judging by Dion's beaming grin in the selfies, they were having a grand time sporting silly reindeer antlers and flashing red noses.

Yvanda pressed her about how the physical momentum had stalled.

"Okay, seriously, Khara, spill it. What is happening?"

"I can't get out of my own way! The only reason I wasn't ready before was because he didn't know the truth of my identity. He does now and there's nothing in the way."

"But you're still not ready."

"If I can't say yes without hesitation, I'm not. He's okay with that. He didn't sound upset, just matter of fact."

"That's because he respects you, *chérie*. Now tell me about these new plans for New Year's."

Yvanda was flabbergasted when Khara explained.

"Khara, what are you thinking? You're going to leave him alone in your apartment? What if he finds your goodie drawer? Aren't you nervous?"

"It's not that big a deal."

"It is." Yvanda was undeterred. "You never even left your fiancé in your apartment alone. In fact, if I remember right, you never even had him *in* your apartment."

"What are you talking about? Of course, I... well."

"Exactly. It was important that you have your own space."

"It still is."

A comfortable silence settled between them as they savored another sip of their rich, chocolatey concoction. The fire crackled softly in the background.

"He's not Gary. I don't have enough cuss words to describe what a shit Gary was. Friend to friend, woman to woman here, Khara. Why are you really hesitating?"

Khara thought of Riddick's outrage upon learning Gary had left her in the middle of her cancer battle. Then she recalled the intensity of Riddick's passionate kisses that left her aching for more.

"Khara, what's the hesitation?"

"I'm afraid he'll be disappointed," she admitted. "I don't want to get hurt like that again."

"Let me amend. Gary doesn't deserve to be the litmus test. Anyone who makes a *slide presentation* for their fiancée on ways she can improve her sexual technique is a bastard. A controlling, unsupportive bastard who booked when you needed him most. Fuck him."

Khara still remembered the pangs of humiliation she'd felt sitting there in the darkened living room with Gary pointing out all her sexual shortcomings. At the time, she wondered why the hell he hadn't just talked to her. Instead of putting the effort into making a slide show, he could have handled it a different way. He'd done it to make her feel small. It had worked.

The worst part was that this lecture took place after she started her treatment for breast cancer. Her beloved kinky coils of hair had already fallen out. While she was depressed and overwhelmed and insecure, her fiancé had ambushed her with a multi-point guide on how her fellatio needed work. Khara distinctly remembered seeing the word "fellatio" on a slide in big, red letters.

Yes, that had been just the thing to help with her stress. The prick.

He was the only lover who'd ever complained, but those feelings of inadequacy remained. As much as she wanted Riddick, Khara couldn't bear the rejection of him thinking she was a shitty lover. She was so self-conscious after Gary's betrayal. She'd had enjoyable sex since Gary. Why was this getting in the way with someone she really liked?

She and Gary had had a very public, very formal courtship. She thought it was sweet then. It seemed silly now when she looked back on it. There had been no spark, no passion with her ex. He'd been *acceptable*, which appeared to be the pinnacle of what she could expect at this stage in her life and in the public eye. Why had they even decided to get married in the first place? She would have been bored out of her mind in no time. Their breakup gutted her, but she suspected that had more to do with the timing.

"You could just tell him, you know. Tell Riddick. Then he'd know what he's dealing with."

"It's not his problem. It's my issue."

"Don't you think he'd want to know so he could adjust? He's not going to want to trigger you."

Considering, Khara dunked a decorated snickerdoodle into her drink. "It's so humiliating. Mortifying."

"You have to be honest with him. *Chérie*, don't protect yourself so much that you push an opportunity for joy away."

"I think...," Khara choked back a sob, an odd thrill fluttering through her belly. "I think I'm falling in love with him."

Yvanda patted her hand, wearing a brilliant grin. "Oh, *chérie*, that ship sailed so long ago it's docked again."

By the time she climbed into bed, Khara questioned what she thought she felt. Or didn't feel.

Chapter Twenty-One

T HREE WEEKS.

His bag sat packed well ahead of time, and Riddick was impatient to get to Lytua.

Holiday season obligations kept him busy, but he looked forward to experiencing Lytua and Khara in her natural environment. Two weeks off to soak up the sun, sand, and alone time with his woman? Riddick felt relaxed every time he thought about his upcoming trip.

Fortunately, nothing major had gone wrong in the two days Riddick was dealing with the kidnapping and aftermath. Lena hadn't batted an eye when Riddick gave her a heads-up about who Khara was and that the press may get involved. She'd simply arched an eyebrow, cocked her head, and pinned him with that no-nonsense look.

"Well, you don't hear that every day," she'd declared, then moved on with her work. Typical Lena—taking anything he threw at her in stride.

Official photos from the State Dinner had appeared in the regular news outlets, but he wasn't in more than a couple of wide shots of the room. The journalist held up her end of the bargain.

A pair of Lytuan Guards combed over Riddick's home, office suite, and car to assess for any security concerns. No one knew what the third person in the kidnapping scheme planned, so all hands remained on deck. After a serious discussion, Jaden decided Brixton Calhoun and Quincy Stanford would remain assigned to Riddick for the short term. If nothing suspicious happened in the meantime, they'd reassess once he got back.

Riddick returned to his regularly scheduled, early morning gym time with Eric. They met three times per week to push each other's fitness performance and chew over office matters.

They'd just started cooling down when Riddick asked if Eric had a minute for something serious.

"You finally asking Khara to marry you?"

The resistance band Riddick had been using to stretch his quads snapped from his grasp, shot across the alcove, and bounced off the mirror. "What the hell, man? No." He went to retrieve the band, his entire face burning. "And what do you mean 'finally'? We've only been dating a few months!"

Eric shrugged one giant shoulder and toweled sweat from his bald head. "Just calling it like I see it. You'd be a damn fool to let that woman get away from you."

The jackass had the nerve to smirk. "Well, I did want to talk to you about Khara, but it's not that."

"You're moving in together?"

This time, Riddick gave his business partner a side-eye that bordered on a death stare. "Jesus. Knock it off."

"Encouraging you to consider your future with a fantastic woman in it? You might want to get on that."

Riddick closed his eyes. Khara *was* fantastic, but he was nowhere near ready to think about setting up house together or... getting married. He swallowed hard. Jesus.

Now Eric was humming "Single Ladies" and recreating the iconic dance moves from the video. "You won't be the only one to recognize that treasure. Seriously, friend, start thinking ahead before it's too late. For real."

"Okay, okay, enough of that. I don't know how Maya puts up with your meddling ass shenanigans."

With a final enthusiastic hip twerk, Eric wiggled his eyebrows. "I do have many admirable qualities. What's up? What do you have to tell me about Khara?" Serious now, Eric gave Riddick his full attention.

Scrubbing at the back of his neck, Riddick huffed out a breath. "Ah, you might want to sit down."

When Eric merely gave him a huge smile after he told him the truth about who Khara was, Riddick's brow furrowed. "Did you hear me? An honest-to-God Queen, Eric. I'm serious."

"I heard you. We already knew."

"You— How the hell did you already know? How long have you known?"

Eric recounted how Maya had discovered Khara's secret: she'd recognized Khara as Queen Lillianna from a morning news show appearance months earlier.

"Jesus, am I the only one who didn't know?" Riddick groused.

"Oh, no, my friend, no. You don't get to bitch. Maya thinks it's the most romantic thing in the world. Anything I do is going to get compared to this forever, so thanks for that."

Riddick slapped him on the shoulder. "You'll just have to up your game, man."

"This is a big change from single, smoldering Riddick who had women throwing their panties at him."

"That was *one* time."

But Eric was too busy guffawing.

Chapter Twenty-Two

The Riddick & Sloane holiday party was always an elaborate to-do and one of Riddick's favorite things. While he and Eric made sure their employees felt appreciated year-round, they reserved the last few weeks of the year for extended festivities.

He always delighted in making merry with everyone's families, but this year, he was feeling a little off-kilter, wishing Khara was with him. Riddick didn't bring dates to the company holiday party; Khara would have been the first. Maybe she could attend next year? No doubt she'd charm the hell out of everyone. Then maybe he could get her alone in his office under some mistletoe. An unfamiliar hopeful feeling sparked at the thought.

Long-term relationship planning wasn't something Riddick did.

Eric's marriage talk must be getting to him.

Despite missing Khara, Riddick celebrated enthusiastically with R&S families, friends, and associates. It was a particular delight to catch up with Lena's wife and son. The kid was growing like a weed and slaying the high school drama scene. Riddick took the ribbing about his uncharacteristic behavior in stride. According to the staff, he'd been more jovial than usual and out of the office more often.

Riddick let out a good-natured laugh when a junior architect ventured, "We thought you might have gotten a girlfriend or something!"

The knot of people standing nearby nodded their emphatic agreement.

"Actually, I did, but she's been on travel."

He joined in when they toasted his new lady and expressed the hope that she would join them next year.

Riddick was puzzled by how acutely he felt Khara's absence until it dawned on him that they hadn't been apart more than a few days since meeting. They'd grown accustomed to spending time together and he missed that. Missed *her*. The sensation was unexpected—not unpleasant, just... baffling.

He'd only ever heard how challenging, lonely, and unfulfilling long-distance relationships could be. That wasn't his experience at all. Sometimes their daily conversations were short, five-minute affairs. Other times, they talked for hours over text or video chat.

The whole situation was going smoother than expected. It felt so natural, Riddick wondered what that meant on occasion. Then he reminded himself to enjoy the here and now and quit catastrophizing.

Chapter Twenty-Three

A CAR MET HIM at the airport; Khara waited inside, out of view behind tinted windows. He kissed her with enthusiasm, then pulled back to scrutinize her face. The bruises had faded, and the cut healed. He touched gentle fingertips to the scar she carried on her cheek, as though it might still pain her. Anger rose in him.

"I'm alright," she assured him, cupping her hand over his. "Very happy to see you."

Riddick took a deep breath and let his anger go. Nodded.

Khara asked the driver to take the scenic route so that Riddick could get a preview of the island with her playing tour guide. Lytua was breathtaking—sun-drenched and vibrant. Beautiful people dressed in colorful clothing. Pastel buildings.

The eclectic architecture fascinated Riddick. Khara explained that the freed and runaway enslaved people who founded Lytua had come from many different lands, bringing their unique visions of community with them. A myriad of styles and influences were represented in the silhouettes and intricate flourishes—African, Dutch, Moorish, baroque, neo-gothic. Roman columns were everywhere.

Khara pointed out the palace, or the Hubbard Building—the Hub for short—that housed her office. It was a sprawling complex of pink stucco.

The car slowed to enter the secured garage of a charming three-story building just outside the capital city of Augustus, near a large verdant park.

"Where are we now?"

"My home."

"I was under the impression there was an official residence of some sort."

"There is. But that's not my home. I lived here before I was elected and fought to stay here. I needed a sanctuary, an oasis where I could regroup and truly be off duty. Privacy is a precious commodity, and I knew I wouldn't get it in any sort of official residence."

"Let me guess. You were the first Queen to want to live off site."

Khara's laugh was almost musical. "Guilty. I thought Jaden was going to murder me. It wasn't secure, and I insisted he make it so without inconveniencing the other residents. There's a sweet older lady who's lived here for decades—Ms. Bloom—I made sure she was involved in the planning."

So, his woman was a maverick, as well as a monarch? That figured. Riddick wondered what else she'd given her handlers hell over.

Chapter Twenty-Four

K ITCHEN ENVY WAS REAL.

Khara gave Riddick a tour and said she'd meet him in the kitchen once he got settled in. She disappeared into her bedroom and reemerged in full casual—face washed free of makeup, lightweight shorts, and an oversized T-shirt with the word "Kween" on it. In bare feet, her curls restrained in a messy ponytail, and no jewelry, she was relaxed and adorable. The off-duty Queen at her leisure. He spotted more of those freckles he liked so much. The only time he'd seen her this way was right after the kidnapping.

"I like my comforts at home. It's my sanctuary."

"As a home should be. I like it. Love the shirt."

"I picked it up from a street vendor in New York. Couldn't resist."

He snagged her around the waist and drew her to him. She wrapped her arms around his neck. "I missed you. Missed being able to do this." He kissed her soft unpainted lips, brushed his nose against hers.

"I missed you, as well."

After a few kisses to get re-acquainted, Khara set to throwing together a quick vegetarian stew for a light dinner. "I had hoped to have this ready, but my meeting ran late."

"What time's your flight?"

Khara grimaced while stirring the potatoes she was sautéing. "Oh-dark-thirty, sadly. I hate to leave you on your own so soon, but I'm going to need to turn in early."

"It's no problem."

She declined his offer to help with the cooking but tasked him with setting the table on the terrace so they could dine alfresco. The heat of the day had passed, leaving behind balmy breezes as they ate. Between the soothing sound of the waves pounding the sand and the fabulous view, Riddick was as relaxed as he'd been in weeks. The stew was spicy and delicious, perfectly complemented with a Shiraz and a loaf of crusty bread.

Khara's apartment was on the third floor, a bright and airy unit with an ocean view from the balconies. The building was small, just six units, with all the amenities. When Riddick remarked on how it looked like a resort, Khara explained that if it hadn't been for the inheritance from her parents, she'd never have been able to afford it. Lytua was like many other Caribbean countries in that real estate was pricey.

"If I'm ever doing something you don't like or you want done differently in bed, I expect you to let me know."

Where did that come from? Riddick sat his spoon down, wiped the corners of his mouth, and regarded his companion, who was looking out at the surf. Sitting across from him, Khara had one foot tucked under her in the rattan chair. Her tone had been casual and pleasant enough, but there was something close to the surface here. *Careful.*

She wouldn't look at him, but her mouth was tight. They hadn't talked much during the meal. He'd thought they were just enjoying the food and the view. Come to think of it, she'd been quieter than usual since he'd arrived. Riddick didn't like that something troubled her, and he'd missed it. He said her name softly.

There was wariness in her eyes he couldn't decipher when her gaze met his. Almost like she was waiting to be disappointed.

"I will."

"I mean talk to me about it, not...." Shaking her head, Khara got to her feet and grabbed her bowl. "Never mind." She disappeared inside.

Riddick followed and found her scraping the rest of her dinner into the sink with jerky movements. That was unusual. Khara didn't waste food. Riddick took the bowl from her hands and set it aside on the counter. "'Not' what?"

"This... this is new for me. I don't want you to tell me down the line that you've been dissatisfied the whole time."

"I would tell you if something wasn't working for me. You'll do the same, right?"

Something wounded swirled in her eyes, like a frightened animal caught in the act of darting away from a predator. There was an unhappy story here, and he was pretty sure he'd want to kick someone's ass when he heard it. Riddick suppressed the anger that tried to swell within him. He rubbed his hands up and down her forearms in what he hoped was a comforting gesture.

"If you need me harder or longer, my tongue a little to the left or me to not pull your hair so hard, whatever. Just tell me and I'll adjust. Give me all the directions." She smiled a little at that, some of the tension drained from her shoulders. "I don't ever want you *enduring* anything with us. I want you enjoying the hell out of it and counting the minutes until we can do it again."

She pulled in a deep breath. "Alright. You can pull my hair as much as you want. I like that."

His eyes darkened, just as he hardened. "Duly noted. What's bringing this on now?"

She shrugged and waved her hand. "Just a good talk with my bestie. She urged me to talk to you about any concerns or reservations I had."

"Solid advice. I'm glad you told me."

Later, as she was trying to decide how to launch into the whole sordid Gary tale, Riddick provided her with the opening she needed.

"What were you about to say earlier? 'Not' something. Did someone do something other than level with you?"

Khara frowned. She should have known he was far too clever to have missed that slip. It was embarrassing, but she told him about the slide presentation and wasn't prepared for his vehement reaction.

His voice hardened, like he was holding onto his patience with both hands and a heartbeat from an angry outburst. "What kind of childish, passive-aggressive—? He should have his neck wrung for hurting you like that."

He'd gone rigid on his lounger and was shaking his head. "No one should get blindsided by things they aren't doing 'right' in bed. It takes a special kind of asshole to make an entire fucking slideshow. That's bullshit, Khara. Petty, selfish bullshit."

"Well, he *is* a lawyer."

"So are you, but you're not petty or selfish. Why the fuck didn't he just talk to you?"

Khara shrugged. "I suppose it was easier to humiliate me. More satisfying, too, I expect."

"I can promise I'll never do something like that. If I ever see this guy, it's an automatic ass whooping."

The relief that exploded in Khara's breast threatened to overwhelm her. Thank goodness she could trust Riddick to never do something so terrible.

Chapter Twenty-Five

L ATER, RIDDICK SAT PROPPED up against the headboard in Khara's guest room bed, hands behind his head and deep in thought.

He hadn't trusted himself to speak right away after hearing about that fucking lowlife fiancé. Her words had been cautious, artificially light, but the hurt was still lurking, and he'd be damned if he let that stand.

Listening to that shitty presentation must have been excruciating. Riddick couldn't even imagine the torture.

Disgust with how Gary's behavior fouled things up lingered. He was up against that horrid memory whenever he touched Khara. That stain needed to be wiped from her memory, and he vowed to make her forget.

Khara was a room away from him and hearing her move around sent awareness zinging through his senses. He froze when he heard the shower turning on and groaned, imagining water sliding in rivulets over her naked body.

He lay awake for over an hour, wound tight as a coiled spring, trying not to imagine her under him or above him in this bed. If she was ready, she would have sought him out. He would wait if it killed him and it well might.

A thud and muffled curse drew his attention, and he went to investigate. "You okay?"

"Yes. I just... knocked something over." Her voice came from down low to the left, in the hallway's direction. "I'm sorry, did I disturb you?"

"I was still awake." He spotted her hunched near the wall a split second before she flicked on the overhead light. She rushed by him into the kitchen, filling his senses with the subtle scent of whatever she used to keep her skin so supple.

A pretty vase—miraculously unbroken—laid on the colorful runner covering the hardwood. Water was spreading. Khara returned with a dish towel just as Riddick picked up the vase. Their hands bumped as they both reached for the scattered flowers. "I got it."

Khara dropped to her hands and knees to blot the spreading water. Riddick sat the vase on the console table it must have toppled from and did a double-take when he glanced at Khara again. He could see right down the neckline of her nightshirt, to her breasts swaying with her scrubbing motion. One luscious brown nipple was visible, hardened and prominent.

Fuuuuck.

Blood rushed to regions south. She caught him looking, and a blush suffused her cheeks. In that moment, she was so enticing that his engorged dick almost got the better of him.

The polite thing to do would be to avert his gaze, but God help him, he wouldn't have been able to tear his gaze away if his life depended on it. And Jesus, it was the left one, the one that had retained sensation after her cancer surgery. He wanted to tug that neckline down so he could lick and kiss and suck that perfect little nipple until her back arched. And then all the rest of her. Whenever he got his mouth on her, he was going to savor every single part of her body.

She caught her lower lip between her teeth as her eyes came to rest on the erection his loose-fitting lounge pants were doing a piss-poor job of disguising. He made no move to conceal anything. Let her see how much that curvy body of hers turned him on, how much he wanted to fuck her right then and there. All down the length of the hallway.

"Riddick," she said at last, sitting back on her heels.

He crossed his arms over his chest and felt a sliver of pride when her focus drifted to linger on his biceps and shoulders. His old gray Howard T-shirt—faded and soft from its many trips through the laundry—fit close to his upper body in a way that clearly pleased her. Excellent intel. "Yes, beautiful Khara?"

"I can't—I can't stop thinking about us."

"In what way?" Did she have any idea how fucking sexy she was to him? If he touched her even a little, he'd be stripping her naked and getting his tongue all over her. Her heart was pounding.

"The things you said. About us. Making love and fucking." She got to her feet.

"Hmm. Yes?"

"You look at me like... like you can't wait to devour me."

"Sounds about right."

"I want to do all of that with you. Right now."

"Then why are we just standing here?" The question was almost a growl. He was ready to throw her over his shoulder and make for the bedroom. Hell, the couch or kitchen countertop would do at this point he was so turned on.

"But not yet. What if it messes everything up?"

That sobered his lustful thoughts. *Fucking Gary.* "Let's take a time out and have some tea."

Once they'd settled on the love seat with steaming cups of hibiscus tea, Riddick broached the subject. "You shared a big secret, one you worried I might not be able to get past. But you being the Queen is fundamental to who you are."

She nodded.

"You told me what it's been like for you and you're not sure if I'm going to head for the hills or not, which makes you apprehensive."

Tears swam in her eyes as she nodded again.

"This is my fault."

"What? No, it's not."

"I don't think I've been clear enough in how much I want you."

"You have."

"No. You wouldn't have any doubts if I was. Only when you're ready. Yes, I still want to spend time with you, even when sex is off the table. That's what people in relationships do, or so I'm told. I've mentioned I don't actually know. You're selling yourself short if you believe I'm only hanging around for the sex we may have. Sweetheart, I've only just gotten to know Khara. This part, this build-up is so delicious."

"What if it's disappointing?" She blurted the question out and Riddick knew right away this was her true fear.

"Not possible." But she was looking at him uncertainly, her concern clear in the wariness in her eyes, the way she worried her lip. Damn that fuckup ex for this. If Riddick ever saw that dude, it was curtains. "But let's say for the sake of argument it is. What do you think we should do?"

"Um." She gulped. "Go our separate ways?"

He chuckled. She was precious. "Wrong answer."

"I don't know, then."

"We should try again. And again, until we get it right."

Her lips formed a perfect little o.

"You're coming. That's my only objective."

"What about *you* coming?"

"Oh, I'll get mine. Let's get you to bed. You've got that early flight. And I don't trust myself."

They shared a few molten kisses by her bedroom door before Riddick told her, "Goodnight, beautiful Khara." He breathed the words against her mouth. "With kisses like that and how hard we've both come with foreplay, I don't think we'll have a problem."

Khara went back and forth with herself about if she was ready to make love. She was feeling a little raw after talking about Gary, the schmuck. She'd thought of little other than Riddick in the intervening weeks and, now that he was here in her space, her hormones were raging out of control. It was an ideal time, but that couldn't be the deciding factor. If she couldn't say "yes" without any hesitation, then the time wasn't right. Ultimately, she masturbated, fantasizing about him instead. She still had difficulty getting to sleep. She realized she still didn't know what he wore to bed. Then she had to masturbate again.

Though unburdened after talking about the humiliating slide deck, nerves plagued her. Yvanda had been right in encouraging her to talk to Riddick about her worries. She slept better that night, even as she fell asleep thinking about Riddick in the next room, with just one wall separating them.

Riddick kissed her out the door so enthusiastically in the morning she had difficulty remembering where she was going.

Chapter Twenty-Six

Khara was so stunned at the cozy, domestic sight that greeted her when she opened her apartment door on New Year's Day that she could only stand there gaping. Weather grounded her flight the previous day and they'd missed their planned celebration. She'd texted that she would be getting in late, yet there was Riddick, wearing one of her over-the-top frilly aprons over a T-shirt. Mellow jazz had him swaying as he stirred something on the stove. Her heart was suddenly in her throat.

Riddick caught sight of her and flashed a dazzling smile that made her pulse skitter.

"Welcome home," he called and came striding toward her. He greeted her with a thorough kiss that curled her toes, then took her bag. "How was your trip?"

"Long and hard. It smells delicious in here. You made dinner?"

"Just a quick pasta. Wasn't sure what you'd want."

I want *you*, Khara almost blurted. She looked around at the beautifully set table, the fresh flowers adorning nearly every surface. "It's late. You didn't have to—"

"I know. I wanted to."

"Thank you. That's very thoughtful. I'm sorry I missed New Year's *and* your birthday. I am the worst girlfriend."

He placed a gentle kiss on her forehead, right where she was frowning. "You're not and you can't control the weather. Go refresh yourself. Dinner will keep."

"I have a parliament committee meeting in the morning. Once that's done, I'm off for two weeks," she called over her shoulder as she started toward her bedroom.

Khara smiled in the shower. She'd never had someone waiting for her, preparing any sort of homecoming for her. Never had anyone cared whether she ate after a long day of traveling. It was marvelous. Had she been too guarded before, or had it just not occurred to her previous partners? She didn't need coddling, but it was exhilarating to have someone *care*. This was what she saw between the Elites and their spouses. Every one of them was capable and a whole person on their own, yet they were so sweet and considerate of each other.

It didn't diminish her to enjoy how Riddick treated her so thoughtfully and with tenderness. Riddick wasn't afraid or jealous of her. He was confident enough in himself. She would never have to downplay who she was or what she did with Joshua Riddick. He'd meet her exactly where she was, without trying to manipulate any of it.

Khara took a good, long look at herself in the mirror and recalled Yvanda's encouraging words.

Don't push an opportunity for joy away.

If she wanted Riddick—and, oh, boy, did she—she'd have to trust that he wouldn't behave like Gary. Khara wanted Riddick. She was ready to make love with him.

Should she put on some lingerie? Just go out and tell him? Gah, why wasn't she more prepared for this?

She'd thought of little else while she'd been away.

Keeping her mind on her work had been impossible. She was climbing the walls in sexual frustration. Masturbation had hardly made a dent in the white-hot need coursing through her all the time lately.

She'd wanted to fling her rollie bag aside and leap into his arms. Would they have made love right there in the entryway? The kitchen?

No one had ever made her crave them the way Riddick did. She wanted that simmering tension between them to boil over. When he touched her, she melted, felt like a live wire. She wanted to release all concern about how she felt, what was happening, what the future might hold, and just give in to want. Worry about all that another time.

Her body was on fire just being in the same room with him. She couldn't think straight.

Time to do something about that. Was she brave enough to seize that pleasure for herself? To just ask for what she wanted? He'd made it clear that he wanted her, was only waiting for *her* to be ready. Once she said the word, it would be on.

Khara searched her thoughts, looking for hesitation or uncertainty. All she found was impatience that she hadn't gone out there and jumped the man already. A blush heated her face, prompting a smile to go with the ripple of anticipation in her belly. Time to go for it. Get her hands on his body and unleash all the damn lust that had her tied up into the tightest of knots.

All she needed was to get moisturized and keep the nervousness from interfering. Oh, yes. This was it.

Joshua Riddick would be all hers tonight. At last.

Chapter Twenty-Seven

SHE LOOKED BEAT.

Riddick wanted to feed her, to draw her a bath, to put her to bed. Where had this come from? He'd never felt the urge to take care of a woman before, but he'd do whatever he could to put that sweet, surprised smile on her face again, like when she first came in. Tension was evident in the set of her shoulders—something might not have gone well on this trip. He'd ask her over dinner.

There was something in her eyes when she looked at him, something almost… hungry. Had she been thinking about him the way he'd been thinking of her? He hoped so.

Being surrounded by her belongings, her soft scent—Riddick spent most of the last few days hard as a brick and missing her. She favored bright, bold colors and soft textures. Being in her private space felt like a privilege. Tons of photos decorated her home—friends and family, loving parents.

He'd been drawing almost non-stop, doing his best to capture the beauty he was immersed in. Lytua was a paradise. Hot as hell, but he'd acclimated.

Riddick poured himself a glass of wine and settled down to wait for her.

He found her sound asleep after her shower, wrapped up in a fluffy bathrobe, on top of the covers. His heart kicked seeing her there that way—relaxed, vulnerable. Exposed.

"Get into bed, sweetheart," he whispered, then felt a small flare of panic when she shrugged out of the robe. To his relief, she was wearing a tank top of some sort. Riddick wasn't sure what he would have done if she'd been naked.

He tucked her in, got her settled, and once again wondered at this urge to care for her. No woman had ever affected him this way. He leaned over to press a soft kiss to her forehead and was straightening to go when she caught his arm.

"Stay," she mumbled sleepily.

"Just for a while. Let me put the food away and I'll come right back."

She curled in close when he returned, exhaled a breathy little sigh that melted his heart.

She murmured in Lytuan, then English, "Sorry about dinner."

"Shh. No worries. Get some rest."

But she was already asleep again.

Chapter Twenty-Eight

R IDDICK DIDN'T EXPECT TO fall asleep and woke during an early morning thunderstorm, surprised to find himself curled around Khara's back. He'd shucked his pants before lying down with her and now they were both on their sides, limbs intertwined. Her bare legs were smooth against his own, tantalizingly so. He knew down to the marrow of his bones that this warmth, this peace, was right. Before he could examine that further, Khara stirred in his arms as the rain spattered and pounded on the roof. Riddick brushed his lips against the fine hair at the nape of her neck and kissed her there.

She turned to face him, snuggled into his side a little.

"You stayed." There was just enough light to see her face.

"You asked me to."

What else would he have given if she'd asked? Probably everything. He let the unspoken promise hang there.

Khara stretched, brushing up against his body in a way that tested his resolve.

"Sorry about dinner."

"No worries. It'll re-heat."

Khara slipped a hand under the hem of his T-shirt to rest on his bare stomach. Desire raced through him at her touch, at how she was looking at him. She shifted closer, turned her face into his chest. "You smell very good."

When she stroked the skin beneath her thumb, Riddick caught her hand in his and rolled so that he arched above her, his lower body pressing down on hers. He'd gotten hard the moment she touched him, and he made no attempt to disguise it. His eyes drifted to where the neckline of her tank top dipped into a V. Light as a whisper, he used his thumb to trace the exposed inside curve of her breast, where he knew she was sensitive. He lowered his head, pressed the lightest of kisses there, and watched in fascination as her nipple hardened. Christ, she smelled delicious. Her heart was hammering, just as his was. *Good.* He gave in to need and sucked that left nipple into his mouth, right through the shirt material.

Khara arched into him, cried out. "Riddick—" She broke off with a gasp when he sucked harder, pushing her hips up into his. It brought her in contact with his prominent erection.

Riddick slid a knee between her thighs, to where he could feel the heat of her. *One touch,* he promised himself. Just one touch and he could leave. One touch and he'd be momentarily satisfied. Maybe. God, he needed this. *You will not rush her,* he commanded his dick sternly.

Riddick swallowed hard. "Khara, being honest here, I want my hands and mouth all over you more than I can say." His voice was strained, and he didn't dare touch her further. He was hanging on by a thread as it was. "If you're not ready to make love, I'm gonna need to get the hell out of this bed right now."

She slipped her hands under his shirt, splayed them along his sides, making his dick twitch. He couldn't stop looking at her mouth and his last control was unraveling fast.

"I had grand plans to seduce you last night," she breathed. "But I fell asleep."

The thrill of something that wasn't quite fear, but adjacent to it, shivered up his spine. Anticipation, yes, but something more. Perhaps exhilaration?

He cupped her cheek, fought valiantly to remain still, even though every muscle was tensed. Even if it killed him, *he would not rush her.* "Be sure, sweetheart."

"Oh, I'm sure."

"Thank Christ," he murmured, then brought his mouth down to hers in a searing kiss. She made a sound deep in her throat and gave him her tongue. He let her nudge him onto his back with a push to his hip.

She climbed on top to straddle his lap. It felt like a furnace branding him and she rocked against his hardened cock. She slid both hands back under his shirt and sank her nails into his sides a bit. Riddick's breath caught. *Oh, Jesus.* He didn't realize until that moment just how much he'd wanted her touch. Just craved it. Thought he was going to lose his mind without it.

"Are you ready for me? It goes both ways."

"Yes. I'm ready. This means something."

"It does. Thank you for not rushing me."

"Don't thank me for that. You always have the space to decide what you really want."

"Thank you just the same. What I really want right now is you, Riddick."

Those words triggered something. Riddick had never wanted to belong to someone, but damned if he didn't want this woman to claim him. "I'm yours." He didn't understand it, didn't know where it came from, or why it felt so critical to voice that truth at that moment.

She leaned down to kiss him, stopped just short of their lips meeting. "I can't wait another single moment."

Riddick brightened, recalling the exact moment when he'd said that to her, as well as what he'd said right after. "'Then we're in business'. Khara, you're fucking killing me. Come 'ere."

It was a kiss hotter than any they'd shared so far. Just as Riddick was taking control, Khara sat back and fingered the hem of his shirt. "You're overdressed."

He tore his T-shirt off and tossed it on the floor. The pleasure that lit in her eyes as her gaze roamed his bare upper body—that was heady stuff. But it was the lip bite and the sound she made—something like a contented purr—that almost did him in. Her fiery gaze on him was everything. He wouldn't be slacking off from gym time anytime soon.

Khara kept that succulent lip caught between her teeth as she took him in, sending warmth spreading through his belly. "If you keep looking at me like that, you might just get thoroughly fucked."

She let out a seductive little laugh. A slow smile crept over her full lips. It was filled with mischief, maybe a few secrets. "That's not much of a deterrent, I'm afraid. I'm going to get thoroughly fucked, anyway. You, Joshua Riddick, don't do anything halfway. I don't expect this will be any different."

Her words tugged at something primal in his soul. Riddick grinned and barked out a laugh. Any lingering doubt about having finally met his match faded away.

He'd expected to be the one to start things and here she was—as always, it seemed—knocking him off balance. The lazy pattern she drew across his pecs and down over his abdomen left his skin tingling like fire had ignited under her touch.

Then her breath hitched, and her expression changed from one of *come hither* to mild alarm, the flirtatious smile slipping from her face. Her eyebrows came down in a frown as she fingered the twin scars from the attack in Istanbul. The sutures had left behind only the slightest of ridges.

He took her hand from his side and brushed his thumb over her palm, then kissed her fingertips.

"I'm fine."

His reassurance did little to chase the worry that tinged her features away. "You could've been—"

"I wasn't," he told her, his voice firm.

He sat up and cradled the back of her head so he could look into her eyes. The hint of sadness there gutted him. Something like possessiveness flooded him. Or was it protectiveness? Maybe both. He didn't want any part of her to be uncertain. "I'm here, Khara. Exactly where I want to be."

She nodded and closed those expressive hazel eyes for a moment. When she opened them again, that glimmer of doubt had been extinguished. Desire was all that remained.

His kiss wasn't gentle, it was demanding. Right until the moment she pushed at his chest so that he lay down again. Bossy, just as he'd suspected.

The muscles in his stomach jumped when she traced the light, crinkled hair of his happy trail. When she hooked her fingers into the waistband of his shorts, he was so surprised he didn't respond right away. Khara cocked an eyebrow at him. "You going to make a girl wait?"

He needed to catch up, but he was enjoying her playfulness. It was uniquely her, a mixture of verve, boldness, and a sweet vulnerability. He lifted his hips for her to tug his boxers down and off.

Khara gasped when his cock sprang free. "Well," she breathed in wonder, then licked her lips. "Wow."

She took his cock in her hand and gave him an experimental stroke. Then again, with more confidence.

Riddick groaned. "Sweetheart, we'll be finished here before we start if you keep that up."

She gave him a siren's smile and tightened her grip and kept stroking, clearly enjoying his reaction. "I haven't had many chances to touch you yet."

Shit. His eyes widened. "Next time," he gritted out.

"Ah-ah." She moved before he could reach her and settled to where she was kneeling between his legs, her palms resting on the outside of his thighs. "I still think about all those dirty, dirty things you told me you want to do to me. I wanted everything you said. All of it. But I didn't get a chance to tell you the things I'm going to do to *you*. Let me rectify that."

She scratched her nails down his thighs with just enough tantalizing bite to make his ass muscles clench. "Are you listening, Riddick?"

"Yes," he choked out. He was hanging on her every word, hypnotized by how her sexy voice curled around each one. She was giving him extra accent.

Khara pushed up so that she crouched over his lower half on all fours. She wrapped her hand around the base of his erection and stroked. She made an appreciative sound at the back of her throat that made him throb in her grasp.

"So big and hard for me. I want to be fully dressed and made up, standing there ready to walk out the door, but tell you I need one more thing. Then unfasten your pants and get down on my knees to take this beautiful cock out. I'm going to tease and suck you slowly, as if no one is waiting on us. You're going to watch. Then, after I swallow you down, I want you to wipe the corner of my mouth and tell me what a good girl I am."

Riddick almost spilled into her hand right then.

"Then I want to get up and go out like nothing happened. Not a hair out of place. And when you look at me all night while we're out, all you'll be able to think about is how much you want to see me down on my knees for you with my lips wrapped tight around your cock again."

He was going to have to bury his cock in some part of her soon before she made him explode. This hot, passionate Queen of a nation was throwing down some serious game.

She'd pumped him lazily as she spoke. Foregoing any more teasing, she licked up the length of him and looked right into his eyes as she swirled her tongue around the crown, keeping her tongue flat to cover more surface area. Riddick lay transfixed as she kissed the slit at the tip, swiped her tongue over it. All while holding his gaze. "Do you want my mouth, Riddick?"

"I want your everything."

She sucked his entire length into the hot velvet cavity of her mouth. Riddick let out a soft groan, followed by a curse. His eyes narrowed to slits. No one woman's mouth should feel this good.

Her head bobbed as she worked her mouth up and down his shaft oh, so slowly, curling her tongue around him. She was enthusiastic and thorough, lavishing every bit of him, massaging and sucking his balls.

Riddick let out a hiss, grabbing the sheets. He forced himself to keep his hips still, fighting the urge to piston them upward. Ruthlessly refusing to give in to the temptation to tangle a hand in her curls because it would be a short jump from that to holding her by her hair so he could fuck into her wondrous mouth. And fucking hell, she wanted to swallow him down. *Good girl, indeed.* Riddick let his eyes drift closed, surrendering to that glorious thought and visual for a few moments as she worked him over.

Not yet, he admonished himself. *Too soon.* He'd destroy her with his eagerness. But soon, she'd get down on her knees for him, fully dressed just the way she'd described, and look up at him with those eyes while she did it. "Jesus, Khara—"

He was in over his head and there was nothing for it. She could do whatever she wanted to him. Torn between wanting her to stop and hoping she'd continue, he feared both. How was he wound tight as a drum, and he hadn't even touched her yet? If he didn't act, he'd explode.

Riddick pulled Khara up from the best oral anyone could ever hope to have. His cock came out of her mouth with a juicy-sounding pop. This woman. He flipped her over onto her back and followed so that he arched over her. The little minx was *laughing*.

"I haven't finished teasing you yet!"

"If you tease me anymore, you'll be swallowing me down right *now*. As hot as that would be, we'll need to come back to that filthy mouth of yours. I need to regain control of the situation at hand here."

She raised her eyebrows at him. "Oh, I see. You thought you had it all figured out, did you?"

"I did, yeah." The admission surprised him.

"Bet you thought you'd take charge in bed and leave me a quivering ball of need. Why should you have all the knee-weakening fun?"

Then she looked up at him with those gorgeous hazel eyes, sparkling with desire and humor.

Riddick couldn't help it. He laughed, thoroughly bewitched by her. How could he be this turned on and having fun with Khara being a smartass? Had he ever laughed in bed before? Wasn't this supposed to be serious business?

Something tightened in his chest when she beamed at him. How many nights had he dreamed about having her with him like this? "You're so beautiful." He brushed his nose against hers. "And you're also overdressed."

She sobered, her mirth dying away. She covered his hand and shook her head when he made to lift her tank top. "I have scars," she whispered, her eyes going wide with nerves. With fear? Panic? Self-consciousness? Not quite a full-scale retreat, but close.

Riddick released the shirt's hem and cupped her face, stroked her cheek. "And they mark you as a warrior who kicked breast cancer's ass."

That made her smile, but she wasn't convinced. "I'm a fraud. For all we promote body positivity and open discourse about sex...." She bit her lip, a furrow forming in her brow. A far cry from the vixen she'd been a moment ago.

His sweet girl thought he'd call it off right here. Oh, that would not stand. Not *this* day. Khara Therin wouldn't be having even one single moment of doubt if he had anything to do with it. He'd prove he could be trusted with this, to hold this for her, ease at least some of the worry. "Leave it on, then, beautiful Khara. And let me get to work here."

He skated a fingertip down over her covered left breast to circle the nipple with just a glancing touch.

Then he took his time and looked at her. He'd known she was stacked, but knowing and seeing were two altogether different things. "Such gorgeous brown skin." He drew his palm downward over the side of her breast, pausing to cup its weight, down over the flare of her hip, then her thigh. "Beautiful," he murmured, spreading an open palm over her soft belly. He shook his head in disbelief at how lucky he was. "A masterpiece." He met her gaze, let his appreciation of her loveliness show. "Lush and full, the way a woman should be."

He called her name softly. When she looked up at him, he uttered a single word, "Mine." It came from the far reaches of his primal mind. Thunder crashed, sounding close.

Then he set about showing her just how beautiful he thought she was. He discovered and caressed, scattered reverent touches down to her toes and back up to her hips. When he brushed his fingers over the thin blue cotton covering her, he smiled upon discovering she was damp.

"You going to make a man wait?" He gave her playful words back to her with a teasing smile.

"Never," she sighed, then lifted her hips enough for him to ease her panties down and off. He cast them aside and returned to his prize, nudged her long legs open to admire the neatly trimmed curls.

"Lord, I've been wanting to taste you," he told her, then bent his head to the task. Soft, sweet kisses up the inside of her thighs made her shiver. Thunder rolled again as if punctuating the sentiment. The outer lips of her pussy were glistening with her arousal. He lapped and nibbled and sucked until she was on the cusp. The taste of her was even better than he remembered and so much sweeter from the source. His hands holding her hips, he moaned his appreciation. "I could stay here all day."

That was when he curled a finger inside her and sucked her clit at the same time. He found the spot that made her weak, knew it when she gasped and grabbed his shoulder. He slowed his motion to where just his fingertips fluttered over it with a barely there stroke that had her squirming.

She trembled beneath the tender onslaught, the tension tightening within her like a corkscrew, her breath coming out in short little gasps. "*Riddick—*"

"Hell, yeah, Khara, *come*." He licked up her seam with an almost lazy slowness. "Squeeze my fingers like you'll squeeze my cock. Come for me." He knew the signs, her little tells. She was close. He kept his finger buried in her, feathering against that spot, while he sucked her clit, circled it with his tongue.

She *erupted*. The orgasm bubbled up, and she came hard for him, loudly, entirely without inhibition. With the sheet clenched in her fists and her back bowed off the bed, she was unfettered—crying out and moaning her pleasure. The sight of her unbound was breathtaking. She said something in Lytuan that he thought might have been pleading.

Taking more time to savor her would have been lovely, but it was futile. They were both too on edge, too eager. No way he could hold out with her so wet and looking like a whole damn fantasy come to life. She grabbed the foil packet from where she'd placed it next to the lamp the night before and ripped it open. Gave it to him.

"I can't go slow," he apologized, getting the condom on in record time, his eyes roaming all over the lusciousness waiting for him. His hands were shaking. This was more than casual desire. This was pure, all-consuming need. All he knew was that if he didn't get inside Khara, he was going to cease existing. He couldn't wait another minute if the world was ending around him.

"Slow the second time, remember?" She smiled up at him as she said it, spreading her legs wider to give him room, waiting for him, inviting him.

He grinned, lifting her hips, then paused with his cock pressing right at the edge of her entrance, sliding through the abundant wetness his attentions had caused. "Let me see those pretty brown eyes, Khara." It was equal parts command and entreaty.

He held them there, quivering at the edge of life and world-changing. When her gaze met his, something powerful locked into place, like a bond being sealed or a promise fulfilled. Riddick had a split second to appreciate once again how damn lucky he was before he surged inside her and sank home to the hilt. And that's just what it was, coming to the place where he was always meant to be. This. Her. Right here and now. "Fucking *hell*," he hissed. It shouldn't have surprised him. He dropped his forehead onto hers.

Khara gripped his biceps hard, arched her body up against his. "Oh, yes," she purred, twining her legs around his and tucking her face into the crook of his neck. "Riddick, *yes.*"

Every love song, every poem, every awed word that ever spoke of this act with reverence rang true to Riddick right then. *This* was what made men go to war to protect.

God, he wanted to absorb her. He pulled away and slid back smoothly, then again. She groaned and tightened around him.

He could feel the tension building in her. She resisted every withdrawal, her breath hot fanning across his neck and shoulder.

Riddick sat back on his heels just long enough to shove his elbow under one of her knees. The change lifted and opened her to him, giving him just enough room to reach between them.

"Wanna feel you come around me this time, Khara." He got his fingers circling her slippery clit and thrust deep. That was all it took. Khara bucked beneath him, thrashed and moaned, clamped her knees around his hips as the pleasure overtook her once more. It was a gorgeous sight, one he knew he'd be remembering every day for the rest of his damn life. Khara melting beneath him. "So fucking beautiful."

The wonder coursing through his body was reflected to him in the dazed expression on her flushed face. He made another circle of her clit with his thumb. She jolted, sensitive after such recent orgasms. She tried to close her legs, to run from too much sensation. But he was everywhere, his body rubbing over hers with each thrust. His thumb was insistent.

"One more," he ordered, not letting her go. "Let me feel that again."

Khara wasn't sure if she wanted to push him away or ask for more. Her body decided for her. Her thighs shook, and she blossomed into a sudden release, grasping him tight inside and out. She threw her head back and shuddered with it, crying out his name and growing even wetter. Her sheath, so slick and tight and hot as she rippled all along his cock, almost made him lose his mind.

He didn't let up—kept touching her, stroking her, prolonging it for them both. The storm grew louder, wilder, wind-whipped rain lashing against the windows and roof.

"*There. Oh, right...* there." She urged him in Lytuan, one ankle hooked on the side of the mattress as an anchor, the other wrapped around his thigh. Khara clung to him, every one of her fingers dug into his ass cheeks to pull him into her as she raised her hips to meet each powerful thrust. With his dick riding over her sweetest of spots, she lapsed into incoherence.

Riddick gave her everything he'd ever had.

Jesus, she was soaked. Her moans and cries and motions grew frantic and desperate. He pounded her hard, hitting his target with each heavy, world-shattering stroke and using every filthy word he knew to encourage her. Then she was chanting his name and *yes* in Lytuan over and over like a mantra and ripping the fabric of his world apart.

She came so hard she almost dislodged him.

Khara was breathless and beautiful and wild, uncontained and *his*. She was still coming when he plunged deep and let go, seizing heaven for himself. A groan ripped from his throat as he kept thrusting until he was empty, with nothing left to give her. By then, he was sure his heart was about to give out or he was going to keel over. Because nobody could survive this level of unbridled pleasure and not die from it.

They lay tangled together in an exhausted heap, weak and panting. He'd driven her up the bed and had her just about pinned against the headboard. They both moaned when he slipped out of her to shift so that he wasn't crushing her. They lay side by side while their breathing and pounding hearts slowed. He didn't want to get up, wanted to stay right there forever, but alas. "Be right back."

Catching sight of himself in the bathroom mirror, Riddick grinned. Looked a lot like he was glowing.

He found Khara drowsing on her stomach when he returned after dealing with the condom. He pushed her hair aside to kiss her bare shoulder. She said something in her native language, and he could hear the smile in her voice, even without understanding the melodic words. He loved hearing her speak Lytuan.

"What was that?"

"I'll be wanting you again later for 'slow'."

"Me, too."

They nestled together and let the soothing sound of the rain lull them back to sleep.

Chapter Twenty-Nine

RIDDICK WANTED TO STAY in bed with Khara, but his internal alarm clock was insistent. With her back tucked to his front, their limbs were intertwined again. The warmth and exquisite softness of her curves were exactly right in his arms. All was quiet, but for the far-off trilling of unfamiliar birdsong. The rain stopped; the storm now spent like they were. Her curls draped over his arm, tickling some. Riddick didn't move right away, letting the moment's peace soak in.

She didn't stir when he finally extricated himself, rose, and tucked the coverlet over her. His body humming with pleasure, Riddick dressed for the gym, unable to keep from stealing glances at Khara's sleeping form. She lay on her side, facing away from him. Heat rushed to his groin recalling those throaty cries of pleasure, his name on her lips. He brewed coffee with an irrepressible smile on his face, and brought her a cup.

Though watching a woman sleep was not something he'd ever felt compelled to do, Riddick swore he could watch Khara's peaceful face forever. He stood in her bedroom doorway with his arms crossed, already visualizing how he'd capture that muted glow of the rising sun in the sketch he'd do of the scene later. She was beautiful and disheveled, looking as though, yes, she had been thoroughly fucked. Completely and thoroughly fucked to within an inch of her life. The thought made him smile. He'd never had so much fun in bed. He called her name, shook her bare shoulder.

Khara rolled onto her back with a languorous stretch. She gave him a lazy, satisfied smile that made his heart squeeze. Not painfully, more... curiously.

"Good morning again."

He sat the mug on her nightstand, leaned in and gave her a light kiss. "Good morning, beautiful Khara. Here's coffee. I'm gonna head down to the gym so you can have your silence."

"What time is it?"

"You don't want to know."

When Khara groaned and pulled a pillow over her face, Riddick laughed and told her to drink her coffee while it was hot.

Damn, she felt *good*.

Khara sat cross-legged in bed, sipping the coffee and smiling, replaying their lovemaking in her mind. It was perfect. The best she'd ever had. She was tender from being stretched and a sticky mess, but she wouldn't change anything.

Still sitting there daydreaming when Riddick returned, she did a double take at how he appeared dripping with sweat, his T-shirt clinging to the hard muscles of his chest and arms. Her mouth went dry. If this was what her man looked like every morning after working out, Khara might turn into a morning person after all. Just so she could lick up his abdomen and those impressive pecs.

Her man. Riddick was *her* man. Her lover. A fluttery feeling invaded her belly, bringing a smile to her lips.

Lord, that body had done all kinds of magic to hers.

She was tempted to go with him when he disrobed and headed for the shower, but the thought of her scars stopped her. She shook the fear off, refused to let any negativity into this solace. One day, she might be comfortable enough to let him see her, but not today.

It had been such a relief the sleep shirt she still wore hadn't gotten in the way at all. Her need to keep it on to feel comfortable hadn't fazed Riddick. He'd taken that in stride and kept the good stuff moving. That simple act meant more to her than she'd ever be able to express.

And then he gave her the coffee and quiet. Yvanda was right. The man was a dream. And a hot one at that. Could she be any luckier?

Chapter Thirty

RIDDICK ALMOST BURNED THE eggs when she came into the kitchen wearing his favorite Howard T-shirt, her nipples outlined against the gray fabric. *Shit*, he thought, his gaze sweeping over her.

She bit her lip, uncertainty creeping into her eyes. "Is this alright?"

Riddick turned the heat off and slid the frying pan from the burner. It wouldn't do to burn her house down. He stepped close, pulled her up against him, and kissed her deep, letting her know without words that he approved.

"Are you wearing anything under this?" She was downright edible.

When Khara just smiled, Riddick let out a theatrical groan. "Eat. Before you get carried back to bed hungry to get even more thoroughly fucked."

Her bare legs distracted him as they ate. She was all soft and dreamy, radiating pure contentment like a satisfied cat. He'd done that, he realized—and it pleased him like nothing else.

"This is delicious, thank you."

She was delicious sitting there in his too-big shirt. Riddick was too busy staring at her mouth to eat. Remembering the feel of those succulent lips and that tongue had him rock hard and wanting her again. He forked up some eggs. If he didn't get control of himself, he was going to end up shoving the dishes aside and fucking her right there on the kitchen island. "Did your meeting get canceled?"

"What meeting?"

"I thought you had a parliament committee meeting."

Khara glanced at the wall clock and jumped up with a cry of, *"Valscht,"* prompting a chuckle from him.

"Pretty sure that was a Lytuan cuss word," he called after her.

"It was!"

He watched with a bemused expression as a harried Khara rushed to get dressed and do her makeup. Riddick sipped his coffee and enjoyed the spectacle. He could get used to her walking around in her underwear, although if he was being honest, he preferred her out of it.

Riddick answered Alene's knock at Khara's shouted request. He offered his greeting in Lytuan, *"Good day to you, Ms. Alene."* He stood back to invite her in.

Alene grinned at the warm welcome. *"And a good day to you, as well, Mr. Riddick."*

"Ready," Khara called as she breezed toward the door, fastening her earring.

"Khara, shoes." Riddick held up the nude pumps she'd picked out.

Khara glanced down at her feet and laughed. She'd almost left barefoot. Steadying herself with a hand braced on his shoulder, she stepped into the shoes he held out for her. "This is becoming a pattern."

Riddick ran a hand up her calf and flashed her a rakish grin. "You did say I make you forget yourself."

That evening, after a repeat performance of the morning's festivities, Khara presented Riddick with a small cake and a few gifts she'd hidden away in the butler's pantry.

"Happy belated birthday, Riddick," she sang as she sat the cake before him. She pecked his cheek. "I'm so sorry I missed the actual day. You have the luckiest of birthdays. New Year's babies are considered very good luck in Lytua." He pulled her into his lap and opened the presents.

His heart clutched glimpsing her luminous smile. Right then, Riddick felt lucky.

Chapter Thirty-One

FOR TWO DAYS, THEY stayed at her home—teasing, laughing, enjoying each other all over her damn house—everywhere from the sunroom to the kitchen island. They were insatiable.

They cooked and ate together, often with the news playing in the background, still dubbed in English. When the newscaster said something about Senator Richardson's new proposal, Riddick perked up. So this was the guy. He wanted to limit leave time for elected officials.

"No way that gets through," Khara said, her tone dismissive. "That won't even make it to committee."

"You're not worried?"

She shook her head and took another sip of her coffee. "That's just a dig at me. He takes one at least once a week. Always seeking some way to undermine me, or say I'm not suitable to lead. You'd think it would get boring."

"That's the kind of politician I'm used to hearing about. Does he think he can do a better job or something?"

"He's convinced. He's all about grandstanding. Do you know he once said I wouldn't be suitable because I didn't have a spouse to host and entertain? Ridiculous, right? As though I weren't smart enough to hire a planner."

"Ridiculous," Riddick echoed.

"Always digging for something to use against me. Honestly, I think he'd use something from my childhood if he could get away with it."

Riddick thought of his own childhood—at how someone petty like Richardson would relish a juicy story like that. He seemed like just the type to use someone else's misfortune against them like a wrecking ball. Prick.

Even though Khara seemed unconcerned, worry took root within Riddick. The disdain in Richardson's voice unsettled him. He hated bullies. The whole thing almost put him off his French toast.

After he'd fucked Khara into an orgasm-induced slumber that evening, he decided to learn more and discovered that some of Richardson's positions were gaining steam. Most of his attacks were so trivial it just made him look foolish, but Khara was right. Almost every week, Richardson was leveling some silly accusation against her. He stewed on it for a few minutes, then put that loser's shenanigans out of his mind. Riddick had much better things to think about.

Chapter Thirty-Two

THE AIR TURNED COOL as they sat in the wicker loveseat on the terrace after dinner. Khara retrieved a throw from the storage ottoman and draped it over them. It was marvelous to have him hold her while they gazed at the night sky together, listening to the waves crashing on the shore. Peaceful.

Riddick's voice brought her back to the present. "So, tell me about these dating rituals you mentioned earlier."

"Much of it is symbolic in nature and derives from the traditions of our West African ancestors. Everything is about family. There are ceremonial dances, lots of singing, playing pranks. There's Knocking when you call on the family to present yourself as a prospect. Then there's the formal tea with the female elders. Bridewealth is like a reverse dowry, where the groom-to-be offers his most prized possessions to the elders and convinces them the woman he wishes to marry is more valuable and that he will provide for her and any children they have. If the elders accept him, they re-gift his possessions back to him, for him to honor his beloved with them when he proposes."

They meandered inside to refill their wineglasses. "What happens if they don't accept him? They just keep all his stuff?"

"Remember, it's symbolic. They'd work something out or take liberties with the tradition to fit the situation."

"How do you mean?"

"A widow with adult daughters might ask them to have the tea. I acted as a ceremonial elder for Alene. Her mother and grandmothers died when she was young, and she only had the aunt who raised her."

At the interruption of an urgent-sounding knock on the door, Khara called for whoever to come in. A Guard Riddick didn't recognize swept in and gave her the traditional greeting, then nodded in his general direction.

"*Avlah*, Mr. Riddick. I'm very sorry to intrude, but do either of you recognize this man?" She held up a tablet displaying a photo of a man's face.

Both Khara and Riddick shook their heads.

"Who is it?"

"Someone we've noticed hanging around. Nothing overtly suspicious, but it appears he's watching the building. We'll check him out."

Khara was heading back out to the terrace when Riddick's voice stopped her. "How are you completely unfazed?"

"Because it happens. That could have been a training exercise for all I know."

Riddick lifted his gaze from the garden sketch he was working on when Khara approached him on a sunny afternoon, clad in her favorite green satin robe.

"Are you up for a shower?"

A frown creased his brow. "Together? That means—"

"I know." She tossed the words over her shoulder as she left the sunroom.

He set the charcoal and pad aside to follow. She waited for him in the en suite.

"You don't have to—"

"I know," she said again, stepping in front of him. "Would you mind getting naked first?"

He'd respected her boundary—never pushed, never tried to coax her into baths or showers together. She wore a camisole, nightie, or tank to bed, and he treated it like the most natural thing in the world.

He kept his eyes on her face as he undressed, dropping his clothes aside. His movements were careful, measured, as though he didn't want to startle her.

Khara steadied herself and loosened the robe with trembling fingers.

"Hang on." Riddick sat and motioned her closer. "Let me be near you while you do this."

She straddled his thighs, cradled his face, and kissed him. Her palms spread over his chest as she closed her eyes, and breathed him in—his heartbeat, his warmth, the solid feel of his hands on her hips—she drew strength from all of it. The contact grounded her. Centered her. Helped her gather the last bit of courage she needed. When she opened her eyes, admiration glimmered in his.

She untied the belt and let the robe slip to her elbows. Instinctively, she covered her scarred breasts, shoulders curling inward.

Riddick only slid his hands beneath the hem to rest on her thighs, a silent reassurance. No rush. No pressure.

Her choice.

Her heart pounded. She inhaled, then lowered her hands.

One small shimmy and the robe whispered to the floor.

She sat naked before him.

The Queen of Lytua—bare before her lover.

Riddick's mouth tipped in a soft smile. "Beautiful *and* brave."

He curved his hand along her cheek. She covered it with hers, her throat tightening.

He studied her, tracing her torso with reverence. "You kicked cancer's ass, didn't you?"

"I did."

"A warrior," he murmured. "You see scars. I see strength. Victory. Christ, Khara." He kissed her gently. "You're beautiful. Inside and out."

His lips brushed over her scars. The sight of his bent head undid something inside her. Tears burned behind her eyes.

"You have freckles everywhere," he whispered. "The same shade as your—" He looked up and stilled. "Shit, honey. Don't cry."

"You're not repulsed?"

"Honey, no." He drew her closer. "Does this feel like I am?"

She felt the proof of his desire and her breath hitched.

She wiped her tears and framed his face. "Kiss me, Riddick."

"Gladly."

She rose and turned on the shower. Steam soon curled around them as the water warmed. He let her catch him looking as they stepped under the spray, never hiding his awe.

He pressed a kiss to her forehead. "Thank you for trusting me."

"Thank you for being close when I did. That made a difference."

She left the bathroom without reaching for the robe, aware of his gaze, his knowing smile.

Chapter Thirty-Three

S UNRISE WAS BREAKING WHEN Riddick woke Khara with his tongue. Then they moved together, hands and mouths all over each other. He touched her everywhere, made her feel precious, like the rarest treasure.

The instant he was safely gloved up, he took her chin and kissed her as he sank himself inside her, all at once. Khara let out a heartfelt sigh as she twined her arms and legs around him.

They glided together in the hazy morning light, in perfect sync. Riddick rested his weight on his elbows so that their bodies touched as much as possible. The sweet, openmouthed kisses he left at her hairline and all over her neck teased her higher.

It was so intimate and loving, Khara almost broke down. She loved the feeling of him against her as he moved with deliberate gentleness. The sight of his muscles flexing was a feast for her hungry gaze. She rolled her hips up into his and clenched her inner muscles and delighted in his sharp intake of breath, how his grip tightened on her ass. Pleasure rippled over his handsome face, stealing her breath. Her whole body was zinging beneath his touch, embracing the fullness.

There, in her own bed, Joshua Riddick, the American architect who'd wooed her so thoroughly, made love to her with the sweetest tenderness she'd ever known. It humbled her, left her weak and in a floating dreamlike state. Riddick was everything she'd ever wanted. More than she'd ever dared to hope for.

Something cracked open inside her, and tears blurred her vision. She clutched him and cried out, the emotional overwhelm taking her by surprise. It was

"

almost too much sensation, a heaviness, an intensity that was almost more than her heart could bear.

With his eyes burning into hers, he breathed her name, and she'd never heard anything more exquisite.

Demonstrating a startling knowledge of her body, Riddick took her to the edge multiple times, then backed off the angle and intensity she needed to get across the finish line. After the second time, when she made a protesting noise and chased him, straining toward that release, he pulled back and whispered into her ear. "Not yet, beautiful. Let it build."

He entwined their fingers, raised her arms above her head, then caged her wrists in one of his powerful hands and pinned them there to the mattress. Her eyes went wide, and Khara did something she'd never done. She surrendered. She surrendered to the riot of emotions churning through her body, leaving her almost dizzy. Riddick brought her within a heartbeat of bliss again and again, then letting it fade back until she was almost out of her mind with the need for release.

Just when she was positive she couldn't take anymore, he told her in a husky voice, "Come now, Khara." His lips were a warm brush of velvet against her ear. He slipped his hand between them to gather some of her wetness and rub and tease her clit with firm circles of his thumb. "Come. Look at me and come, baby."

The sensations, the command in his voice, his ardent gaze boring into hers—it all coalesced. What started as a low moan grew into something more primal.

Khara didn't just come, she *splintered*. Heat spread out from her core, and she used her legs to cling to him, pulling him tight to her as wave after wave washed over her. She'd never experienced anything like it and just barely kept from screaming her pleasure.

Tears she couldn't stop leaked from the corners of her eyes. It was joy, just utter, uncontainable joy. She loved him so much, with all her being. She let the love cascade all through her as they rocked.

His lips were warm and velvety as they kissed her tears away. The moment he released her wrists, she cupped his face in both hands and let what was flowing within her come tumbling out.

"*Chu schwe shala*," she gasped and drew his mouth back to hers. There was no way for him to know what she'd said, but it was momentous nonetheless. He pressed a kiss to the corner of her mouth, and she sighed her contentment.

But Riddick was just getting started.

When he commanded her onto her knees, Khara didn't hesitate. She scrambled into position, gripping the headboard tight. He trailed his fingertips down the long, tantalizing expanse of her bare back, leaving her shivering. Riddick fitted himself to her and slid home, holding a long moment once he'd seated deep with his hips flush to her ass. This was heaven.

He took her slowly from behind.

With his hands running over her luscious body, he gave her all the words, told her how damn good she felt, described how many ways he wanted to take her, how much he'd been wanting this, how they fit so well together. He felt her deep moan when he gathered a handful of her curls and pulled until her back arched. He had to fight hard to keep his orgasm at bay as she tightened around him, trembling and keening breathlessly.

Riddick dropped kisses along her back, nipped at her shoulder. He reached between her slick thighs to find her clit again and she was so wet his fingers slid over it with ease. She was so aroused her juices were running down the insides of her legs.

He sat back on his heels and brought her with him so that her back was to his front. No material between them this time.

She was naked now. All his.

An arm across her chest steadied them as he ground into her welcoming warmth. She let loose a guttural moan and reached behind her to grasp the back of his neck. They gazed into each other's eyes as they rocked together, the connection almost too intense for them each to bear. But neither looked away. Their sweat-slicked skin gliding together brought with it a staggering intimacy. He cupped her cheek, accepted the remarkable gift she was giving him. She was laying herself bare in a way he instinctively knew she never had before. Hell, he was, too. He'd never felt so exposed, so connected. There was only this, and he leaned into it.

She grabbed his locs as she hurtled over the edge, gasped more words his brain didn't understand, but his body seemed to interpret. Something snapped inside him, something deep down and irrevocable. He gripped her hip tighter and sped his thrusts, gave himself over to the voracious need. He felt her respond—tightening and growing wetter still. There was no defense against this. No holding off anymore. He rode it with her, not letting up, so that her orgasm was ferociously hard and long. Only once it was nearly done did he let himself follow, pounding her through it until they were both spent and weak.

She felt like putty when he was done with her—a combination of sated and spent, overwhelmed. She collapsed down to rest in a child's pose with a heartfelt sigh as he withdrew from her. Riddick went to deal with the condom and when he saw she hadn't moved from where he'd left her asked, "You alright?" He'd brought her a warm washcloth. She let out a long sigh when he wiped her thighs clear.

"I've never come like that. So...."

"Neither have I. You were soaked."

Khara straightened out to lie on her stomach, gave a luxurious stretch. "Is that pride in your voice I hear?"

"Hell yeah." He kissed up the enticing expanse of her naked back to nuzzle her neck, pleased she hadn't felt the need to throw a shirt on.

He gathered her in his arms after tossing the washcloth into the sink. While Khara dropped off back to sleep, Riddick's mind was busy trying to understand what the hell had transpired between them. He hadn't been prepared for it—that deeper connection. That had been something more than sex. More like his soul had unraveled, then intertwined with hers. And he didn't even believe in metaphysical shit like that.

Chapter Thirty-Four

DAYDREAMING AGAIN.

Sitting in the rumpled bed with coffee Riddick had made for her before another early morning workout, Khara gave a huge, bone-cracking yawn. Riddick was wearing her out in the best possible way.

Muscles she'd never known existed were complaining, and she loved it.

Riddick was a giving lover, attentive. He displayed a mastery over her body she would never have believed possible. And to think she'd been worried about him being terrible in bed.

She'd never cared for being taken from behind, as it always felt like she was being conquered, and not in a good way. But this was quite different. Riddick dominated her, yes, but this felt affirming, loving even. His words and movements were intentional, full of care. She was exposed, out of control, and turned on like never before. Quivering on the edge of something unknown.

Revealing her scars, letting him take her from behind—it was so much intimacy. He'd held it, seemed to understand how momentous it all was. No one beyond her medical team had seen her scars. She hadn't been naked with a man since before cancer. The feel of their bare torsos together, the hot skin of his chest rubbing over hers was such a turn-on she could hardly stand it.

She'd also never been much for anal play, either, but the way he'd teased the sensitive skin with his thumb without penetrating her had been hot as hell. Almost too much sensation. She'd never come so much in her life. Khara squirmed just remembering it.

She hadn't intended to call out that she loved him, but the emotional release burst forth in her first language. While he'd heard her, he hadn't understood what she'd said.

"Twice in one week. He's in rare form."

Riddick caught Khara rolling her eyes over Richardson's ranting during a talk show appearance that morning while they washed the breakfast dishes. The Senator offered scathing criticism of Khara's vacation time, railing that she was irresponsible and lackadaisical with her duties. Who the hell even still uses the word "lackadaisical" nowadays? *Pretentious ass.*

The last time Khara had taken off was years before; she'd taken very few days off in her entire tenure. Yet Richardson was bitching about her lack of commitment. From everything Riddick had seen, Khara was as committed as could be. Indignation made him frown. "That's completely unfair. Why didn't you tell me he was after you like this?"

"No need. This isn't new. He's like a crotchety old man who wants everyone as miserable as he is."

"But—"

Khara offered reassurance with a smile and a kiss. "I can handle myself. I'm good at what I do. Please don't worry about him. He's forever looking for dirt, digging into something and trying to spin it."

"I can't tell if you're really this unconcerned or if you're downplaying it for my benefit."

"Really, his shenanigans don't bother me. He's been looking for a chink for a long time. Speaking of time, let me scoot so you can get ready for your call with Dion."

She kissed him goodbye, scooped up her tote, and headed out to the neighborhood farmer's market.

Yet the worry continued to gnaw at Riddick.

When they were lying close together in her bed later that night, satisfied and replete, Khara turned to face him. "Riddick," she started.

"Hmm?"

She spoke a few words in Lytuan that puzzled him.

"I think you've said that before. What does it mean?"

"That I'm in love with you."

He faltered where he'd started lazily stroking her side. His eyes popped open, and he gaped at her.

She laughed. "If you could see your face. Don't think I'm saying this to pressure you in any way. I wanted you to know how I felt. I couldn't hold it in anymore."

Riddick had to remind himself to breathe. He stared up at her without speaking for several long moments, then cupped her face in his hand. "Khara, you don't—"

"I do. You don't think I know my own heart and mind? I love you."

She cut off his protests with a kiss.

He rolled them so that he was above her. Fire blazed in her eyes, so intense he couldn't look away. "I love you, Riddick," she said with more conviction. "With all that I am. Deal with it."

Something tightened in his chest.

This woman. This *fucking* woman loved him, as unbelievable as it was. Damn her gorgeous, brilliant ass. Desire rocketed through him. Just like that, he wanted her again. He needed her in a way he'd never wanted anyone else. Riddick fumbled to put on a condom and then he was spreading her legs wide and arrowing into her deep and hard. She was open and ready for him, welcomed his possession with raised hips, parted lips, and a soft cry. The way she smiled....

Khara loved him. The thought filled him with heat. She was his, all his, and goddammit, she loved him.

This perfection, this... *everything* was going to split him in two. There was no holding back, unhinged as he was with affection, lust, wonder. Hell, he couldn't identify all he was feeling. Her back bowed and she broke apart beneath him, her breath snagging on his name. It pleased him so much to see and feel her lose control, knowing he'd been the one to make her do so. He brushed her hair away from her face to take it in both hands. She did the same, her eyes locked on his.

I love you. She mouthed those incredible words to him with the sweetest smile curving her lips. It undid him. Riddick erupted with a helpless groan, spearing deep again and again until it waned.

He was weak after, disoriented, too depleted to rise right away.

"I love you, Riddick," Khara whispered. "I do. No matter what you have to say on the matter, I'm in love with you."

There were tears on her lashes when she faced him. Riddick's heart clutched. He reached for his woman, gathered her to him, and kissed her shoulder. They'd figure it all out later, but for right now, he needed her to know she was heard. His breath caught in his throat when droplets of wetness fell onto his chest. All he could do was will his fingers not to tremble as he stroked them over the satiny length of her curls.

Chapter Thirty-Five

H E WAS UP BEFORE her, as usual. Riddick went to work out, and hit the machines hard. He needed to keep his mind busy for a bit. Too busy to think about what she'd said, what it meant. The feelings it evoked.

When he was honest with himself, he must have known on some primitive level that she'd told him she loved him. He'd responded with more vigorous strokes, more sensation, just *more*.

I love you.

He hadn't been able to fully take it in. He didn't comprehend what these words were doing to him, making him feel. With so much swirling inside him, it felt like he couldn't catch his breath.

He'd bailed before this point in previous relationships, and he knew he'd been on the right track. This shit was... uncomfortable. Sticky. He was used to being in control of things—his work, his life, his feelings. Things ran much more smoothly that way.

But this, this was messy. He wasn't sure he liked how Khara had upended his ordered life. Even though he'd tried to push back against it, tried to be upset about it, he couldn't quite get there.

It was weird to have his first thought in the morning be her. Unnatural. He hardly knew himself anymore. Yet, when he thought of her now, it wasn't irritation that things had changed; it was humility.

Riddick shrugged off the thought, not quite ready for it. *Relax*, he told himself. No need to panic. Nothing changed, he reminded himself.

For fuck's sake, *everything* had changed.

Her bravery in telling him how she felt lay between them. It was something he both admired and feared. This was dangerous territory, and he had no idea what he was doing. Once more, he told himself to relax.

He'd just returned to the apartment when a text came from Dade telling him to call as soon as possible. After making sure Khara was still asleep, Riddick stepped into her office and closed the sliding doors. Dade picked up on the first ring.

"I've got shit news. Maybe nothing, but just a heads-up."

An old teammate of theirs died two weeks ago in Miami under suspicious circumstances. They'd worked together on a single mission—the last one—and grown apart, then lost touch.

Morgan had battled addiction for years. All signs pointed to his death being related to that.

After thanking Dade for letting him know and disconnecting, Riddick put it out of his mind and got cleaned up. He'd think about it later when his thoughts weren't so crowded.

He cooked breakfast, set a beautiful table. Khara's kitchen was a marvel he rather enjoyed creating in.

"You could spoil a girl like this."

"Maybe a girl deserves to be spoiled." Truth be told, he did like spoiling her. He didn't even know himself anymore.

"I didn't plan on it, you know. Loving you. I didn't want to. God, I tried so hard not to. I don't know what to do with it now."

Her uncertainty made his blood run cold. *He* didn't know what to do with it now, either, but he didn't want her to be unhappy over this turn of events. Words failed him, so Riddick leaned over and left a gentle kiss on her cheek instead.

Chapter Thirty-Six

THE ALARM THEY HAD the following morning was not a training.

Two burly Guards met Riddick at the gym and instructed him to stay put until a potential threat was dealt with.

When they received the all-clear, Riddick bolted to Khara's apartment. She was standing in the kitchen near the coffee machine when he burst in. "What happened? Are you alright?"

Khara yawned as she got two mugs down from the open cabinet. "An intruder in the building."

"An—" Riddick stopped himself and pulled in a steadying breath. His heart was galloping as though he'd been for an extended run.

"Riddick, you look like you've seen a ghost. Everything's alright. He didn't get far."

Folding her into a tight hug was all he could manage when his words failed him. The heart-clutching terror of that moment stayed with him all day.

Later, he took Khara to bed and loved her as though his life depended on it. He couldn't seem to turn off the intensity since she'd told him she loved him. Every time they came together, it was more and more explosive, but this—this time felt shot through with urgency. He kissed away the questions and confusion in her eyes.

Sleep was impossible for Riddick that night after he received worrying news from Dade. The tripwire on Riddick's military records had been triggered. Someone could be looking for him or at him. That alone wasn't cause for much concern. But that, Blandon's release, and Morgan's death—were these things connected?

While uneasiness kept him wide awake, Khara had no apparent trouble. She slept like a lamb at his side, oblivious to the dagger she might have hanging over her head.

It could all be unrelated, but so close to Blandon's release…. Trepidation settled over Riddick. Was he putting Khara in danger?

When she'd noticed that Riddick seemed to be withdrawing into himself, Khara attributed it to cabin fever. It would be different in Nevis when they could go out and do things together. When doubts tried to assert themselves, she nudged them away with confidence. Then she saw him staring at a news report on Richardson with a dark expression. It evaporated when she called his name, but it troubled her.

Outside of bed, he'd grown quieter—reticent, even. But in bed, he made love to her with an almost desperate edge, like he couldn't get enough of her and was afraid he'd never get another opportunity to try. He had no answer when she asked what was wrong beyond a lot on his mind. Then he kept distracting her until she couldn't remember what she'd been concerned about in the first place.

Even though the worry lingered, Khara refused to let it rob her of the euphoria she was experiencing. They just needed to get to Nevis.

Chapter Thirty-Seven

A NIGHTMARE WOKE HIM, and a devastating truth came with it.

Khara slept in his arms, trusting as a child. Guileless. She stirred a little, mumbled something in Lytuan as she burrowed closer to his heat, but didn't wake. Riddick soothed her, pressed a kiss to her shoulder, his thudding heart heavy with indecision. He lay there in the dark, listening to the rasp of her breathing and marveled.

His sweet, feisty, beautiful Khara. Making love to her had unlocked something within him. She'd made herself so vulnerable—by revealing her scars, by receiving him with such enthusiasm, by relinquishing control. By loving him.

She didn't wear anything to bed anymore.

It almost hurt to breathe when he looked at her now. And yet, when he did, an optimism he'd never known swelled within him.

I'm in love with you.

Riddick shut his eyes now remembering. He'd scarcely been able to breathe for the happiness that had filled him at her words, the conviction. For the space of a single heartbeat, he'd been foolish enough to believe. To hope. That moment had sung with a clarity and beauty so pure it undid him. And it had been glorious before he clamped down on it. No, she didn't love him. How could she? She didn't know who he truly was, the wounds he carried on his soul. What an embarrassment he could be. How dangerous it could be to be with him.

He'd been so damn naïve to think he was better than he was. He knew better than to think he would ever be able to escape his past—any of it. No matter how hard he'd worked to elevate himself, he couldn't change the fact that he would always be Evelyn and Jordan's gutter rat.

Thief.

Killer.

Guys like him didn't get happy endings.

The terrible truth was that shouldn't have gotten involved with this woman. He'd always known deep down. Just having fun and keeping things light and superficial was different. This had always been borrowed time.

Lytua needed her. All he'd ever be was a liability.

The way Riddick saw it, there were two major problems plaguing him.

Well, three, if he counted Khara being in love with him as a problem. If not a problem, it was... a complication.

Problem number one, the most pressing, was that he wasn't sure if Guacamaya Roja was coming after him or not. He'd witnessed what Sergio Blandon did to the people his enemies cared about.

If someone wanted to hurt him, striking Khara was a surefire way to do it. And with Lemmy's trial coming up, she'd be splashed all over the media again. The Elites would protect her, but he couldn't bring danger to her doorstep. Sergio Blandon did his worst to the significant others of his enemies. Torturing the one left behind with images and recordings. If he got to Khara....

Just the thought made him want to bolt from her as fast and as far as he could. He quelled that impulse so he could try to be rational.

If she wasn't around, though. More accurately, if he wasn't around her, Blandon wouldn't have a significant other to strike at. If she didn't seem important to him, there would be no leverage in harming her.

His absence could ensure her safety.

Problem number two, which could help him with problem number one—this Richardson prick. He was a petty tyrant, and if he wasn't willing to let his animosity go after six years of Khara being Queen, he wouldn't hesitate to go after her about Riddick's past.

Richardson wouldn't stop.

He would keep going until he found an Achilles' Heel to exploit. And he, Riddick, was that Heel. He'd be handing Khara's enemies ammunition. Once Richardson found out about his past, that the Queen was in bed with a former foster care kid, a criminal, a killer, he could whip up a public outcry. He would question Khara's judgment, maybe her fitness to serve as Queen. Her career as Queen might be over.

Riddick would never forgive himself if Khara lost the most important thing in her life because of him. Eventually, she'd resent him and the complications he added to her life. How could he do that to her? He'd been so damn stupid.

He had to end it before word got out. And before Blandon discovered she mattered to him. He needed to disappear from her life.

She thought she loved him, and she was stubborn; she wouldn't give up on them easily. He would have to be unforgivable. The thought of hurting her, though, breaking the trust she'd placed in him, was gut-wrenching.

She'd doubt everything once he shat all over their time together. She'd been nothing but near perfection. Open, honest, giving. He didn't deserve her goodness.

If he cared about her at all, he had to do what was best for her, even if it destroyed him. And he did care. The best way he knew how, which he realized was inadequate.

He didn't belong here. He needed to return to his world and leave her to rule in hers.

Better she hated him and lived than lose her life for loving him.

The Elites would keep her safe from whatever still threatened her. He wouldn't be able to live with himself if someone hurt her because of him.

He got up and dressed, then grabbed his duffel and opened it.

Chapter Thirty-Eight

RIDDICK TOSSED CLOTHES INSIDE his bag but paused to watch Khara sleep for a while—debating himself. He didn't want to break up with her. His heart wanted—*no*. It didn't matter what his damn heart wanted. He needed her alive and living her vibrant life. That was what mattered.

He was so engrossed in his worry he didn't realize she'd woken up until she spoke. "You're deep in thought."

Riddick took a long look at Khara's smiling face, hating that this would be the last time she ever smiled at him. He'd hold this memory close. He'd stolen all the moments he could. It was time.

"I've been thinking," he started, regret already twisting his stomach into knots. He sat on the edge of the bed.

Khara slid her arms around him from behind, nuzzled his earlobe. "Yeah? What about?" Her voice was husky with sleep, sexier than usual.

Riddick steeled himself, hardened his heart before he gave into the temptation to sink into her embrace. "I'm gonna head home." He unwound her arms from him and rose to his feet.

Khara was frowning. Then gasped when she spotted the duffel. "Did something happen at home? Oh, God, is it Maya? Dion?"

Dammit. Of course, she'd be concerned for his people. Christ, he didn't deserve her concern. "Not that. Look, it's been good and all—great, really—but this isn't working out." He made his voice as emotionless as he could, despite the anguish roiling inside.

"What?" Khara threw on her robe, furiously tied the belt. "No. I don't believe that. What's really going on here?"

He looked away from her lusciousness. He had to or he'd lose his resolve. The robe stopped barely at mid-thigh—thighs he'd become well-acquainted with in the last few days—and, by God, did he want to bury himself between them again. He shut it down. He had no right to want her. None. Not when he was doing his level best to shatter her heart. She was looking at him levelly, though, that too-perceptive gaze speculative.

He hated seeing her cover up. She'd been so open with her body once she'd revealed herself to him. "This isn't working out," he repeated lamely.

"Is this because I told you I love you? If I scared you or overwhelmed you—please be assured I didn't say it to obligate you. I've never felt about anyone what I feel for you."

That hit him like a gut punch. "What, did you think we would get married, have kids, live happily ever after?"

"The thought crossed my mind, but that seemed premature."

Fuck, she was being too reasonable about this. She wasn't nearly upset enough. He respected her for it, that she was as level-headed as ever, even as he was cutting a fool. Riddick floundered for a moment, then purposely recalled the horrifying image of another woman Sergio Blandon had tortured and mutilated to get back at her husband. That strengthened his resolve. He had to come up with something that would throw her off completely. Needy? Clingy? She was too strong and self-possessed to believe any of that weak shit. "Just mail my stuff to me."

"What did I miss? The last thing I remember is you telling me to get some rest because you weren't through with me. What changed between then and now?

"You're moving too fast," Riddick forced himself to continue, despite the self-loathing. She trailed him into the living room. What he was doing to her was reprehensible, but he had no choice. He couldn't leave any doubt. He had to make her believe. "We both got what we wanted. Time to get back to the real world."

She gasped. The hurt that crept into her eyes turned his stomach. She grasped the lapels of her robe together in one hand. "Why... why would you say something that hurtful? This is not like you."

He hated the anguish and uncertainty in her voice. He savagely shoved his concern aside and went for the kill. "We had a good time; that's all it was ever going to be. This being cooped up isn't really my thing."

Reducing what they'd shared to such raunchy, disrespectful terms felt akin to blasphemy. He'd never spoken to anyone in such a cavalier manner as this, even in his worst breakups. Khara looked stricken. And who could blame her? The love they'd made not three hours ago had been tender and sweet. His lovely Khara didn't deserve this goading. "I think we both got what we wanted—it was simmering for a while; just can't deal with all you have going on."

Khara took a step backward and closed her eyes. "You said you didn't mind—I couldn't have misjudged you so."

Using the slide deck was the last resort and Riddick thought hard about it but decided against it. He couldn't hurt her to the core that way. He wasn't that much of a bastard. "For fuck's sake, Khara. It's over. Have some dignity."

That did it.

The words landed like a blow, and in that moment, Riddick despised himself. Confusion brimmed in those beautiful, expressive eyes. He'd killed the joy, the sparkle that usually resided there. The color drained from her face. He watched Khara gather herself, straighten, struggle against the urge to say more. Her back was ramrod straight as she strode to the bedroom. A moment later, she was speaking in Lytuan to someone on the phone. She returned, looked at him from the doorway. "Cenn will pick you up in ten minutes and get you home."

The hollowness of her voice concerned him. Riddick wasn't sure if he'd gone too far or not far enough. Maybe he'd gone too far. "Khara—"

She raised her hand to stop him. "You don't need to say another word. I heard you loud and clear. You can see yourself right out of my life."

"Can I—" He had no idea what he was going to say.

Now it was anger that sprang into her eyes. "You can go straight to hell, Joshua Riddick."

Riddick grabbed his duffel by the handle and walked out.

Chapter Thirty-Nine

R IDDICK BRACED HIMSELF OUTSIDE her door with his eyes closed, leaning against the frame and unable to get enough air into his lungs. She was crying. Hearing his Khara cry almost made him lose his nerve. He balled his fist, wanted to kick something for how he'd cut her so deep. He couldn't leave her wounded like this. And yet, he had to. This was for her own safety, for her future. Better she hated him and stayed alive and whole and continue to rule. Her sobs tore at him, adding to the already painful pounding of his heart. He felt ill.

No dramatics. No hysterics from his Khara, even as he'd been a grade-A asshole. She had maintained every bit of her dignity despite his words to the contrary. How he wished he could yank the terrible words back into his mouth and leave them unsaid.

"Oh, I beg your pardon. You must be the person whose correspondence makes the Queen light up."

Riddick opened his eyes and turned to see an elderly woman with snow-white dreads behind him, holding a canvas grocery bag. Riddick straightened, mumbled an apology in Lytuan, and fought the urge to slink out of the building. This must be Ms. Bloom. Rotten timing. He said nothing else, just left her standing there as he got in the elevator.

He forced cheerfulness into his voice when Cenn pulled up.

"Is everything alright?" Cenn asked, reading something in his face.

"Why wouldn't it be?"

"You seem... off."

Off? Good God, his entire world was upside down. Consumed by flames. "Nope. Everything's fine. Just ready to get home and back to work."

She wasn't buying it, but she didn't say more. He and Khara were supposed to be flying to Nevis in two days. He kept the belligerent act going until she dropped him off at the airport, assuring her he was fine to wait the two hours until boarding. Once on the plane, he dropped his head into his hands and let out a long, low curse. *I'm sorry*, he thought, morose and disgusted with himself. He'd meant it when he'd promised her that he wouldn't say ugly or hurtful things. Then he'd gone and done just that. His word was important to him and he'd broken it in the worst way possible.

He was the lowest of the low. He'd seen the hard-earned trust she'd placed in him crumble right before his eyes. It was the most heinous thing he'd ever done.

Her life wouldn't be in danger anymore, though. Her career wasn't at risk. Which was all he wanted for her. She'd be safe and eventually happy. She would be neither of those things with him.

The jagged ache in his chest told Riddick he'd just destroyed the very best thing that had ever happened to him. He'd never had anything better, and he never would again.

Goddammit, was he ever fucked.

Ms. Bloom had watched the tall young man go, a little concerned. After putting her groceries away, she still had a niggling feeling of worry in the pit of her stomach.

She received no answer when she knocked on the Queen's door, but Ms. Bloom could hear crying. Between that and the gentleman who had all but skulked out, Ms. Bloom grew alarmed. Returning to her home, she activated the call button the Elite Guard had equipped her with years ago.

Chapter Forty

K HARA PRESSED A HAND to her heart after the door closed with devastating finality, sinking to the couch when her legs wouldn't hold her. It hurt to breathe. They'd just had a good time. She'd been so, so naïve. Why had she believed this would be different? The tears came in a flood, wouldn't be held back.

She heard knocking, Jonnis' anxious voice, but couldn't bring herself to answer, even knowing she'd worry.

"*Avlah*?" Jonnis breathed. She'd used the emergency override key and found Khara sobbing disconsolately on the couch. "Are you hurt? Have you been threatened?"

Khara turned away, her voice trembling and unconvincing when she said she was fine, just not feeling very well. She tried to get control of herself and only ended up sobbing harder. "I'm okay. I'm okay. Just give me a moment. Please, God, just give me—" Khara dissolved into a heap of tears. "Please, just leave me alone. I need a—"

Instead of leaving, Jonnis came closer. "*Avlah*, I—"

"Please, just *leave*!" Khara lashed out, her voice raised uncharacteristically. "Everyone is always in my business. Can't I have one fucking minute on my own?"

Jonnis was stunned, she could only stand and stare. Mortified, Khara slapped a hand over her mouth, ashamed to have said something so terrible to one of her Elites. "Oh, my God, Jonnis, I'm so sorry. I never—I—"

Tears were already blurring her vision. She couldn't contain the sobs.

The shock on Jonnis' face gave way to compassion. "It's alright, *Avlah*. If you don't need any assistance, I'll leave you for now." Flummoxed and unsure of what to say, she departed.

Drawing her knees up to her chest, Khara wrapped her arms around herself and rocked.

What a fool she was, entrusting Riddick with her heart. She'd almost dared to believe they'd spend the rest of their lives together.

Khara rested her cheek on her arms and bawled out her heartache.

Chapter Forty-One

K HARA WASN'T A CRIER. Not usually. But she couldn't seem to get through an hour without sobbing now. She was so damn foolish. She cried through the night between fitful bouts of sleep and into the next day.

Her face was puffy and hot; she didn't dare look in the mirror. She hid in her apartment, afraid she wouldn't be able to stop crying.

A pounding headache forced her back to bed, where after getting herself under control, she burst into tears again. Disgusted with herself, she stomped out to the living room to snatch the throw from the sofa and gather it around herself, berating herself all the while.

She was a fool. A whole, entire fool. Her stomach was too upset to eat, although she considered getting drunk. Ultimately, she decided against it. Then she'd just have a hangover on top of heartache.

After switching a security briefing to virtual format, Khara got herself muted and the camera turned off in time before the dam gave way. She'd never been like this. Not after her cancer diagnosis, not even after her parents' deaths. This was agonizing, unfamiliar territory.

She'd thought Riddick was different, but she should have known better. Just because they connected before he learned her identity didn't negate the fact that no one wanted her as she was.

Nevis offered the perfect hideaway. She'd already packed for the trip, so she didn't have to worry about that. She could wallow in self-pity all she wanted there.

Joanne arrived to escort her to the airport the following morning, took one look at her, and gasped. "Oh, no. *Avlah*. Khara? What happened?"

Khara shook her head and reached for the handle of her suitcase. "I should've known it was too good to last. It doesn't matter." Somehow, she twisted her mouth to say such things when she was dying inside.

While she'd been desperate to get out of her apartment where everything smelled like *Riddick*, the couples-only resort she'd chosen was a nightmare. Much too quiet, too much space. She'd forgotten all the romantic surprises she'd added the day she and Riddick made love for the first time. The couples' spa treatments and chef-prepared dinners were awkward. Even the sunset cruise with live music was survivable. But she was ready to run screaming from the resort when the catering staff arrived for the champagne and chocolate tasting. Her sobs had subsided into desultory sniffles by then, but the rose petals strewn everywhere broke her open again. Riddick probably would have hated every moment of this, since she didn't know him at all, it seemed.

She had to get out of there. She needed to do something to occupy her mind and her time, she decided. Then she'd have no choice but to pull herself together.

God, she had to stop *crying*.

Chapter Forty-Two

JADEN RETURNED FROM HIS long-overdue vacation relaxed and refreshed, but it was short-lived.

He went straight to Khara's office to check in when his family got back. He took Dorian along with him, for she adored the Elites' children, and it was mutual. The flight exhausted his pregnant wife, who needed a nap. The Queen was full of warmth and smiles when greeting his son, scooping him up into a big hug with lots of kisses. Dorian chattered non-stop about the trip, even presenting her with a prized shell he'd found on the beach.

Even though Khara listened and asked questions of his son, something felt off. The vibe was... unsettled. She wouldn't meet his eyes. Jaden re-directed Dorian to the selection of toys and coloring supplies Khara kept in her office for her youngest visitors and turned to face her full-on.

She buzzed around, telling him she'd changed her mind about going to a conference in Casablanca.

"Should we invite Mr. Riddick?"

"That won't be necessary, thank you. We won't be seeing him again."

The casual way she made the pronouncement didn't quite conceal the pain, but she wouldn't look up, was suddenly very busy rummaging through her bag.

Jaden frowned at the top of her head. "*Avlah—*"

When she met his eyes at last, she wasn't quite able to smother the misery and grief before he glimpsed it. She gave a small shake of her head, declaring the subject off-limits.

Her shoulders held tension, the sleepless nights visible in the sunken cheeks and fatigue lining her face. What the hell? She'd been walking on air the last time he'd seen her. The joy had now faded from her eyes.

"You want to talk about it?"

Panic at the very thought crossed her expression. Jaden didn't press, just gathered Dorian to take him home.

"Why is *Avlah* sad, Daddy?" he asked in the car.

"I'm not sure, son." But he was sure as hell going to find out.

"Cenn, what the hell happened?" Jaden demanded as soon as he was back in his office.

His lieutenant shrugged from her seat in front of his desk. "I honestly don't know. Before you ask—it happened about a week ago. We weren't going to spoil your vacation. They were fine—like two peas in a pod—and then he wanted to get back home to work, he said. *Avlah* hasn't said a word about him since, like it never happened, almost."

Jaden thanked her for holding the information instead of telling him immediately when it happened. She was right; it would have torpedoed his family's vacation.

Cenn crossed her ankles, her expression turning apprehensive. "Sorry to hit you with more, but Lemmy Barbenoit is dead. Ruled a suicide, but I don't know what to think."

This just kept getting worse. Jaden frowned, filled with uneasiness. "He was our only lead. We'll never get to the bottom of that whole thing. Shit."

"We've been on high alert, but there's nothing to report. We'll stay vigilant."

"What did Mr. Riddick say when you picked him up again?"

Another shrug. "Not much. He said he needed to get back to work."

"I thought sure those two were skipping toward the altar."

"As did I."

Jaden drummed his fingers on the desk and sat back in his chair. "Well, couples break up all the time. *Avlah's* a big girl. It's none of our business."

"None whatever. But...." Cenn looked pained. "She cries at night. Jonnis and Link have both heard her."

A wave of anger for his friend swelled within Jaden. He let out a deep sigh. "Shit. He broke her heart. That son of a bitch."

"That's my guess. But I don't know anything."

The heaviness in her demeanor concerned Jaden. Was she remembering how awful it had been when she'd broken up with her husband before they were married? It had devastated her. Jaden schooled his face, willing the frown away. "We'd better let her sort it out."

It didn't sit well with either of them or with any of the team.

Chapter Forty-Three

RIDDICK'S FUCK-IT-ALL BRAVADO HELD up for eight days.

Calling in sick allowed him to hide out at home, away from curious eyes that knew him too well. As surly and out of sorts as he was, heads would've gotten bitten off if he'd gone to work.

What had he been thinking, getting involved with her like this? He wrestled with his conscience nonstop, thought he'd feel better knowing he'd made the right decision. He'd known it couldn't last. He should have called it off as soon as he found out she was the Queen.

He fingered the pair of inch-long scars on his side. The ridged flesh hardly registered anymore, but he remembered her concern when it happened. How she'd resigned herself to him walking out on her. And didn't he do just that? Didn't he leave her? He'd failed so spectacularly.

The weeks crept by, and he remained a hot mess. He wanted to explain. He didn't want to leave it with Khara hating him. Whenever the temptation to reach out surfaced, he locked it down with ruthless efficiency by reminding himself that he was doing this for her future. She would get over him and get on with her life. She didn't need any lame explanations from him. Perhaps she would thank him one day. There was no way they could have worked out with his past. Any of it.

And he would never get over her.

Riddick ran for miles at a time several times a day, took himself through punishing workouts, anything to keep the gnawing ache away. It didn't matter that he was risking injury if he kept it up. He deserved worse.

He figured his best bet was to get drunk and party until he could forget about Khara for a while. The first part of the plan—getting shitfaced—went off without a hitch. Then his brilliant idea stalled. The idea of partying was repugnant. Thinking of Khara was excruciating. She shined bright in his memories, though, and thoughts of her consumed him. Her laugh, her voice, her smile. How she felt under him, clenching and clasping around him and gasping his name as she came to bliss.

How she'd worn nothing to bed after revealing her entire self.

The feel of her fingertips trailing down his spine.

What it felt like when she'd looked at him like he had no equal.

Being held in her high regard had been indescribable. Riddick hated that he'd damaged that.

Those days they'd spent in her bed were the best days of his life. There was no way around it.

He dreamed of her. Kept reliving their last conversation. He found he was sketching her face everywhere. It was all he could do just to get through each day.

She'd recoil and turn away in disgust if she knew the truth, the things he'd done to survive. There was no place for that in her world. So, he'd lied to her. Insulted her.

And he'd done it right before her big parliament session, too, he realized. There had to be a special corner in hell waiting for him. It was torture to watch the livestream, but it was a car crash he couldn't look away from. Khara was beautiful and as poised as ever, which just provided further proof that she didn't need him or his baggage.

Then a box arrived from Lytua.

A fresh wave of remorse engulfed Riddick at the sight of Khara's precise handwriting. He stood in his foyer, tracing his finger over the return address. She'd used her own name, not her title. For a moment, he wobbled. He missed her so goddamn much.

It took him the better part of a day to gather the courage to open the box. The scent of her wafted out and assailed him, hitting him like a spear in the belly. He let his eyes drift closed. It was a mistake to do so, for the image of her lying next to him in bed came to him, every detail in sharp relief. The freckles he'd counted with kisses, her hair tangled because she'd forgotten to wrap it. Riddick shoved the images away. He couldn't take the piercing ache in his chest that came with them.

But the truth would no longer be denied.

It came blazing into him right then, without any sort of warning. Riddick sucked in a ragged breath with the realization and the agony it brought.

He'd gone and fallen in love with the woman. Damn it all to hell.

He loved her.

He loved Khara.

The thing he never thought himself capable of. The *only* thing.

He had to grab the edge of the table to steady himself. Riddick needed to sit with that for a bit before he could go through the box's contents. Inside were a few items he'd left behind, including the copy of his house key he'd had made for her. There was no note—shocker. Something colorful at the bottom of the box caught his attention. It was one of her scarves. It must have gotten mixed in with the rest of the items. He bunched the scrap of fabric in his fist, the melancholy swelling within him, even as he brought it to his nose. Her delicate scent almost broke him.

Just like that—the bravado wavered. What the hell was he doing? He didn't think he'd ever be able to love someone, to fall in love. And yet... he simply loved her. Guilt soon eclipsed the wonder he felt.

He'd broken her heart, made it impossible to forgive him. He'd done the right thing, hadn't he? Who was he to think he could give her anything other than broken shards of his tortured soul?

Let Blandon come for him. There was nothing left of him to hurt.

Chapter Forty-Four

T HE NEXT WEEKS WERE like Khara was sleepwalking. She threw her-self into her work, despite being on vacation. Filled her schedule to overflowing to leave as little time as possible for thoughts of what couldn't be. She couldn't bear the sympathetic looks from Joanne and the others. It put her teeth on edge.

She attended the requisite functions and put on a brave face.

When she was off duty, she kept to herself and fell into bed exhausted every night. She did everything she could, tried to keep her mind busy and off the fact that she'd been unceremoniously dumped by the man she was sure she loved. She was miserable and hated it. Her brain wouldn't let her rest, kept replaying memories and images of their happy times together until Khara thought she'd scream.

She hadn't been able to pack his things to send him right away. It was still too raw. Then she found herself snatching things up from all over her home in the middle of the night when she couldn't sleep again. She forced herself not to smell a T-shirt he'd left behind, even though her heart had longed for it. The sooner she got all traces of him gone, she could start to put herself back together again.

One thing was for sure: she was officially through with romance. She'd be a proud spinster Queen, dedicated to her work. Maybe if she worked hard enough, she'd stop dreaming of him coaxing her to come again right before he did. She'd been right about him being relentless in pursuit of her pleasure. He'd never left her unsatisfied.

Just brokenhearted. The bitter thought burned.

She tried to reason with herself that she'd just gotten swept up in the moment. Carried away. Extraordinary sex could do that to you. And it *had* been extraordinary.

His drawings were everywhere, far too beautiful to discard. She packed those up, too. She found one he did of her smiling in her sleep right before their breakup. Another of them laughing together hung on the refrigerator. She snatched it down and gasped when the sheet almost split in two. It was like a wound ripping through her soul. Just like that, she was weeping again. She couldn't bring herself to throw it away or repair it and just put it back up.

She told herself that she didn't care, but.... What man was ever going to want to be second banana? Gary hadn't, although he was an absolute dick and shouldn't even count. Riddick hadn't, and she'd thought he was different.

Thinking of Gary—asshole that he was—led Khara to remember how Riddick had turned her on with some very sexy talk and directions, but never once said the word "fellatio." God, was anything less sexy than that clinical term? Oh, he'd had plenty to say about her mouth on his cock, though. *Plenty.*

Khara cut that thought off abruptly as the too-familiar tingles started in her core. Why did she keep thinking about the fun times?

She couldn't help who she was. And she wasn't going to change for a man, no matter how she felt about him. Now, if she could just get her heart back onboard with all that, she'd be fine. Maybe. At some point.

Chapter Forty-Five

R IDDICK OPENED THE DOOR expecting his food delivery and got the shock of his life seeing his mother standing on his doorstep.

"What the hell, Ma?"

She wasn't due home for several months. He'd emailed her a couple of days ago that he must have caught a bug on his trip and had a ton of work to catch up on. In answer to her question about how Khara was doing, Riddick said she was fine. It hurt to type the words. He didn't consider it a lie, more like wishful thinking.

"What happened?" she asked.

He dodged the question. "Aren't you supposed to be in, what, New Zealand or something?"

"Tahiti, actually. My son needed me, so I came home."

"You cut your trip short?" Riddick was agog.

"There's something wrong with my son. Of course, I cut my trip short."

With that, all the bravado left him, and his throat closed. She'd planned this trip for *years*. "How—?"

"You've never been sick a day in your life and you haven't sent an email that wasn't gushing about Khara for months. Then she's 'fine' suddenly? Eric and Maya emailed me. They're worried about you."

Shit, Riddick hadn't thought of that. His feelings of guilt swelled.

The real delivery person arrived then. Riddick accepted the bags but couldn't even remember what he'd ordered.

As soon as she saw him, Parie knew something drastic had gone wrong. The entire ordeal was written in the misery on his face. She set about making tea. Joshie slumped up onto one of the kitchen counter stools, paying no attention to the delivered food. It had taken three planes and thirty-one hours of flight time to get to her son.

She placed a steaming mug of chamomile before him and sat down next to him. "What happened?"

"We... I broke it off. She thinks she's in love with me." He laughed, but it was brittle.

"Is that so unbelievable?"

"She's better off."

"Are *you*? Do you think you bring nothing to the bargain?"

Shock rippled through Parie when her all-his-shit-together son crumpled in on himself. "What did she say when you broke it off?"

"I didn't give her much of a chance to say anything. I was too busy insulting her and trying to make her hate me."

Parie pressed her lips together in disapproval. Joshie needed her support right now, not her judgment. "Why don't you start at the beginning?"

The story came pouring out and Parie kept her face as neutral as possible. Though she sensed he was hiding something, she didn't push.

"Call her, Joshie. Seriously. Tell her the truth and you might still have a chance."

"I buried any chance I had."

"I know you were trying to protect her career, but you didn't give her a chance to decide for herself."

Riddick said nothing, just fiddled with his mug.

"Dammit, Joshie. Why? What you told me about her—she doesn't sound like the type to judge."

"Because I love her. I'm afraid for her."

Astonishment lodged the breath in Parie's throat. *Dear Lord.* Joshie had never, ever said he loved a woman. Not once. Never even believed he had the capability. He'd always kept that vulnerable side of himself so closed off and guarded. Of course, he must have been freaked out, trying to sort through all the newness. Some part of him was probably scared to death. "You deserve her. You deserve every good thing, including her."

"I don't." He was shaking his head.

"Did she tell you that?" Affront bristled through her.

"No, nothing like that. It was all me."

"I don't think you're giving her or yourself enough credit. You might be making a mistake."

"My mistake was getting involved with her in the first place."

He didn't believe that. Not really. Parie kept the sentiment to herself. He was grieving, the wound still fresh. "What you had—it wasn't worth fighting for?"

At this, Riddick turned away, offered nothing to defend himself.

Being who she was, Parie had not been the least bit impressed with Khara's identity until Riddick had explained how the Lytuan government worked.

She discovered some of his sketches, took a moment to examine them. The care and attention to the details were breathtaking. Love was evident in how he'd captured Khara's face, her posture. It was all but springing from the page. He really was an amazing artist. "Oh, Joshie, these are beautiful. So is she."

Parie kissed her son's forehead and told him she loved him. "You have to stop punishing yourself."

"This isn't about—"

"Of course it is. This is complete self-sabotage."

His frown confused her. Was it possible he hadn't considered that?

Parie wasn't sure what to think. Should she say more? Or talk to Khara? She dismissed both thoughts. Parie's heart hurt for her son, but he'd have to work through this himself.

Parie looked at the exquisite drawing of Khara in her hand. The half smile she looked back over her shoulder with was flirtatious and intimate. So much love in the rendering—in the curve of her lips, the mischief in her eyes. That he could feel this deeply for a woman brought her profound joy. She wanted to meet this woman who seemed to have broken something open inside her son. Hoped she would get the chance.

Her heart ached for Khara, too. She must be so hurt and confused.

Despite what Joshie had said, Parie didn't believe the situation was hopeless. Perhaps with time, he'd realize that and do something about it. Right now, he had some grappling to do. Until then, all she could do was encourage him. Parie sent up a prayer to the universe to help these two kids find their way back to each other.

Chapter Forty-Six

"A VLAH, A MOMENT?"

Richardson approached Khara as the other committee chairs filed out of the conference room after their meeting. Did he want to berate her for another perceived infraction?

Khara shoved her irritation aside. He never offered the slightest variety. "Yes, Senator?"

"May I speak with you in private?"

Her impulse was to refuse, for surely no good would come of this. But she was a servant leader. She nodded her assent, waved off the Guard stationed outside the room, and waited for Richardson to close the door.

"I, ah, know we've never gotten along, but I need to ask a favor."

That's one hell of an understatement. It intrigued her, though, despite her misgivings. The man had some nerve to ask her for anything given his crusade to make her professional life miserable. "What is it, Senator Richardson?"

He was squirming. "Would you consider going out with Cyrus just once, then saying it didn't work out? It would make him and Trina so very happy."

When she stiffened and simply glared at him, Richardson grimaced, tugging at his collar. "I know it's an unusual request—"

"It's an inappropriate request. Entirely." He smelled of liquor.

"Would you try? Please?"

"This preposterous conversation is over."

He blocked her path as she attempted to leave the conference room. "Just hear me out."

"I will do no such thing." Outraged, Khara moved to push by him, but he caught her arm and pulled her back. "Remove your hand from me at once!"

"I will in a—"

His sentence ended in a coughing sort of gasp as Khara rammed the heel of her hand into his solar plexus. He dropped his hold on her and stumbled back into the wall.

At the thumping noise, the conference room door flew open, and the room Guard reappeared, her face grim and a hand on her weapon. "*Avlah*?"

"I'm fine. I was just leaving."

Richardson clasped a hand to his chest, was still coughing when she marched out. Khara forced herself to calm as she walked with purposeful strides toward her office. She'd regained control of her demeanor after just a few steps. It wouldn't do for others to see their leader storming about.

The temerity of that man. Propositioning his sovereign as though she were a dating app. Or an escort.

She might be brokenhearted, but she hadn't fallen so far that she would consider such a request. Why would she care about what would make his wife and son happy? That wasn't her responsibility.

It hadn't been regal to strike him, but he most certainly should not have behaved in such a manner. So un-Senatorial. She should have kneed his balls into his throat and let the Guard arrest him.

How about some public shaming for making Cyrus and Trina happy?

Chapter Forty-Seven

THE ONLY THING RIDDICK roused himself from his funk of self-pity for was his regular meeting with Dion. Nothing would get in the way of that relationship. No matter how sorry he felt for himself. They were still healing from their earlier rupture.

Dion shot surreptitious looks at him during their study session at the library.

"So, what happened to that chick you were seeing?" Dion finally asked.

"Not poultry, Dee. Remember? Khara and I broke up."

"Shame. She was a fine piece of ass."

"Hey." A fine thread of irritation wreathed the single word. "We might have broken up, but I still think the world of her. A real man doesn't badmouth someone because things didn't work out. That's common and you are anything but. Trash-talking says more about the person doing it. Don't be that guy."

Dion grunted. "You love her?"

"Yeah, I do. I know this might seem hard for you to believe right now, but it's not a weakness to love a woman. It can... make you want to be the best version of yourself."

Sitting back in his chair, Dion slanted a hard look at him. "Yeah? Is this the best version of you? You look like you got mugged and slept in the gutter. Why'd you break up?"

Because I'm an idiot, Riddick thought ruefully, but didn't say. "It's complicated." He did not want to talk about his dumpster fire of a love life, but Dion wouldn't let it go.

"You sleep with her? Did you knock her up? You *are* whipped! Damn, man, I thought—"

The teen came to an abrupt stop at the obvious disapproval in Riddick's expression. He dropped his gaze, mumbled an apology.

Riddick laid a hand on Dion's shoulder and gave it a gentle squeeze, waited for him to meet his eyes again. "I made love with her. Not at all the same thing."

"You use a condom like you always tell me to?"

"Yes. Every time. Safe sex protects both partners, Dion."

"Did you mess it up?"

Riddick's sigh was heavy with self-recrimination. "Yeah, I messed it up. Bad."

"Can't you make it right?"

Riddick shook his head. "It's for the best. She's too good for me."

"Fu—bump that. If you love her and you messed up, why ain't you fighting for her, then?"

"Like I said, it's complicated. That's enough about that. Let's see some more work on this science project."

Dion peered at him with eyes full of skepticism, then surged to his feet. "No. What you've been telling me for years is when it's something you believe in, you don't go down swinging, you swing hard enough to not go down in the first place."

Great, he was a hypocrite on top of everything else now, too. So much winning. Riddick slapped that sentiment back. He didn't get to be glib after the shit he'd just done. His face had turned stony. "I don't have an easy answer here. Sometimes couples break up."

"Yeah?" Dion crossed his arms over his narrow chest. "You looked at her like she was the best thing in the world."

It was true. And it hurt like hell. "She was. Just not my world anymore."

"I knew you were full of shit."

"Hey," Riddick showed some temper at that. He'd never gotten pushback like this from Dion before. He'd let him down, too, he realized. "That's not fair."

"You always said fuck fair. Well, fuck *you*. I thought you were gonna marry her and move and never come back."

He was making a damn mess out of everything. "Even if I did move, I'd still be here for you. You're always going to be a part of my life, Dee."

Dion wasn't having it. He shrugged away from Riddick when he tried to put a hand on his shoulder again. "Don't fucking patronize me!" He gathered his things and left, leaving Riddick to his misery.

Because he couldn't help himself, Riddick went to the *Augustus Herald* website and almost dropped the phone when a picture of Khara standing next to some guy came up. They were standing close together, both dressed up, and she was wearing a crown he hadn't seen before. Not only that, but she was also wearing that blue gown she'd worn to the White House, the one he'd touched her in, had damn near made love to her in the back seat of that goddamn limo in. She'd looked like an angel, a precious feast spread before him. He'd never taste that sweetness again. His memories would have to be enough.

Riddick felt an almost violent reaction to the picture. He didn't read enough Lytuan to understand what the picture caption said, but he could guess. Something along the lines of *Avlah's out on the town after piece-of-shit American dumps her.*

He texted Dion a little later, figuring he'd had a chance to cool off.

Riddick: I'm not in a good headspace right now, but I'm not mad at you.

He watched the three dots showing Dion typed a response, but nothing came through right away. Frowning, Riddick dialed Dion's number.

He answered with a sullen, "Hey."

"You know I'll always listen if there's something you want to say."

The kid's breath hitched like he was struggling not to cry.

"Dee?"

"Is this... is it my fault? Like I could maybe talk to Khara and tell her."

God, this kid. Riddick's heart couldn't take any more strife. "Dion, no. It was not your fault. It had nothing to do with you and everything to do with me. Khara is...." He couldn't find the words to describe what Khara meant to him. Couldn't make a teenager understand how damn much it hurt to breathe without her.

"My dad told me it was my fault. If I hadn't been so bad, my mom wouldn't have left—"

"That wasn't your fault, either. Adults make stupid choices sometimes." Riddick's throat was burning. If Dion's dad wasn't already out of the picture for good.... "It's easier to blame someone who can't fight back than it is to take responsibility for your own shit."

"You would tell me, right? If it was my fault."

"No. Because it can't be your fault."

By the time they hung up, Riddick reassured Dion, but Riddick himself was as hollow as ever.

Chapter Forty-Eight

COREY RICHARDSON WAS IN her face again.

This time, disheveled and smelling more strongly of liquor. He stood in front of her desk, wearing a shamed expression. If Joanne hadn't announced him with, "He says he's here to apologize for the other day," Khara wouldn't have let him in.

"I want to apologize. I was completely out of line." It must be killing him to say it, but he sounded sincere.

Her personal cell chimed with an incoming text from Yvanda, but she ignored it. Khara didn't dare take her eyes off this man.

Why did he hate her so?

He let his mask slip a little, and she glimpsed the exhausted man beneath it, wearing an air of defeat. He was looking at her with imploring, blood-shot eyes.

"Thank you for not pressing charges. I'm in your debt."

Something softened in her the tiniest amount. "There is no debt owed."

The man was swaying on his feet. Khara bade him sit down. He sagged down into one of the chairs in her seating area and squeezed his eyes closed.

The Senator's behavior the last week in Parliament had grown erratic and now he was here before her, drunk again. Khara asked Joanne to get Deputy Chief Krove on the line.

Trina's voice on the phone was hesitant when Khara greeted her.

"Deputy Chief, your husband is here in my office. I don't want to say too much, but I'd like you to please come and join us as soon as possible. How quickly can you get here?"

She sounded far more confident when she said, "Thirty minutes, give or take."

"Very well. I'll let Joanne know to expect you."

The Senator had roused himself enough to look horrified. "You called Trina? She's coming here?"

"Senator, this is the second time you've come to me in an intoxicated state. It is worrisome. I'm going to give you a choice. I can order you to a rehab facility, which would rob you of the choice to do so on your own."

"Or what?"

"You know that if you refuse that order, you can be recalled and charged with treason. On the other hand, you can make your own decision to go. As a professional courtesy, I will allow this to remain private between the two of us. You can tell your family, your constituents, whatever you wish."

Richardson collapsed back into the chair, a worried expression creeping over his face. He'd fallen asleep while she worked and when Joanne ushered in Deputy Chief Krove. Their son, Cyrus, was with her. Trina's open, buoyant expression transformed into horror when she caught sight of the state of her husband.

"What have you done to him?" she snapped at Khara, hurrying to his side.

Before she could answer, Richardson woke and started crying, moaning how sorry he was. Trina gathered him in a hug and shot daggers at Khara, as though she'd harmed him some way.

"I'm s-sorry, Trina."

Khara looked from husband to wife, unsure what was happening.

"You look pretty today, *Avlah*."

Khara was startled when Cyrus spoke from beside her. She'd been so focused on the unfolding drama between his parents that she didn't hear him approach. "Oh. Oh, thank you, Cyrus, that's very kind. It's nice to see you again."

Cyrus reached to hug her, but she transformed it into a handshake with practiced ease.

"We thought you were calling with good news. That you might want to—"

"Cyrus!" Trina hissed. "Hush now."

Cyrus shrank into himself at his mother's scolding tone of voice. Khara flushed with sympathy. It shouldn't feel like she was intruding on a private matter when it was *her* office.

Trina helped an openly weeping Richardson to his feet. Cyrus rushed to assist.

Compassion made Khara take a step toward them. "Shall I—"

"I don't want your pity." Trina looked at her with something behind her eyes that sent a frisson of fear up Khara's spine. It was gone in an instant, her polished, professional veneer back in place. But Khara had seen it. Woman to woman, she felt moved to empathy. Did she herself not know what it was like to be disappointed by the man you loved?

Khara whirled around and strode to the window, willing the sudden tears burning at the back of her eyes away. She would never cry in front of a political enemy, but God, she was tired. So damn tired of putting on a brave face. She wanted to stay in her apartment and wallow in ice cream and potato chips.

"I wasn't offering it," she said, still facing away from the family. It wasn't until long after their departure that the tense muscles in her shoulders relaxed.

Chapter Forty-Nine

R IDDICK OPENED THE DOOR a few weeks later to Jaden on his
doorstep, seething with barely concealed fury. Jesus, he never knew
who he'd find at his door these days.

Jaden's astute gaze assessed Riddick, the greatest threat to the happiness
of the woman he'd sworn to protect with his life. Jaden noted the tired
eyes, the dejected slump of his shoulders. Oh, there was a story here, and
he intended to get it. He suppressed the urge to shake him. "You look like
shit."

"Well, I feel like shit. Might as well come on in."

They sat on the back deck, sipping bottles of beer in silence until Riddick broke it. "Who's the asshole in the picture?"

"Which picture?"

"You know damn well who I'm talking about, man."

"You don't get to know that when you broke her heart."

"That's fair. Now tell me anyway."

"Her ex-fiancé."

"The motherfucking asshole that left her while she was in chemo? What
the fuck is he doing back in the picture?"

Jaden crossed his arms and gave Riddick another withering look. Riddick couldn't hold his gaze.

"The Speaker's son showed up sniffing around, too."

"What. The. *Fuck*? That clown Rufus?"

Jaden left out the part about Khara refusing to see him. In fact, she'd been so distressed that she'd retreated to her apartment until he left the island. "It shouldn't matter to you what she does."

Riddick couldn't shake the irritation he had no right to feel. Wasn't this what he'd wanted, for her to move on? The thought of her giving that brilliant smile to someone else, though, made him feel ill.

"You here as the Sentinel or her friend?"

"The Queen is always fine. It's my friend I'm worried about. She didn't send me. She'd twist my dick off if she knew I was here. Aimee might have a problem with that. She hasn't said a single unkind word about you, although God knows I suspect you deserve it. She hasn't talked to anyone about whatever happened between you."

Riddick frowned. He'd thought her friends would support her, that maybe they'd go get drunk and trash him. He didn't like the thought that she'd been alone with it.

"I don't make it a habit of being wrong. I gave you shit when you showed up, just like I do everyone. Suitors come sniffing around her all the time in all sorts of guises, like you wouldn't believe. But those assholes weren't interested in her as a woman, only as a prize.

"When she realized you didn't know who she was? I let her talk me into keeping up the charade, even though I thought it was a terrible idea. And you know I was suspicious. But you *were* interested in her as a woman. I have never seen her so happy. She was lit from within when I left. I did not expect to come back home and find her brokenhearted. You hurt her."

It was excruciating to hear. Thinking of her now, Riddick rubbed a hand over his chest, trying to soothe the ragged ache there. How was his heart still beating when it was walking around in Lytua? "It's... just the best for everybody."

Jaden scoffed. "Don't insult me. There's something else in play here you didn't tell her."

Mild alarm flared in Riddick's eyes. *Ah.* Jaden was on the right track. Time to twist the knife a little. "She cries at night when she thinks no one can hear her."

That bit of knowledge had the desired effect. Riddick closed his eyes and drew in a sharp breath, anguish rippling across his features. "I'm not worth her tears."

"You tried to protect her some kind of way, didn't you?"

Riddick said nothing, but his jaw tightened.

"Whatever you think you're protecting her from, is it worth losing her love for?"

"Nothing will ever be worth that," Riddick snapped.

"Then what the hell are you doing?"

Riddick thought of the awful things he'd said to Khara. The lies he'd made her believe. The hurt, disbelief, and betrayal. His broken promise. He pictured the devastation on her face before he'd turned to leave her. That look haunted him. "I was... protecting her from Richardson and people like him."

Jaden's eyebrows came down as he frowned. "*Senator* Richardson? That blowhard's been after her throne for years. You don't need to worry about him. It's *my* job to protect her from him."

Then Riddick was up and pacing. "He'll exploit any weakness and I'm a danger to her career. I'm that weakness. I didn't tell her... my past could sink her career. Richardson would use it against her, I'm sure."

"You're not giving her enough credit. She can handle herself if someone gets catty about her boyfriend's past."

"You know it's more than that." Riddick only hesitated a moment. "I don't want any of that touching her, getting in the way of whatever she's trying to do."

"No one will judge you for growing up in foster care or for anything you did while you were. Or for defending yourself as a kid from what, by all accounts, was on its way to being a fatal attack from an adult. Do you think she would fold to people gossiping? You think so little of her fortitude? What do you take her for? She loves you. She would never tolerate shit being slung at you about your childhood."

"I'm worried about her reputation, her career."

"Wait, you thought her career needed saving?"

"Protecting, not saving. She's not some helpless damsel in distress."

Jaden laughed until it hurt. He knew he shouldn't, but the notion was absurd. Riddick's disgruntled expression made him laugh harder.

"And what's so goddamn funny?"

"You're worried about protecting her career? Is that all? That's adorable. Oh, sit down. You can be forgiven for not knowing and being protective. But this is the epitome of ego. You didn't grow up in Lytua and you don't know her as Queen. Let me tell you a few things about Khara Therin, Riddick.

"She overhauled our entire legal system, evaluated every single law on the books one at a time. If it wasn't consistent with current Lytuan values and morals, she got it updated. That was just in her first year. She brought about a lot of social change.

"Khara's built quite a reputation. The citizens love her. There's a reason she's so respected. She takes zero shit and doesn't hesitate to put her citizens' needs first. Every time. Even when it comes at great personal cost. When she took a beating in public opinion about an unpopular decision in a high-profile case, never once did she waver. No hiding or prevaricating or making excuses. She faced it head-on, got right out in front of it. She stood up to a bunch of assassins who were mistreating hostages. Like an avenging angel, even covered in the blood of the PM they'd assassinated right next to her."

Damn, Riddick thought as he digested this. "So, what you're telling me is that she's a badass?"

"Yeah. That's precisely what I'm telling you. You have no idea how strong she is, how she's had to be. She doesn't need you to protect her. She needs you to love her, to accept her."

"What the fuck was I supposed to do? Let her go down in flames? Lose everything? I'm not worth it."

"You were supposed to trust her. She knows what she's doing, and she's good at it. You think she got to where she is by being a pushover?"

"I'd embarrass her, and she'd end up resenting me for it."

"You think you're the only guy who's ever messed up falling in love?"

Riddick gawked at the unexpected pivot.

"I was a dickhead and fucked up my own best thing. I hesitated in telling Aimee how I felt. No good reason either. It left her vulnerable to the lies someone else with an agenda peddled her. She was nearly taken from me before I got my shit together and got it straightened out. If it hadn't been for Cenn—I told you before she saved her life—I wouldn't have had another chance to tell her how I felt.

"Khara doesn't know that you were trying to protect her. All she knows is that the man she loves hurt her. She doesn't even know why. Get your head out of your ass and fix this. Tell her the truth. You fucked up. You underestimated her and let Richardson come between you. He'd love that, by the way. You made a huge mistake. You already know that. Are you brave enough to fix it?"

Riddick shook his head in answer. "I can't fix it. I made sure of it. Even if I could, I wouldn't risk her future. I'm not worth that."

"That's the second time you've said that. That you're not worth it."

"I'm not."

"Until *you* believe you're worth it, you won't be. You *can't* be."

Riddick was silent, obviously dug in.

"You were already with her. The damage would have been done, if that's what you're trying to sell yourself."

Still, Riddick said nothing, leaving Jaden frustrated and angry.

"So, the coward's way out, then?" Jaden stood and looked Riddick over with a mixture of sadness and contempt. "Then that's that. You're an utter fool and you never deserved her. I'll see myself out."

Jaden turned back near the door to the house. "The man who attacked her is dead. Hanged himself in his cell. Ruled as suicide, no reason to suspect otherwise, but I don't like it."

"We know there was at least one other person involved."

"Right. If they wanted her dead, she'd be dead. Best we can tell, it was a ransom scheme."

A chill went through Riddick at the thought of Khara dead. "You don't believe that."

"None of us do. The shooter will either try again or they got scared off. But she won't be frightened into seclusion. She has work to do and a country depends on her. Her words. And that's the essence of the woman who's in love with you, asshole."

Jaden chucked his empty beer bottle into the recycle bin and left Riddick to his stubborn regrets. He had a hand on the sliding door when he turned with one last parting shot. "You're no different than her shitbag ex-fiancé. It would have been kinder if you left after learning who she really is."

At this, Riddick shot to his feet, his fists clenched and fire in his eyes. "Fuck you, Jaden. You don't know shit."

Now this was more like it. "You want to try dropping the bullshit and telling the truth, then? You didn't dump her for Richardson. That's insulting and no way in hell is that the real reason. Or the *only* reason. There's something else. Something serious enough for you to fuck up the best thing that ever happened to you."

"Goddammit!" Riddick exploded. Cornered and embarrassed about being called on it. Why couldn't he make anyone believe he was just that much of a dick? "You wouldn't have risked Aimee's life if you had the power to avoid it, wouldn't you?"

"This isn't about me and Aimee, but there's nothing I wouldn't have done to keep her safe."

"Including leaving her?"

"What the fuck is going on?"

"I don't know how much you know about Central American drug cartels, but they hold grudges, and I didn't want Khara targeted because I care about her. Do you get it now?"

Jaden sobered, switching to Elite mode in a heartbeat. "Is she being threatened by someone from your Ranger days?"

"Not directly, but I won't take chances with her life. Dade is on it."

Riddick gave up all pretense and told Jaden what he could of the Blandon story.

After Jaden had given a heightened alert code to his team, he regarded Riddick and spoke to him in a subdued voice. Almost as though he were afraid to spook him. "That's very different from the Richardson crap. And you still won't—?"

"No. I will never put her in danger. This should be easy for you to understand."

The bitch of it was, Jaden *did* understand. He understood perfectly now. In all likelihood, he would have come to the same conclusion and done something similar. He whistled, long and low. "You are fucked, man."

"Yeah, no kidding."

Chapter Fifty

THE SUMMONS TO THE Queen's office hadn't gone the way Trina hoped. After hanging up with the Queen, she'd stopped to get Cyrus. *This was it*, she'd thought, and love and gratitude filled her knowing Corey had made it happen somehow.

Her heart had plummeted the moment she laid eyes on the sleeping Corey. It had been years, but she'd recognized the posture. He'd fallen off the wagon. Five years sober and he was drunk in the Queen's office. Bitter disappointment tasted like ashes in her mouth.

She'd left with as much dignity as she could muster. She would never forgive Corey for that humiliating moment. She'd have dragged him out by his ankles before she accepted that woman's help.

The car ride home was miserable as Cyrus yammered on about how pretty Lillianna had looked wearing a dress in his favorite color and Corey blubbered with apologies.

He'd slept it off, then gone to work the next day without a word, as though he hadn't yanked the rug out from under her. It troubled Trina as she wondered what signs she'd missed. He'd mentioned being worried about reelection next year, but would that cause him to throw away all the hard work battling his addiction?

They needed to have a serious discussion.

Being in the Queen's presence had enraptured Cyrus. Trina escaped to the relative peace of her office and immersed herself in staff evaluations. Reading her mood, her secretary rescheduled her appointments and made sure she had something to eat for lunch. Fabiola was an excellent secretary and Trina was lucky to have her. She didn't miss Fabiola's concerned expression, even as she turned away from it and shut it out.

Chapter Fifty-One

RIDDICK WAS USELESS AT work, doing a half-assed job of telecommuting. Mindless busy work was all he could handle. He'd emailed Lena when he got home and asked her to cancel his appointments for the foreseeable future. He sat at his laptop and puttered, accomplishing very little.

Out of patience at being blown off, Eric came to his house looking for answers. He found his best friend haggard, unkempt, and hungover when he finally answered his pounding on the door.

"What the actual fuck is going on with you, Riddick? You've never blown a deadline. You left me tap dancing for Copeland. Are you still sick? Why haven't you answered my calls or emails or texted me back?"

Instead of answering, Riddick retreated to the sofa. He was disappointing everyone. "I'm sorry."

Without invitation, Eric sat in the wing chair opposite him. "Talk to me."

"Khara and I broke up."

"Yeah, I figured that part out. What did you do?"

Riddick hesitated, then gave him the abridged version with Richardson as the reason, which left Eric baffled. "Why didn't you just tell her the truth? She didn't strike me as shallow."

When he didn't respond, Eric was even more perplexed. "That can't be all. You couldn't have been dumb enough to let that incredible woman go over that. What else happened? The woman who was with you at Thanksgiving seemed like she's well worth fighting for."

"It's not about worth."

"No? I don't get it. Was there no other way you could have handled this? It's not like you to just... sell yourself short."

"I was afraid for her. I just didn't want her to get hurt because of me."

"How would you being in foster care hurt her now?"

"It could hurt her professionally."

Eric gave him a puzzled look, sensing that there was a lot left unsaid. "Look, man, I've always known you had more happening than you let on and I've never pushed. Seems like there's some additional layer of turmoil going on here. There's more to this than you're telling, isn't there?"

Riddick nodded, sadness in his eyes.

"If you'd been honest with her and she rejected you, that'd be different. She deserves the truth, to know the real reason you broke it off. You're selling her short, too. Maybe she wouldn't care. You took her choice away, and that's not cool. You'll need to answer for that."

"It's not that simple."

"Figure it out, man. Call her. Write to her. Something. Maya's worried about you. You know we've been through it and I'm always going to have your back." He was almost out the door before he gave a dramatic sniff. "And for fuck's sake, man, take a shower. You stink to high heaven. This vagrant-chic look isn't working for you."

While he was standing under the hot water spray, Riddick switched focus. He needed to pull his shit together and get moving again. This pity party had gone on long enough. No matter how crappy things were for him in his personal life, there were still people depending on him, responsibilities to fulfill. He didn't get to just clock out. Eric and Lena would have had to carry everything, and he regretted leaving them in a bind.

Eric had only told the staff that he was on leave and given no further explanation. Folks were glad to see him back and offered warm greetings. Lena's hard gaze flicked over him when he entered his office suite, but there was sympathy there, too.

"Back with the living, are we?"

"Sorry I left you hanging."

"Are you alright?"

"No, but I will be while I'm at work."

Instead of asking about what had transpired, she said, "Let me talk to you for a moment like you weren't my boss, like we're just Lena and Riddick. Just two people who've known each other for years."

She stood up behind her desk, leaned over the high counter to place her hand over his.

"I've never seen you the way you had been, and it was a joy to see. Not just happy, but... invigorated. When someone affects you like that, you work it out. Do whatever you have to and don't let anything stand in your way." She squeezed his hand and smiled at him. "You've been good to me, and I would hate to see you go anywhere, but I'd cry tears of joy if it was because she was the One. And then I'd dance at your wedding. You know how I can get down."

Riddick blinked, his throat clogged with emotion. "Lena—"

But Lena was already back in professional mode. She released his hand and sat down. "Now, you have quite a few important phone calls to return, Mr. Riddick, so let's get on it." She gave it away with a quick swipe under her eye.

"Thank you, Lena."

She flapped a hand to send him on his way, declaring the subject closed.

By the end of the day, Riddick had a new appreciation for the term "emotional exhaustion." The day felt weeks long, leaving him wiped out and ready to collapse into dreamless sleep for a month.

He managed to keep his head in the game to get caught up at work, but his mind wandered to Sergio Blandon, 3,000 miles away. His thoughts refused to stop swirling around his Khara and the threat Blandon could still pose to her and the men and women who protected her. That was an unacceptable risk he couldn't tolerate. His woman might hate him, but he couldn't—*wouldn't*—chance Blandon getting to her.

What if leaving her wasn't enough? Had he left her vulnerable?

When he woke up drenched in sweat in the wake of another fever dream of Blandon lying in wait to pounce on Khara, Riddick choked back the rage and sense of helplessness. He thumped a fist into the mattress. That was it. No more of this shit. This level of uncertainty couldn't go on. A preemptive strike was in order.

It was time to take the fight to Sergio Blandon.

<h1 style="text-align:center;">Chapter Fifty-Two</h1>

RIDDICK DIALED DADE, WHO sounded downright chipper for it being the middle of the night. Didn't the man ever sleep?

"What's up, *hermano*? How's life in paradise?"

"Send me all the stuff you have on Sergio Blandon's release and last known whereabouts."

The pause that greeted his request spun out. At length, Dade addressed him with caution. "You're not going down there, are you?"

"I'm not leaving him as an unknown variable in Khara's life."

"That's quite the declaration there. What's going on?"

Riddick gave him the capsulated version and was relieved when Dade didn't ask a slew of invasive questions.

"When are you going? I'll meet you there."

"No way. I'll—"

"You're not going in there alone, all scorched earth and everything. You'll need backup. What's the plan?"

Gratitude swelled in Riddick. He emailed Eric and Lena.

Three days later, Dade picked him up at the Managua airport. He clasped him in an embrace and slapped him on the back. "Reached out to a contact still at work here. Didn't want to announce our presence. Got a place to lay low, get supplies, etc."

The memories cropped up faster than Riddick could process. The smells, the oppressive humidity. Riddick let his facial hair grow out and covered his locs so he would blend in better. The two still stood out, but less like retired military and more like bros looking to carouse.

Dade looked better than he had on video during the kidnapping. Riddick told him so.

The other man shrugged off the praise. "Started with some basic research, but you were already in the air."

They hunkered down to review what Dade had gathered, talked through scenarios. Riddick had to level with his friend.

"This won't be a turn him over for questioning-type thing."

Dade didn't even blink. "I figured. I feel you. If Ana were still alive, I'd be worried about the same thing you are."

Only a touch of melancholy tinged Dade's voice now at the mention of his wife. Did this mean he might, at last, be moving on after her death?

"Melanie Goodnight said you were cocky." He hadn't meant to go blurting that out. His own heart might be broken, but Riddick was pretty sure he wasn't the only one who recognized their connection.

"Yeah?" A grin took over Dade's grizzled face, genuine humor lighting in his deep-set eyes. "She's not wrong. I mean, her stuff was great. I'm just better."

The phone dinged a notification, interrupting before Riddick commented further about the tech. Their informant had found something.

The informant was a clerk at the Supreme Court of Justice's criminal division. They met him in a seedy restaurant and listened to his report with rapt attention. A rival cartel had bribed corrupt officials to orchestrate the release of Guacamaya Roja's leadership. Blandon and all his lieutenants were taken out in a series of ambushes.

The Ocelotes Muertos rose to power long after the Rangers' job. They killed off their biggest potential competitor in one fell swoop and made examples of them. The remaining members of the routed gang were low-level foot soldiers who did the sensible thing and switched loyalty.

Riddick remained silent for a long time, considering. The orphaned members would be busy proving they could be trusted. They'd be worried about saving their own skins, not settling old scores of dead *jefes*. If they knew about the Rangers, they wouldn't be willing to say anything.

And cartel kingpins didn't confide in their lackeys.

Leaning in close, Riddick spoke in a low, deadly voice. *"Estas seguro?"*

The informant gave a shrug and an unconvincing smirk.

Lightning fast, Riddick's hand snaked across the table, knocking aside cups and bowls to grab the man by his grimy shirt collar. He hoisted him out of the chair to shove up against the wall and pinned him there. All attention in the room turned with the ruckus. Riddick ignored the shouting, confident that Dade was watching his back.

"I swear to Christ, I will track you down and hurt every person you've ever known if you're lying to me."

Dade placed a restraining hand on Riddick's shoulder. "Easy, bro. No scorched earth, remember?"

Riddick shrugged him off and tightened his grip on the scrawny man. He let him see in his eyes the horrific death that would be coming for him if he gave false information. *"Estas seguro?"*

The informant's eyes grew wide with terror as he tried to shrink away. *"Por mi familia. Te lo juro!"*

Mothers were sacred here. Khara wanted to be a mother someday.

Of their own accord, Riddick's fingers unclenched. He stepped back and let go, gestured toward the door with his chin. The informant hurried out of the restaurant without a backward glance. Riddick offered apologies to the proprietor and tossed money onto the table—enough to cover the damages.

Dade stood nearby, staring at him with a raised eyebrow.

Riddick gave a terse shake of his head. "Later."

They didn't speak on the long, dusty, bumpy ride back to the other side of the city.

Only once they were in their dingy hotel room with the door locked behind them did Riddick allow the relief to flood his system. Lightheaded with it, he stumbled over to the dresser and slapped his palms flat on it, gulping in great lungsful of air. The wild beating of his heart thundered in his ears.

He stood there shaking while Dade used two other contacts to corroborate the informant's story. Dade was as excited as Riddick had ever seen him when he delivered the news.

Safe.

His Khara was safe.

Every part of him sagged. Riddick slid to the floor when his legs wouldn't hold him. His entire body felt feverish, and he was having a hard time getting enough air. He brought Khara's smiling face to mind. His breath hitched. The burning ache in his chest for her grew.

Swallowing hard, Riddick looked up into the concerned face of his friend. He'd been so desperate to keep her safe he hadn't been thinking straight. He could have done this without hurting her, but he'd taken the coward's way out, just as Jaden had accused.

Riddick wasn't living without Khara, he was surviving. Barely. How had he convinced himself of the lie he didn't need her to breathe? Was there a way to fix this?

"I might've made a mistake. In fact, I know I did."

Dade's eyebrows shot up. "Is it something I can help with?"

"Thanks, but no. This is shit I gotta shovel myself."

Chapter Fifty-Three

"I'M SORRY I LET you down, Trina. Okay?"

Sitting across from each other at the dinner table, a wave of sadness rolled through Trina searching Corey's earnest face. She'd been dreading this conversation. How many times had he sat in that exact place and said those exact words?

Resentment clawed at Trina's insides when he looked at her with an expectant expression. Was he waiting for her to say it was okay? Didn't he realize nothing was okay and that she couldn't bring herself to utter those words one more time? Trina swallowed the rest of her wine and said nothing, refusing to give him absolution.

A frown wrinkled Corey's brow. This conversation wasn't going according to the script he'd prepared. Trina didn't have the energy or the inclination to care at the time. She wanted to smash something and knock that phony look of humility off his face.

"I have news."

Trina sighed and didn't respond until she'd poured herself another glass of merlot and taken a healthy swig. "And what's that?" If he noticed how emotionless her voice was, he didn't say so.

"I'm checking into a rehab facility in Toronto tomorrow."

"That's wonderful, Corey." It had been Los Angeles last time. And London before that. She couldn't remember any of the places before those two.

"You don't sound very happy. Don't you want to know why?"

Trina snorted and had another gulp of wine. "Not really, but I'm sure you'll tell me. We've been here before. Several times, if you recall."

Heedless of her disdain, Corey plowed on with the story. Trina listened with half an ear until she lost the thread and had to ask, "What choice are you talking about?"

"The Queen. The Queen gave me a choice. She showed mercy I didn't deserve and allowed me to decide what to do. I could relinquish responsibility and only go because she ordered me, or I could decide to go on my own. Going on my own is much better, I think, don't you?"

So smug, so proud. Sure that this whole thing was a mere inconvenience. Now Lillianna was his ally, his savior? Something special who hadn't destroyed their family? Because she didn't throw him in jail? It was too much. Trina's rage overflowed. She was on her feet and yelling before the wineglass she hurled into the wall shattered. She had the satisfaction of seeing Corey flinch.

"*I* was the one to handle everything when you almost killed that family driving drunk. It was me who kept this family together when you were at the bottom of the bottle. I begged you, Corey, pleaded with you to get help. One word from Lillianna and all that counts for nothing?"

She stalked around the room, flinging dishes off the table onto the floor, the walls, the window as she screamed at him. As abruptly as she started, Trina ran out of steam. Standing beside his chair, shaking, tears streaming down her face, Trina stared into the eyes of the man she'd loved and been devoted to for over thirty years.

"Everything I've ever done has been for you," she whispered.

A commotion drew their attention, and they hurried into the living room to find Cyrus thrashing around, much like Trina had been doing. He upended occasional tables, kicking at furniture, and shrieking in frustration.

"What's wrong, honey?"

"They won't—let me see her!"

"Who—the Queen?" Corey asked.

"Of course, the Queen!" Had he always been so clueless about this?

With a wounded bellow, Cyrus punched a hole through the drywall, the crunching sound loud. Trina caught his arm before he could do it a second time, but he shook her off.

Even after so many years of dealing with these episodes, Corey *still* managed to react the wrong way. "You think we'd better call—"

"*No mobile crisis!*" Cyrus shouted, shaking his head and backing up against the front door.

Trina threw her husband an aggrieved look and dropped to her son's side, where he'd crumpled to sit on the floor. "We're not calling them, honey. It's okay. Let's go take a ride like we used to do."

Cyrus looked up at her with watery eyes and Trina's heart lurched. "She said it was nice to see me."

He sounded forlorn. Trina wanted to wrap him up in her arms and make it all go away. "I'm sure she meant it. Sometimes... was her flag flying?"

The clouds cleared from his expression, leaving behind bright hope. "I don't know."

At Trina's imploring look, Corey grabbed his phone and pulled up the island's main webpage. Only the Kingdom of Lytua's flag was flying over the Hubbard Building.

"Look, Cyrus, her flag isn't up. She's not even on the island."

"Really?" Cyrus snatched the phone away from his father to see for himself. He smiled. "She's not here."

"No, she's not on the island, baby, that's all."

The laugh Cyrus let out loosened the tense muscles in her shoulders. "She's not here!" When he caught sight of the destruction he'd caused, he deflated, his shoulders hunched. "I did it again. I'm sorry."

Trina waved a dismissive hand at the mess. "Don't worry about any of that. It wasn't anywhere near as bad as the last time."

"Why don't—" Corey started, then cleared his throat. "A change of scenery always seems to help. I'm going to be on a work trip for a while. Why don't you two pick a city to go explore for a while like you used to? Then, by the time you get back...." He let it hang there.

In that moment, Trina's heart swelled with love for him, and she checked her own ego. It didn't matter why he received the treatment, just that he did. She would do a reset with Cyrus while Corey was in Toronto, and they'd deal with all the rest later.

Chapter Fifty-Four

J ADEN ENTERED KHARA'S APARTMENT after a brisk knock. "So. You want me to kick his ass?"

Khara didn't even smile, just shook her head morosely.

Jaden sighed, disheartened to see his friend curled up in the window seat, looking wretched. How Riddick could believe this devastation was for the best—it was beyond him. Khara was so selective in choosing her lovers. She'd taken such a risk. Would she recover from this? It had been six weeks. His friend was hurting deeply and time wasn't making it any better. Time for drastic measures. Jaden sat next to her, kicked back, and crossed his ankles. "Are you finished feeling sorry for yourself yet?"

A flicker of annoyance crossed her face. It was the first emotion he'd seen in her besides sadness in ages. "Jaden, I'm not in the mood—"

"Too bad. I've given you space. We're doing this. You love him?"

"Yes." The word was miserable, but unhesitating. Her eyes brimmed with unshed tears.

"Then what are you doing here?"

"What am I—*what*?" Khara turned to face him full-on.

"Why are you here instead of giving him what for? I've never known you to back down from a fight."

"There's nothing to fight for. He doesn't want me." Her misery was palpable.

"Oh, he wants you. He loves you."

Khara was shaking her head again. "I was just a good lay."

"Khara, that man loves you so much he chose your future over his own happiness."

"What does that mean?"

Jaden weighed how much he should tell her. "Leaving you was not his best decision, I'll grant you, but one made with nothing but your best interest at heart."

"I don't understand. I will not go crawling back to someone who dumped me."

"He thought he was protecting you. He has no idea how tough you are. I know he hurt you, Khara, and I'm not making excuses for that. I'm just saying there's more to the story of why he did. If what you feel is worth the risk, then go ask the tough questions and get answers, kid. You'd be a fool not to. I know you. You'll regret it if you don't. And what you hear might change things."

Tears streamed down Khara's face by the time he finished. She might be sad, confused, and angry, but she regarded him with suspicion. "You know more than you're saying."

"I do, but I think it's important you should hear it from Riddick."

"You don't even like him."

"Actually, I do like him. I like him a lot. I *don't* like that he's hurt you. And you know my loyalty will always lie with you."

"I'm so angry."

"I know you are. You should tell him so. He should certainly answer for that. Think about it."

Khara paced in agitation, vacillating between indecision and outrage. What could Riddick have been protecting her from? *Did* he love her? She'd been so devastated by his hurtful words she didn't look past them. And here she was, licking her wounds. He'd broken her heart and all she could think about was his smile, the warmth in his eyes locked on hers while they made love. No, they hadn't made love, she reminded herself. The bitter thought left a sour taste in her mouth. They'd only fucked.

She couldn't smell him on her sheets anymore. Ugh, she hated that. And hated that she hated it. She'd loved Riddick freely, fearlessly. Oh, who was she kidding? She'd made love with her heart wide open. She missed him so much. Oh, mercy, how she missed him. Nothing filled the hollowness in her chest.

Protecting her? From what? She didn't need him to protect her. She could take care of herself. Had she not finished law school at the top of her class? Overcome an ugly smear campaign to become the youngest Queen ever elected? Hadn't she handled crises, negotiated on an international level, proven herself capable? Governed a country, for pity's sake? She needed no one's protection. How dare he make decisions about her future without even consulting her? The more she thought about it, the angrier she got. The absolute nerve. Just who did Joshua Riddick think he was?

She chewed on it almost nonstop for two days. Then she called Joanne.

A few hours later, she was ringing the doorbell to Riddick's neat, end-unit townhouse in Alexandria and girded for battle.

<h1 style="text-align:center">Chapter Fifty-Five</h1>

Parie Riddick opened the door to a furious woman. Joshie had captured her beautifully in his sketches. She trembled with anger and looked heartsick, with misery shining in her lovely brown eyes. "Yes?"

"I love him," Khara said, tilting her chin up in defiance, almost daring Parie to disagree.

Oh, Parie adored her already. This woman would fight until Joshie was hers. That was all she'd ever wanted for him. A partner who would fight for him.

"He has a great deal of explaining to do," Khara continued.

"I imagine he does."

"Is he here?"

"No, but he will be. I invited myself over for dinner tonight."

"Forgive my manners. My name is Khara Therin. I've heard much about you, Dr. Riddick. It's an honor to meet you."

"And you, as well, dear. Come on in. I'll go find something to do for a few hours and get out of your way."

After Parie grabbed her purse and keys, she surprised Khara by sweeping her into a tight hug. "Give him hell before you make up."

"I intend to."

"Then I'll see you soon."

"I want to hear all about your cruise."

"You will. I'll be getting back to it soon."

Parie had questions but held onto them. If things went the way she hoped, she'd have plenty of time for that.

Humming, Parie left and dialed her son in the car. His voice was morose when he answered. Parie smiled. She wouldn't tell him he had the biggest of surprises waiting at the house, but she had some strategic needling to do.

Then she'd contact her travel agent to coordinate her return to the cruise.

God help the man when Khara unleashed on him. Fireworks were in the forecast. *Come on, Joshie. Get your act together.*

Khara was too nervous to sit and debated whether she should try to strike a seductive pose. She wandered the living room and couldn't resist going through a stack of Riddick's drawings she found on the counter. So many of them were of her, which left her burning with curiosity. These looked like he cared for her and were at odds with his callous words. What did this mean?

She needed shoring up. Yvanda picked up her call on the third ring. "Just remembered I was supposed to call you."

"Jamal, here, take the baby, please. Where are you?"

"At Riddick's house, waiting for him."

"You're not there to do something ill-advised like seduce him and walk out or anything, right?"

"No, of course not. There might be seduction later, but I'm here to fight for what's mine."

"Hell, yeah. Atta girl! Don't take it easy on him. He needs to know how serious this is."

"I will not be taking it easy on him. You don't have to worry about that. There's something he's not telling me and I'm not leaving until I find out. Then we'll deal."

"Fight dirty if you have to."

"Oh, I will. He's mine."

"Good. You're wearing something appropriately killer, right? Like make him drool, knock his socks off sexy?"

A smile curved her lips as Khara looked down at the armor she'd chosen to don. "Oh, yes. I came ready. I'm wearing that red dress."

Yvanda cackled. "Good on you, *chérie*. Get him, girl. Call me later."

Chapter Fifty-Six

RIDDICK MEANDERED AMONGST THE Saturday afternoon shoppers crowding Whole Foods. There was no rhyme or reason to what made it into his basket for dinner.

He'd gone back and forth for days since getting back from Nicaragua, disgusted with himself and thinking hard on a way out of this mess he'd made. He'd considered, made lists, talked himself into and out of showing up unannounced in Lytua.

He'd already decided he was going to do whatever it took to get Khara back, even before Parie's haranguing phone call. By the time she'd finished fussing him out and hanging up on him, he'd had the come-to-Jesus moment. There was only one thing to do.

Fight.

Fuck all the careful planning, trying to anticipate what she might say, the points he wanted to make. Khara was everything. Everything he could have ever dreamed of in a partner. More than he'd ever hoped to deserve. It wasn't protection that Khara needed. She'd never needed that.

He had to get to her and explain the truth—how he felt, what he'd feared. All of it. If she couldn't forgive him, well, then he'd have to convince her to give him another chance. Start over, maybe?

Khara was as essential to him as air or water. He wanted the messy, emotional creativity she unleashed in him. Nervousness settled in the pit of his stomach as a small part of him tried to raise doubts. Riddick shoved that away. That fear had done enough damage.

Halfway to his car, he realized he was still carrying the filled grocery basket. He hustled back inside to the checkout line to pay, embarrassed to have accidentally shoplifted.

A clerk chased him down in the parking lot after he left his bags and credit card in the machine. *Get it together, Riddick.*

If Khara didn't want to see him—and really, who could blame her—he'd wait. Grovel if necessary. He'd find a way. He'd made a gargantuan mistake letting her go over something that *might* happen. It was a mistake he never intended to make again. No matter what it took, he would win Khara back.

Swing hard enough to not go down in the first place. Riddick smiled at the thought. *And* fuck *fair.*

Unbidden, a dopey smile came over his face. Khara Therin had been his from the moment she gave him the business for hanging up on her. And he'd been hers. God was he hers. He couldn't breathe without her.

He wouldn't breathe normally until his Khara was back in his life and back in his arms.

Where she belonged.

Riddick dialed Eric in the car, caught him at one of Holly's games. "I'm going to be out of the country for a bit," he informed him when he answered, not even bothering with a greeting. "I don't know how long."

"Ah, so finally got your head out of your ass, do you?"

"Head's on straight."

"'Bout time. Go get your woman, then, and don't worry about things here."

"Thanks, Eric. I owe you."

"No, you don't. Didn't you kick me in my ass when I fucked things up with Maya?"

It was true. Riddick had *literally* kicked Eric's ass, although he'd never rub it in his face. "I'll call Lena now."

"I'll take care of it. Go."

Riddick threw the car into park and dialed again, his heart racing. He pounded up the stairs, the phone glued to his ear, trying to make reservations, trying to pack. His head was full of things he needed to do. He swore viciously when he ran down the stairs to toss an overstuffed backpack by the front door, having knocked into the table in the hallway. "Not you, sorry. Hello? *Fuck*." The agent hung up on him. He redialed, cursing again as he righted the table and decorative bowl he'd upset.

By some miracle, he was connected to the same agent. Riddick apologized profusely, didn't try to explain that his language hadn't been directed at her. If he'd had any sense, he would have called the R&S travel agent. Maybe chartering a plane would have been better. Why didn't he think of that first?

"Well, what about standby? I need to get there ASAP." He blanked on his second trip upstairs, unable to remember what he'd put in the first bag. He had some serious explaining to do. Calling wouldn't do. Khara probably wouldn't even take his call and, again, who could blame her? It was his own goddamn fault. Maybe he could convince one of the Elites to—

"Going somewhere?"

Chapter Fifty-Seven

R IDDICK SPUN AROUND AT the unexpected voice. His heart leaped at the sight of Khara standing there in the living room. He took a step toward her, his body reacting before he remembered he'd broken her heart, that she might see it as threatening.

"Sir? Sir? Are you still there?"

Riddick hung up on the airline agent. He threw the phone in the general direction of the table, where it bounced and landed on the floor with a clatter. "Khara, thank—"

She recoiled when he reached for her. The hostility in her expression tore at him. He'd put that anguish in her eyes and would never forgive himself for it. What was she doing here? "Khara—" he tried again. He wanted to bound across the room, sweep her into his arms, and beg her forgiveness.

Khara took another step back. "Don't you fucking touch me, Riddick." She was all but growling the words. "You've no right."

Riddick dropped his hand, though his fingers were itching to touch her. He wanted to kiss her, hold her to him. "I know, I—" He'd only ever heard her drop the f-bomb once before. "I was coming to you. To apologize, to explain, to make things right between us."

"I don't believe you."

Her mistrust stung, even though he deserved it. "Khara, please, I—"

"No. *No.* I listened to all the bullshit you spewed at me. You made me doubt myself, doubt everything I thought I knew. I don't want to hear anything from you until I've had my say."

Riddick nodded and swallowed hard. "Of course." He owed her that much, no doubt.

Khara stalked back and forth like a tiger in a cage before whirling on him. She let loose an angry volley of what he assumed were Lytuan curse words, then lit in. "I thought we were building something together. I brought you to my home. Made love to you in my bed. I've never brought anyone there. I opened my heart to you, my life. My scars.... Do you have any idea how hard that was? I don't jump into bed with just anyone. It's been two blessed years since I've been with someone. I've never told another man I loved him, not even the man who asked me to marry him. It's such a cliché, but I thought I knew you. I thought we had something special. If you felt differently than I did, the least you could have done was be less careless with my feelings. I'm an adult and could have dealt with that. I would never have treated you so poorly. Never would have thrown our time in bed together in your face.

"If I were just a silly conquest to you, you could have had the decency to be honest about that before we went to bed together. I'm a grown woman and can handle disappointment. For all you know, I might have been just fine with that—a fling. That's what I thought I was supposed to be doing in the beginning, anyway. But you bedded me, broke my heart, and then traipsed out of my life like nothing happened. Like I didn't matter. You were dishonest with me and I'm so fucking angry at being played for a fool. I'm not some empty-headed, starry-eyed co-ed, Riddick. I can live without any more of the best sex I've ever had in my life, but you need to explain yourself."

An angry flush colored her cheeks, and she was breathing hard by the time she finished. How was she more beautiful than he remembered? Everything she'd said was a direct hit, nothing but hard truth. Even knowing that, the painful pounding of his heart continued. He couldn't take a full breath with all the chaos inside. "I didn't want to leave you." God, he didn't want to leave her.

"Then why did you? *Jozelin.*"

"What did you just call me?"

"A bastard."

He absorbed the barb. That, too, was deserved. "I didn't want you to get hurt."

"You thought it would tickle to lie to me, humiliate me?"

"No, I—"

"You were cruel, Riddick. You could have broken up with me without being cruel."

"I was protecting you."

"From what?"

"I'm not who you think I am."

"Then who the hell are you?" Despite her obvious anger, she softened her tone. "Tell me. All of it, whatever it is. I need to hear from you. My word I will listen."

Khara sat. And waited for him to begin.

<h1 style="text-align:center">Chapter Fifty-Eight</h1>

RIDDICK TOOK A DEEP breath to calm his thundering heart. Then another. His grand redemption plan hadn't progressed further than seeing her and apologizing. He hadn't thought he'd ever have to tell this tale. But he would. For her, he abso-fucking-lutely would. He would do anything. "I'm adopted."

"*That's* what this is—?"

"But not before a lot of shit happened. This is hard to talk about, so just bear with me, okay?"

"Okay."

Then he told her all of it. No one had ever heard the complete story. He'd given Jaden the highlights—or lowlights—as it were.

Riddick laid it out for her, told her the unflinching, unvarnished truth about his horror show of a childhood. Even the parts he hadn't ever told Parie and Eric. He explained fast and straight, even though he felt raw and vulnerable as he spoke, like an exposed nerve. He paced in agitation in front of where she sat on the couch.

His birth parents had been addicts, in and out of rehab, petty criminals, and grifters who used him as a part of their cons. He was in and out of foster homes from the third grade. They would always find where he was. Every time. They'd have him steal from his placement homes, giving sob story after sob story. When he tried to steal from Parie, she gave him the money and invited his parents to dinner.

"I didn't know how to handle Parie," he said, his voice wistful and full of wonder. He paused his pacing before starting up again. "Older kids just don't get adopted. I freaked out when she told me she wanted me to be hers forever. That's how she phrased it. I freaked and ran away. Was on the street for almost a year." By that age, he was already big and looked older than he was. He'd managed to stay out of major trouble. Petty theft, some break-ins.

"She never stopped looking for me. The day she found me she told me something I'll never forget as long as I live. She said, 'I love you and that means I stick by you when shit gets real. Come home, Joshie, where you belong.'

"From that day on, Parie Riddick was my mother. I was in 11th grade when the adoption was finalized, and I became Joshua Riddick. Terminating parental rights is... difficult, even when there's clear neglect and abuse. It's a long process.

"Evelyn and Jordan—my birth parents—put up a fight, made false accusations. Made promises to get clean. God, it was hell. Through it all, Parie didn't waver in her commitment to me, even as Evelyn and Jordan played all sorts of mind games. It was a hard time. I almost flunked out of school. Eventually, I realized I could either throw my life away waiting and hoping for them to change or I could accept what Parie was offering—love, a home, consistency—and have a real shot at a decent life. I told the courts I wanted Parie to adopt me. Evelyn was surprised. Can you believe it? She got pretty nasty. There were threats, sabotage, restraining orders, arrests, more court. Even arson.

"She attacked Parie. Put her in the hospital. I thought that was it, that she'd be done with me. But she told me it wasn't my fault, and I was worth it. Lying there after emergency surgery, with broken bones, she said I was worth it."

He stopped pacing and settled. "Once the adoption was final in California, they sealed the records and we moved to northern Virginia so I could have a fresh start. A lot of love and a lot of therapy got me on an even keel."

Khara sat listening intently, without interruption. Watching his face, his body language. Instinct had told her they were on a precipice. Whatever he was about to tell her was going to change her life. She'd sensed it. And she'd been right.

When he didn't say more, she guessed, "She's why you go by Riddick." There was an almost reverent tone to his voice when he spoke of his mother.

He nodded and dropped into a chair. "I was Josh—before. My birth name was Joshua Hobarth. Evelyn spiraled after everything was finished. Jordan had died from pneumonia before the adoption. They weren't together. She would have kept harassing us, but I don't think she had the resources to find us. If she knew where we were, she would have. A social worker who worked my case for years pulled some strings to let me know Evelyn had overdosed. Died in an alley somewhere in downtown LA. I wouldn't have to worry about looking over my shoulder for her for the rest of my life.

"I keep in touch with the social worker. He's retired, but he was a rock. You haven't heard the worst of it."

"No?"

"Khara, I killed a man."

"When you were a Ranger?"

"No. When I was on the street."

"As a teen? Tell me."

He told her about the confrontation with Tom and that he went into the Army as soon as he could.

After a moment, Khara touched his forearm, her countenance softening. "Thank you for telling me. I'm sure it wasn't easy."

"I've never told anyone all of that. Parie and Eric know most of it, but...." He shrugged.

Then Khara was quiet for a long time after he finished speaking, considering. Her heart ached for the frightened, mistreated little boy Riddick had been. For the proud, vulnerable, headstrong teenager he'd grown into. How awful to carry that burden of secrecy for so long, alone. He was watching her face, awaiting judgment. Then indignance and a different kind of anger set in. Why hadn't he just told her this? "You thought I couldn't handle that truth?" she asked finally, her voice soft with compassion.

"Dammit, Khara, you shouldn't have to! It wasn't about that. I've done things I'm not proud of."

"Haven't we all? Did you think so little of me? That I would turn my back on you for something you had no control over? None of that was your fault."

"It wasn't about that," he repeated. "The press would have savaged you for this! Their beloved Queen with a foster care kid? Who killed someone? Who was homeless? I've eaten out of trash cans. Stolen. Your enemies would have used it against you and tried to take you down with it."

"That's what you were protecting me from," she mused. "You broke up with me before word got out about you. Oh, Riddick. You infuriating man. Did you think yourself so disposable to me? I wish you'd told me this instead of trying to think for me. Are you not the same man you were before you knew who I am?"

"I couldn't have you lose everything because of my past. I couldn't have Richardson running you out of town because of a scandal about me."

Khara gave an unladylike snort. "I'm not going to lose anything. Would you feel differently if I were, say, American and a senator? Is that not the same thing? Do you only think of a lawmaker in terms of their profession? Do they not have other facets of their personality? Are they not also spouses, parents, neighbors, friends? They have scandals all the time! The Supreme Court is having one right now!"

"Technically, you'd be more like a president, but you're making a damn good argument. Yes, but it would have killed me if they came after you because of me. And it would be easy."

"I want to be clear here. I'm mad as hell, but it's not that you were in foster care or that you had to take a life to defend your own as a child. Of course not. I don't care about any of that."

"But—I've done things I'm not proud of. Things no child should have to do."

But the agitation remained in his features, as though indecision was weighing on him. While he was relieved, his shoulders were still tense and hadn't relaxed yet. There would only be one reason for him to remain wound so tight. "There's more, isn't there?" Those wide, startled eyes told her she'd guessed correctly. "Tell me the rest."

He didn't bother to prevaricate. There was only a slight hesitation before giving her the nutshell version of the potential danger from Sergio Blandon and the Guacamaya Roja. "And that's it. All of it. I thought you'd be safer if I wasn't anywhere near you."

"You think I don't understand wanting to protect someone you care about? Shield them from any unpleasantness? I get you did what you thought was best for me, but you don't get to decide *for* me. That's bullshit. That's not okay. Riddick, you hurt me."

"I know. I'm sorry. Never regretted anything more."

"I understand why you did it. That doesn't make it hurt less. You said awful things. You were insulting and unkind."

"I had to make you hate me. It was the only way I could walk away from you."

"I didn't hate you. I never did. Jaden... told me I'd be a fool to let go of the man who would sacrifice his own happiness to see my future safe. But he didn't say why."

Jaden *defended* him? "I just wanted you to not have to answer for—"

"I would have chosen you, Riddick," Khara cut in. "You just didn't give me a chance to do so."

That stopped him cold. He had never really considered this. Worrying about worst-case scenarios had consumed him. "You would've—?"

"Without hesitation," she said, her voice calm and even. Resolute. "You didn't trust me enough to try, to stand by you and that hurts. None of what happened was your fault and I'll be damned if I lose you because of it. If you'd told me the truth, you would have heard me say the press and every one of my enemies can fuck right off. If anyone wants to come at me about this, let them. I promise they'll regret it. I love you and that means I stick by you when shit gets real. How do you like that? I will always choose you."

Then something clicked. His throat closed. Giving Parie's words back to him—shit. She'd pierced him. She hadn't recoiled in horror. Because she was right. None of that had been his fault. Hadn't he done his best to live a good, solid life? Hadn't he made it his life's work to protect and help others in similar situations? Khara looked at him like she meant business. She was hurt. Enraged. But not disgusted. He'd thought he'd have to convince her to see beyond his past.

He had fucked up.

She cupped his face for the briefest of moments, then stepped back. "I told you I love you and I meant it. What you choose to do with that is up to you. If we're together, I'll fight 'til the end for you, but it can't just be me willing to fight for this. Or trust. That's not a partnership. If we have no trust, we cannot have any kind of future."

When Jaden was haranguing him, he'd alluded to a man's pedigree and politics and money as bullshit. *A man's own actions—that's what matters.*

Riddick kept a part of himself separate, in a self-imposed bondage. He wasn't living what he told others. That grace he extended to others he'd never given *himself*. "That sneaky motherfucker."

"Pardon me?"

"I—your Sentinel. That brilliant, sneaky motherfucker."

"What has Jaden done now?"

"Made me realize something, as he intended, I'm sure."

"What's that?"

"I'm not worthless."

Khara's face clouded. "He said you were worthless? *Valscht,* I'll fucking kill him."

Chapter Fifty-Nine

R IDDICK WATCHED IN ASTONISHMENT as Khara leaped to her feet and whipped her phone out of her tote. She jabbed at the buttons, fury in every movement. Here was a woman whose heart he'd broken in the cruelest way imaginable. Who minutes ago had cursed at him. Who was in the middle of confronting him, for fuck's sake. Coming to his immediate defense against one of her oldest friends.

Shit. Wait. *Fuck*.

She hadn't hesitated. Dumbfounded, Riddick noted that she'd reached Jaden and was reading him the riot act in a rapid, pissed-off combination of Lytuan and English. He watched her pace, gesticulating wildly, threatening Jaden with bodily harm and professional ruination.

Like an avenging angel, Jaden had said. *This* was what he was worthy of—the love of a good woman who would stand with him against the world.

His heart in his throat, Riddick intercepted Khara's pacing and plucked the phone from her fingers. He ignored her indignant sputtering and put it to his ear. "Jaden?"

"Still here," came the amused-sounding reply.

"The avenging angel misunderstood." Riddick didn't take his eyes off Khara. She was steaming.

"So I gathered."

"I'll straighten it out. She's in the middle of telling me off."

"As you so richly deserve."

"Agreed. What you said before? I get it. And I believe it."

"What changed your mind?"

"The fact that she's cussing you out in the middle of cussing me out."

Jaden laughed. "This is going to make a good story, isn't it?"

"Depends on how I handle this next part. Jaden?"

"Yes?"

"Thanks, man."

Riddick hung up, chucked Khara's phone onto the couch, and grinned at her. "We'll come back to that."

"What the hell is so funny?" Her color was high, her accent more pronounced.

"Nothing, not a goddamned thing."

"Then why are you smiling?"

"Because I get it. That you love me."

"Well, yes, but—"

"If you didn't love me, you wouldn't have been so hurt when I fucked up."

"You *did* fuck up."

"I know. Now hush for a moment, so I can grovel properly."

"I don't want you to—"

"Shh." He risked his life by placing a finger over her lips. The outraged look she shot at him was hot as hell, but she stopped talking, flopped down onto the couch, and crossed her arms, then one leg over the other. She arched an eyebrow at him, her expression expectant.

Riddick paused a moment just to take her in. So beautiful. God help him, she was wearing those pointy, leopard print heels again. His dick responded, and he had to look away from them before he ravished her right where she sat. He'd come so close to losing her for good.

With his heart thudding and a dry mouth, he spilled out the words he'd never imagined saying to anyone. "Not going to bury the lead here. I'm in love with you, Khara. Of that, I'm sure."

Her mouth popped open. She snapped it shut. "You—*what*?"

"I'm in love with you." He exaggerated the enunciation of each word. "I didn't think I'd ever be capable of loving someone like this. I always thought I was damaged and didn't deserve it. But I'm not damaged and I deserve the love of the most incredible woman I've ever met. I didn't fully believe you loved me until just now."

"But I *told* you—"

"I know you did. That's not the same as me believing it and that I was worthy of it. But if you didn't love me, you wouldn't have flown all the way here to rip me a new one. You wouldn't have just lit into one of your best friends on my behalf, even as you were rightfully reading me the riot act.

"Here's what's at the heart of all of it: I didn't know how to let you love me. I couldn't let you because I didn't know how to."

Khara sucked in a ragged breath, tears gathering in her eyes. She got to her feet.

"I was wrong and I'm sorry. So goddamn sorry. You're not too good for me. You're *it* for me." He stepped a little closer, took her hand in his. Felt a prick of relief when she didn't pull away this time.

"Khara, I love you. I should have told you about everything and I'm sorry I didn't. I'm so sorry I hurt you, that I didn't trust you. You deserved better than that, how I treated you. I didn't know how to let you love me," he repeated. "You—I don't know what to do, how to love you, but that's not ever going to stop me from trying. I need you in my life to help me figure it out. Being honest, though, you're gonna have to be patient, because I have no idea what I'm doing. I don't deserve your forgiveness—I know that, but I'm asking for it, anyway."

Khara looked down at his thumb stroking hers. "What about the things you said? How will I ever be able to trust you again?"

"Garbage. None of it was true. Not one word. I won't ever speak to you like that again. I *was* unkind. It was the only thing you ever asked of me and I blew it. It was just... desperation to keep you safe. I love you," he repeated. Khara moved away to unbutton her Burberry trench coat. "I promise to not try to think for you again. Your trust? I know I need to rebuild it. I just lived without you for weeks and I'm not going to ever put myself in that position again. Never. I will never break your trust again." He hadn't planned on doing this much extemporizing, but there it was. It seemed he had more to say on the matter than he thought.

Khara finished unfastening the buttons as Riddick spoke his promise. He lapsed into stunned silence when she took her time peeling the coat off. A flick of the wrist and she tossed it onto the armchair. Riddick's nostrils flared as his gaze slid over her body. She was voluptuous personified in the red *pla-dow* dress that almost made him come in his pants the last time she'd worn it. She'd dressed carefully for this occasion, come ready to seduce. Those sexy-ass heels made a sharp sound on his hardwood floor when she returned to him.

"If you ever speak to me like that again, we're done. I will not be disrespected by my partner and certainly not in my home. No trust, no future."

Her eyes were dark with desire and... love.

"Agreed. I'm all in here."

"Me, too."

Riddick pulled her body against his with an arm around her waist. "So, we've kissed and made up?"

Khara was too impatient for him to answer. She took his face in her hands and kissed him with heat. She moaned into his mouth and sank her teeth into his lower lip as she thrust her hands under his T-shirt. "Take this off," she ordered in a low growl.

Instead of obeying, Riddick grabbed the V-neckline of her dress in both hands. "You first." He tore it wide and yanked it down off her shoulders. She gasped at the sound of seams tearing, and he wondered if his manhandling turned her on as much as it had him.

"Jesus," Riddick breathed, catching sight of the lacy red push-up bra she was wearing. "Do your panties match?"

She gave him a wicked little smile. "Panties?"

Riddick groaned. *Fuck me.* "Lose the dress. Or, so help me, I'll fuck you with it on."

When she untied the dress's wrap and loosened it, Riddick gave a sharp intake of breath, his eyes widening. She wore only black stockings with a back seam and garters.

Standing before him with her hands on her hips, Khara looked for all the world like a goddess. Riddick looked from her bare pussy to her fuck-me pumps to her smug expression and stifled a whimper. "Fuck me," he breathed. "Did you wear this to torture me?

"Yes," she said without apology. "I had no intention of fighting fair. I wanted you to know just what you were trying to give up. You were saying?"

He knotted his hand in her hair, and they were kissing again, moving toward the couch. He couldn't wait to take her anyplace else. "Wait. Shit, I don't have a condom. Wait here, I'll be right back." If he touched her any further, then tried to pull back....

He was striding toward the door when Khara called his name. He turned back, and the sight of her stroking herself mesmerized him. Yep, she was trying to torture him alright.

"I still have my IUD. We're protected."

It took a moment for his brain to catch up. When the realization hit, Riddick went stock still. "Are you saying we don't need a condom?"

"That's exactly what I'm saying. It's quite effective alone. I want you to take me with nothing between us."

Riddick had to close his eyes and suck in a couple of deep breaths before he could speak. "I can take you bare?"

"I've never been without a condom. Let's see what the fuss is about."

"Jesus fucking Christ, Khara. I'm going to die right here. I've never been without a condom, either."

She smiled at him. "You'll take me bare from now on. When you make love to me, when we fuck. All the ways."

"Sit down and spread your legs for me, woman. I have to taste you. Then I need to see you take my cock in that heavenly pussy of yours."

And then his mouth was on hers again as he walked her backward. He pushed her onto the couch and was running his tongue up and down her slit the next moment. He shook out of his clothes at the same time. She caught a handful of his locs, pulled him into the undulating of her hips. He sucked hard, flicked his tongue against her clit. She was coming in his mouth moments later, her breathless cries echoing. How he'd missed this. How had he thought he could ever live without her? "I can't wait to feel you coming all around my naked dick."

"Yes, I want that."

"English, love," he admonished, slipping a finger inside her to stroke. He knew the spot and went right for it. No teasing this time.

"Yes, I want that. Everything. All you have to give."

He groaned when she shuddered into her second release. "I love how wet you get for me. You want my cock as much as it wants you."

She climbed into his lap and held him in one hand before she mounted him. She rubbed the head between her lips, around her clit. Taking him inside her just a fraction. The smile she gave him when he grunted bordered on arrogance.

"Don't fucking tease me, Khara. I can't take it right now." His voice was strained with the effort to stay still. "Get on my cock before you make a grown man cry."

The temptress didn't. She took him inside her a little more before coming off and rubbing him against her clit, faster and harder this time as she worked her way to another orgasm.

"Khara—" his voice held a hint of warning in it this time. His grip on her tightened.

She leaned in to brush her nose against his earlobe, then bit it. "So impatient, Mr. Riddick."

They both moaned at the sensation when Khara sank all the way down onto his naked shaft. "I missed this," she breathed. Coming together for the first time this way moved something in them both.

Riddick buried his face in the curve of her breasts, overcome with emotion. He held her hips still when she tried to rise. "Hang on a moment," he said hoarsely, unmoving. "Please."

Concerned, Khara leaned back. "Are you alright?" His hot breath on her had goosebumps breaking out.

He looked up at her then and there was a fire she'd never seen before in his eyes. "Never felt anything so goddamn good in my life."

"Does it feel different to you?"

"You can't imagine how good you feel. So fucking wet and hot and—*shit*." She'd flexed and tightened her inner muscles around him. He groaned. It was too much. "Fuck, I can feel every inch of you. I'm right on the edge, Khara," he gritted out. "I don't think I have it in me to be gentle right now. Your—"

She squeezed again, this time swiveling her hips some. "Take me how you want to. Give me what we both want."

"You're about to get seriously fucked. Not made love to, but just straight-up, thoroughly fucked. Jesus, I don't think I can—"

Khara cut him off with a light kiss. "Make love to me later. Take what you want, Riddick. I'm giving it to you. You once told me I'd spread my legs for you to fuck my pretty brown pussy however you want. Now's your chance. Or did you not mean that?"

Releasing a growl, Riddick reversed them and put her under him on the couch. He pushed her knees to her chest, opening that magnificent pussy to him, then plunged to the hilt and kept going. No lead-up, no easing back into anything after months apart. Just wild, desperate abandon.

She was beautiful beneath him, accepting him, rising to meet him, her hair and pretty bra in glorious disarray. She was moaning almost nonstop in time with his energetic strokes. He strummed her clit with his thumb, made a heavy circle around it. That was all it took to send her flying again. His woman crying out for him in her pleasure made his heart sing. Her bare sheath clutching at him as she came was indescribable, the stuff dreams were made of. "Oh, fuck," he groaned, holding on as she shuddered.

"This is what I said in the car the night we nearly made love. That you'd have me on your sofa and any other way you wanted."

"Thought it might have been something like that."

She kissed him, too lost in the moment to respond.

They fell off the couch, rolled right off the edge onto the floor. He took the brunt of the fall, cushioning her landing. She laughed merrily, and it was the sweetest sound he'd ever heard. He kept hammering in and out of her, her stocking-clad legs pushed wide. He looked down to watch his cock disappear inside her and reemerge coated with her cream. She was soaked for him again. *Hell, yeah.* His balls felt tight already. The garters and stockings were sexy enough, but the added titillation of those damned heels was just more than he could bear. He was going to lose his damn mind.

He fucked her halfway across the room in his enthusiasm, something primal taking hold, knowing he'd be spilling his essence right into her velvet depths this time.

"I love you," he gasped as he emptied himself, coming longer and harder than he ever had, driven nearly mad by the feel of her.

She echoed the sentiment.

Panting, spent, and sweaty, they lay in a tangled heap there on the floor after.

Khara said, "I like how this feels. Being full of you. It makes me feel naughty. Did you like coming inside me?"

"You keep saying stuff like that, you'll never get out of this house. But yeah, I did like it."

Khara just laughed.

Chapter Sixty

"WE OWE PARIE AN apology," Khara murmured from where she'd snuggled into his side.

"For the hard, fast sex we just had? No need."

"For dinner. I ran into her here."

"She canceled on me. Shit, I left the groceries in the car. I don't even remember what I bought."

When she gave a laugh, he heard the quaver.

"Are you crying?"

"Yes. It's been a very emotional few days."

Her hip started protesting from being on the hard floor. It felt like everything creaked when she pushed into a sitting position. "Ow. The floor isn't very forgiving."

Riddick stood and reached out a hand to help her to her feet. "Good thing *you* are. I love you." They shared a long, tender kiss.

"I may never tire of hearing that."

"Nor should you. I'm sorry I tore your dress."

Khara snorted. "I'm not. It was hot. May I borrow a T-shirt, though? I didn't bring any clothes with me. I just came directly here."

The memory of her standing before him flashed into his mind. "You stopped to put on sex goddess attire but didn't pack anything else?" Jesus, was he lucky.

Riddick sent Parie a text and then took Khara to his bed to spend the rest of the day and night showing her how sorry he was. Khara had to remind him about the groceries.

Still later, she told him, "I can't stay long. I must get back to the Parliament session. Do you have time for a quick visit? I've missed you terribly, though I was loath to admit it."

Riddick looked down at her in wonder. She'd walked out of one of the most important parts of her job. Hadn't packed a thing in her haste to get to him. She humbled him. He would never, ever take her for granted.

"I can get away for a few days, beautiful Khara."

When her gaze met his, he stroked a knuckle over her cheek.

"I know it will take time, but I want you to trust me again."

She nodded.

"It's enough for now just to have you back in my life. Let's start there, start again with dating."

They returned to Lytua on separate flights, so as not to rouse suspicion or interest from the press. In no time, they were back in her bed and negotiating future visits.

Chapter Sixty-One

RIDDICK HAD BEEN IN a few contentious meetings in his life. But nothing was as uncomfortable as the hostility he faced from the Elites the next morning in Jaden's dining room.

He'd asked Jaden to arrange for him to speak to all the Elites at once someplace private. Jaden arched an eyebrow, his gaze sharpening. Riddick explained it was better he find out when they did. Now that they were all sitting there, their body language tense and closed-off, Riddick reconsidered. Maybe they should just line up, punch him, and get it over with. Cenn was flipping one of her knives through her nimble fingers, her eyes narrowed and suspicious.

Even without the gory details, the Elites had to know Riddick had been the source of Khara's misery. These fences needed mending. He was going to get read the riot act by every one of them if he didn't get out in front of it. He'd earned their scorn and mistrust, though, and would weather it without complaint.

Instead of launching into his planned talking points, Riddick followed his instincts and said, "I fucked up." He let the admission hang there for a moment before continuing. "I need you to understand why."

He told them the entire story, a fuller, more detailed version than the one he'd given Jaden. Then he detailed what he was attempting to accomplish when he broke things off. By the time he finished, the hostility had given way to compassion. They must have all made colossal mistakes in their own courtships. He was positive they could understand the difficulty in navigating the unfamiliar landscape that came with loving and wanting to protect a partner.

"I need your help," Riddick said. "You put your lives on the line every day for the woman I love. I'm not going to be passive and just allow the Elites to protect her. I need you to teach me what I need to know so that I'm not a liability, so I can *help* keep her safe, not just get out of your way."

Now he was getting nods and affirmative noises, even a tentative smile or two. Cenn had put her knife away.

"I get that it may take a long time to win you over. That's no less than I deserve. I'll work long and hard. Do what you deem necessary. I just ask you to give me six months to let me try. So, as I said, I need your help."

Riddick sat down.

"What's in six months?" Jaden asked. "Why that particular number?"

"I want to plan something special for her birthday and I need to rebuild her trust before I can."

There was a beat of silence, then an explosion of chatter in Lytuan and English. Soon they were making lists and working through training scenarios. Riddick's whistle cut through the noise and the group fell silent and turned to him.

"Sorry to interrupt all this masterminding, but I have a few other ideas I'll need your help with. They're a little sneaky, but in a good way. Hear me out...."

An hour later, Riddick left, feeling lighter. He'd gotten the Elites on his side. No small task. They were loyal to Khara, but rooting for her happiness, too. They would help him. No one scoffed at the caveat that he wanted all of it to be done in secret so that he could surprise Khara.

He'd done his research and knew what his plan required. Time to get on with it.

Chapter Sixty-Two

S IX MONTHS HAD SOUNDED like a lifetime when they were discussing plans. In reality, it sped by in a blink.

It didn't take long for Riddick to realize he needed serious time management help, prompting him to call in the big guns and get Joanne and Lena together. Between that dream team and the Elites, they cobbled together a timeline that included most of what he'd requested.

When Riddick balked about not getting everything in, Lena told him flat out that, unless he could clone himself or teleport, this was what was possible. They haggled until they generated a result he was satisfied with. The plan they put in place required delegating quite a bit more than normal, but, with reluctance, Riddick agreed that might be a good thing. It would allow him to focus his energies.

A large chunk of the time Khara believed he was at home in DC, Riddick was on-island, training with the Elites in secret. It was a lot at once. They were tough on him and, while he relished the challenge, he fell into bed exhausted every night. Juggling work, travel, and training, not to mention a girlfriend he wanted to spend time with, was far different than the single-focus Army training in his younger days. He worked his ass off and hustled harder than he ever had. When he looked at Khara—hell, even thought about her—it renewed his commitment to the course of action.

It was a team effort to get Riddick everything he needed and everywhere he needed to be, without tipping off Khara. They all had to do some fast thinking and hasty altering of plans on occasion. A worthwhile trade-off was the closeness and solidarity the clandestine nature of it all fostered.

Time marched on and with it came three special opportunities for celebration. The Sloanes welcomed a bright-eyed little boy just days before Aimee had a beautiful baby girl. Not long after, Wyn's wife delivered their first child—a daughter. All three babies were born within days of each other.

New life had a way of renewing energy, and this was no exception.

When Riddick explained to Eric what he was attempting to do, he greeted him with nothing but enthusiastic support.

"I knew it!" Eric grinned and thumped him on the shoulder. "I knew it the minute I saw her in our office that she was gonna knock you on your ass."

"The timing sucks, man, and I'm sorry for that."

"We'll figure it out."

"I love this woman."

"I know. You might have been the last to know that, too."

<h1 style="text-align:center">Chapter Sixty-Three</h1>

"Y̲O̲U̲ C̲A̲N̲'T̲ K̲E̲E̲P̲ G̲O̲I̲N̲G̲ at this pace," Jaden advised, as they flew back to Lytua for another weekend of training. "You'll be a burned-out shell if you keep this up."

Riddick slumped into the seat next to his, a civics textbook open in front of him. He released a heavy sigh and considered. "This is harder than I expected," he conceded. "This back-and-forth is sucking the life out of me. I'd take a sabbatical, but Eric's hands are already full. I won't leave him in a lurch."

"If you're open to hearing one, I've got an idea."

"Shoot."

"What about telecommuting? You might have to get licensed to work on the island, though, even virtually. Tell Khara that part, then you won't have to keep up the whole charade. Knowing her, she'll help any way she can."

"That's brilliant." He didn't tell Jaden how well it played into the other plans he was cooking up.

"You'd free yourself up to focus on training and your classwork. You're doing well with the language study. There might be some weird stipulations for the licensure. They tend to be sticklers in that office."

"That shouldn't be a problem. I can check. Thanks for being so supportive."

"As her friend and her Zildrei, there's not much I wouldn't do for her."

The training schedule had lightened up from the brutal first months, but burning the candle at both ends wore on him. Riddick closed his textbook, then his eyes, and gave a deep sigh. "I want to do this for her. She's worth it."

"Understood. No doubt there. No matter how far you get, she'll love that you tried. Starting training after thirty? You're insane. Even I wouldn't try that."

Riddick cracked an eye open to peer at his friend. "Not even to impress Dr. Aimee?"

"Hmm, you might have me there. You sure I can't at least convince you to stop flying commercially?"

"Nope. No special treatment."

"My back hates you, but I respect what you're doing. She's going to be quite surprised and touched."

"I hope so."

When Riddick discovered what the licensure stipulations were, he could have jumped for joy. He presented the telecommuting idea to Khara, couching it as a way to spend more time together, since it would be better than asking her to be away from her duties.

Jaden was right; she was appreciative of his thoughtfulness.

He downplayed what getting licensed in Lytua would entail, only sharing about the required exam. There was a citizenship component, as well, which required Armed Services training, among other things.

For once, the universe aligned for him.

Chapter Sixty-Four

RIDDICK WASN'T ABLE TO test out of the requirements for a Lytuan architecture license and before he could sit for the exam, there was practical work to complete. Applying and interviewing for an entry-level position was a slight bruise to his ego.

After owning his own firm, Riddick had become accustomed to running things. It was challenging and humbling to be at the bottom of the food chain. But he was there to learn, and he got serious about it. His colleagues were welcoming and seemed relieved that he wasn't there to squash them on his way to the top.

He stayed in the barracks with the other recruits during Armed Services training, refusing any special treatment. It had sounded like a capital idea on paper. In reality, it took Riddick all of ten minutes to remember why he didn't have roommates anymore. He was part of a specially-designated unit for folks who couldn't train full-time—the only concession he would allow.

Being an American made him something of a novelty and his bunkmates joshed him about everything. In the process of trying to bring him up to speed on all things Lytuan, they asked if he'd seen their Queen. Riddick told them he had, and there was enthusiastic banter about how beautiful and smart she was. Riddick listened with half an ear until someone mentioned the Queen would pin them when they graduated.

Perfect. The idea of yet another surprise was forming. The younger men and women were already off on a tangent about seeing the Queen up close.

Commenting on her unmarried status and how it was clear she was waiting for one of them to sweep her off her feet.

At this, Riddick got a hearty laugh. "Not sure that's actually true, but you keep dreaming."

The recruits proceeded to extoll their virtues, each seeking to top the others. Riddick was already sending a text to Jaden.

Chapter Sixty-Five

WORDS ABANDONED KHARA AS she found herself face-to-face with her man on the parade grounds stage. He was wearing the uniform of a newly minted Lytuan soldier, having been through the boot camp required to become a full-fledged citizen.

Riddick flashed her a cocky grin and winked. *"Thank you, Avlah. It is an honor."* His Lytuan was perfect.

His surprise came off as planned, and it pleased him that Khara's hands trembled as she pinned the insignia on his lapel.

Riddick and Khara were all over each other in the car after the ceremony and reception. "My, God, you look delicious in this uniform," Khara ran a fingertip down the line of silver buttons at his chest, then leaned in to whisper, "Will you leave it on while you take me?"

Riddick looked down at her like he was fighting the temptation to strip her naked and take her right there. "I'll give you whatever you want." Raising his voice, he called, "Wyn? Would you kindly step on it, please?"

Both Wyn and Khara laughed, but the car shot forward with increased speed.

Riddick nearly dragged her from the car the moment it pulled up. After running up the stairs together, Riddick backed Khara against the front door as soon as it was closed behind them, already claiming her lips with his. Once he got her out of her dress, he pulled back to admire the matching bra and panty set in muted mint green she was wearing.

He left sweet kisses up the side of her neck and across her jaw to nibble her earlobe. "When did you touch yourself last, Khara?" His voice in her ear was husky with desire.

Khara shivered. "This morning. While fantasizing about you."

With that tantalizing image in his head, Riddick ordered her to open her legs wider for him and slipped two fingers through the leg opening of her damp panties and stroked her silken folds. He made an appreciative sound in the back of his throat and told her he'd missed everything about her while he coaxed a release up and out of her.

She exploded, gasping and crying out, not caring if any or all the Guard heard her. Khara grabbed his forearm, panting.

"Do you have more panties like this?"

"Yes. Why?"

"Good." Riddick retrieved his pocketknife from one of his cargo pockets and, with two quick flicks of his wrist, cut the pretty thong off.

Khara gasped a curse in Lytuan, her voice shaky.

"I know what that means now." Riddick re-pocketed the knife, brought the ruined panties to his nose, and inhaled. "Two months never felt so long." He scooped up some of her cream and sucked it off his fingers with a moan of gratitude.

He tossed her over his shoulder and strode toward the bedroom. Her girly squeal made him smile. He all but threw her on the dresser and pushed her legs wide so he could taste her while he got his pants and boxers out of the way. He drove inside her exquisite heat with a sigh and took a heartbeat just to appreciate how good she felt, how perfectly they fit together.

Then he took her *hard*.

Riddick fucked his woman with an enthusiasm borne of prolonged separation. They went at each other like overeager teenagers—all molten kisses and desperate clinging to each other.

Khara shoved the dresser top clear to give them more room, not sparing a thought for whatever was clattering to the floor. Then she grabbed fistfuls of Riddick's uniform jacket and held on, helping to bring him as deep as he could get. His expression was so intense, like he couldn't wait another single moment to have her. He didn't fuck her like this often, with almost wild, reckless abandon, but when he did... it was potent. She'd be feeling him for days, which would turn her on with every step.

He cupped her ass and pulled her up into his forceful thrusts. The glorious sensation of her hot, wet pussy clasping him almost did him in from the start. Their loving shoved Khara back up against the wall and he followed, hooking an arm under her knee to press deeper. He braced a hand under the back of her head to cushion it as their motions rattled the dresser almost violently. Mussed hair, face and neck flushed, pretty bra askew and falling off. The very picture of sexy.

He didn't let up until she was panting and moaning her way through another orgasm as he pounded into her.

"That's it, give it to me." Only then did he give in to the fantastic need and let himself go. Riddick delved as deep as he could and stayed there, groaning and shuddering as he came long and hard. They slumped together, gasping for breath, sprawled across the dresser, a mess at their feet. Somewhere along the way, one of Khara's shoes had come off. Riddick was still wearing his tactical boots.

"Welcome home," Khara murmured. "We're lucky the Guard didn't break in here with all the noise we just made."

"Nah, they knew what was going down. Careful here, I think we broke stuff."

He carried her to bed, prompting a giggle. Her eyes grew soft with emotion when he told her he loved her and had missed her in flawless Lytuan. He was already looking forward to maneuvers, if her reaction to him in uniform was anything to go by.

They'd only been able to video chat for the last two months, as they couldn't align their schedules, so Khara hadn't seen the physical transformation Riddick had undergone with all the training. He'd forgotten about that part until he got undressed to change into casual clothes and heard Khara gasp.

He glanced up at her. "What?"

She'd shot up straight in bed, her eyes hot as she looked him over head-to-toe.

Riddick gave her a slow, knowing smile. There was approval and heat in her eyes as she watched him walk over to the bed. "Khara, you're staring."

Khara swallowed hard, almost a gulp. "I'm going to say something very shallow right now."

"Oh, yeah?" Riddick felt about ten feet tall.

"I've always thought you were sexy, but this—" she waved an encompassing hand to indicate his newly toned physique. "Good Lord, you're... ripped. I know I said I wasn't ready for children anytime soon, but I think I just ovulated."

Riddick burst out laughing. All the sweat and pain had been worth it with that one gasp. He was in the best shape of his life. Better now even than when he'd gone through RASP to become a Ranger. He figured that had more to do with maturity than anything else.

"How did you pull this off? Who else knew?"

"Just the Guard and Joanne. I wouldn't have been able to do it without their help. It wasn't pretty at first. Lots of ice and wrapping and checking my ego."

"*This* is what you've been doing?"

"In part. It was a requirement for taking the exam."

"Goodness, that seems a bit extreme for—"

Riddick cut her off with a thorough kiss. "I missed you. Can't wait to get you to Nevis at long last."

Chapter Sixty-Six

R IDDICK KEPT KHARA OCCUPIED in their suite for the first two days of their Nevis adventure, making certain she knew how much he'd missed her. On the third night, they dressed up for a special dinner he'd arranged.

Khara kept catching him staring at her. "What is it?"

"You're beautiful, is all."

In the moment before they headed downstairs to the restaurant, Riddick drew his fingertips across her bare upper back before splaying his hand across her shoulder. "I don't tell you this often enough, but you...." he trailed off, blinking back the tears that were trying to gather. "You are the best part of my life." His voice was hoarse and choked with emotion.

She teared up and gave him that smile that made him want to grab a sword and slay dragons for her. God, he swore his heartbeat was stronger because of her.

When Khara stopped in front of the restaurant entrance, she was confused when he kept going beyond it.

"Follow me. I have a little surprise for you."

He coaxed her down a hallway that led to the ballrooms and slipped a blindfold over her eyes outside the farthest one before leading her inside.

"Is someone else in here?" she asked, gripping his arm.

"Just a moment. Are you ready?"

Khara laughed. "What are you up to? I'm ready!"

The first thing she saw when he uncovered her eyes was an elegant dining room adorned with balloons and other decorations. She was exclaiming over the sights when Riddick told her to have a look behind her.

A room full of people yelled out, "Surprise!" and threw confetti in the air before launching into a rousing rendition of the birthday song.

Khara let out a joyous cry at finding herself surrounded by family and friends singing. Amid hugs and kisses and greetings, Khara took in the familiar faces of the most important people in her life and marveled that they were all there for her. "Riddick! How did you do this?"

"With help from other people who love you. We rented out the resort for the duration of our stay. The 'public' is all people you know, so you can relax and enjoy yourself without fear of being watched by the press or curious citizens."

Before she'd adjusted to the surprise of her near and dear ones being present, Riddick led her to a table laden with wrapped gifts in every color and insisted she open his first. He plucked a palm-sized box topped with a fluffy gold bow and placed it in her hands.

Khara couldn't stop grinning and rose on her toes to drop a kiss on his lips. "This really is the best gift, Riddick. Thank you! This is the most incredible thing anyone has ever done for me." When he just smiled, Khara removed the bow and lifted the lid. Nestled within the box was an engraved invitation to a citizenship ceremony the following week.

It puzzled Khara. "I don't understand."

"Look closer."

The invitation to the ceremony had his name on it as the soon-to-be citizen. Was he playing a joke on her? "What's going on? Riddick, I don't understand what this means."

"No? I have something to help with that."

When Khara looked up, Riddick was grinning at her. "I love you," he told her, taking her hands in his and kissing them.

Then he sank to one knee.

Chapter Sixty-Seven

EXCITED MURMURING ERUPTED AROUND them.

"What are you—"

"Khara, you crashed into my life like a comet, and I'm thankful for it every day. You showed me what love is, what love does. A year ago, I couldn't have conceived of you. That someone so wonderful would upend my orderly world and become the center of it.

"You had me from the moment you called back because I hung up on you. I don't know how I got this lucky, but I know I never want to be anyplace else other than by your side. You make me a better man just by being in my life. You make me want to be a better man every day."

Khara blinked hard to keep the tears at bay. He continued.

"I had some things to take care of to get to this moment. I needed to earn this, earn asking you to be in my life permanently. So, I learned your language, moved to your island, got my ass whipped into shape while I went through Army training, did my civil service, got my Lytuan architecture license, set up office space. I passed the citizenship exam, which was hard as hell, by the way."

Everyone laughed.

"This was the moment I was working towards. Being good enough to stand next to you, to kneel at your feet and tell you I'm yours forever if you'll have me."

Khara's elder sister, Shanna, and Yvanda stepped forward and, acting in her parents' stead, offered their formal approval and acceptance of Riddick.

Khara was sobbing openly at this point. Someone handed her a tissue.

"Dee?"

Dion, looking dapper in a crisp guayabera shirt paired with linen pants, shot Khara a huge grin and placed a small velvet box in Riddick's hand.

"I know it's not Lytuan custom, but I hope you'll indulge me in an American tradition. I wanted to give you something that represents my commitment to you. To the future we'll share."

Riddick opened the box. Nestled inside was the most beautiful ring Khara had ever seen. Gasps sounded from every corner of the room as the diamonds glittered in the light.

"It's not just that I want you to be my wife. I want to be your husband. *Chu schwe shala.* So, will you marry me, Khara?"

"Yes," she whispered with a dreamy smile, cupping his cheek. "Yes, I will."

With whoops and cheers of their loved ones ringing in their ears, Riddick slipped the ring onto her finger. He lifted her off her feet as they embraced, kissing her long and deep.

Then the party got started in earnest.

Chapter Sixty-Eight

T HE PALACE CALLED A press conference for the following afternoon once Khara and Riddick returned from Nevis. It was standing room only.

"Are you sure you're ready for this?" Khara asked backstage, slipping her hand into Riddick's. "There's still time to call this off."

But Riddick just smiled and tucked a rogue coil back behind her ear. "I've got this."

There was a moment of stunned silence when Joanne announced that Queen Lillianna was now engaged to be married, then a cacophony of rapid-fire questions. It was pandemonium. As always, Joanne remained unruffled and offered answers about who Riddick was, how they'd met. This was big, big news.

"Mr. Riddick is here and will give his own statement and take questions."

Riddick refused an interpreter. He struggled a little more than he would have liked answering in Lytuan. Seeing this, the press corps graciously switched to English. He joked about improving before the next conference. The questions were straightforward and germane.

Riddick shared a highlights version of his history and worked with Joanne to choose a journalist to do an in-depth interview the next day. With his permission, Dade had unsecured his juvenile records; Riddick would be turning them over in their entirety. By getting out ahead of it, they would control the narrative.

"The fact of the matter is your approval doesn't matter one bit. I'm head over heels for your Queen and I'm a lucky man that she loves me. I intend to spend the rest of my life making sure she knows she's the center of my universe. However you judge me doesn't change that."

He hadn't intended to make it a grand gesture, but it was curtains after that.

Khara ran into his arms when it was over.

"*I'm so proud of you!*" She was so overwhelmed with emotion, she reverted to Lytuan.

Beleaguered, Riddick held her with unsteady hands. "Thanks for letting me do that on my own. It was important."

"You're going to have every woman in Lytua sighing over how romantic you are."

"You think so?"

"This Lytuan woman is."

Chapter Sixty-Nine

TRINA VAGUELY RECOLLECTED HAVING an outburst when she saw the news conference. Fabiola came running, alarmed.

Trina offered the young woman an overly sincere smile and waved her off as she closed her office door.

She fumed as she paced, wrestling down the urge to throw something. This insult could not stand. She'd have to do something drastic. Time was running out. After their extended trip abroad, Cyrus was stable again, thank goodness. Corey seemed to have renewed his commitment to her. She'd felt optimistic about things. She'd planned to regroup and reevaluate her options once things were more settled.

Trina forced herself to calm down and get back to work. She'd think about it later.

The wild swing in mood baffled her secretary. Trina gritted her teeth when Fabiola called on the intercom a few minutes later to ask if she was alright. Fabiola was solicitous to a fault and getting on her last nerve with it. Trina couldn't very well fire her for being considerate. She did her best to keep her irritation in check and thanked her for her concern. She was fine.

The same wouldn't be said for that bitch Queen when she was done with her, though.

Chapter Seventy

NOW THAT THEIR ENGAGEMENT was in the open, they were free to go out in public together. Khara wanted to show Riddick so many things. They accepted congratulations everywhere they went. Riddick worried the citizens might be unhappy that their Queen wasn't marrying a fellow Lytuan, but there was, to his great relief, very little of that. The public was ecstatic for her and embraced Riddick.

Khara shared her life—where she'd grown up, the schools she'd attended, the breathtaking waterfalls. Riddick was full of questions and derived just as much pleasure from her excitement. Seeing Lytua through her eyes filled him with joy.

It thrilled Khara when she overheard Riddick chatting with people in Lytuan. His grammar was perfect. She promised him the interest would die down eventually, but he took it in stride. He understood the public was curious about him and he was gracious about it, amping up the charm.

As predicted, Riddick's declaration of love and commitment to his new life garnered female adoration far and wide. Eric and Maya roasted him mercilessly over his heartthrob status. The roasting was sure to go on for a while. Even Dion got in on it.

When they returned to her apartment after a long day of sightseeing, Riddick fake-collapsed onto the couch with a long sigh. Khara sat next to him, chuckling. "When I was first crowned, it was a shock to be 'on' all the time. I know it's a lot right now. You do get used to it."

Riddick drew her across his lap, waited until she slid her arms around his neck. "I will. I said so before, but it bears repeating. You, Khara Witherspoon Therin, you're worth it." He dropped a few kisses under her earlobe, prompting both a shiver and a giggle.

International media swarmed the island in the wake of the news, but their entry was limited, controlled, and monitored. Khara's office was inundated with requests from all manner of American media, from major networks and publications to Riddick's alma maters. Khara was insistent that the foreign press did not turn the whole thing into a tawdry spectacle. Joanne did her best to keep that from happening and had never worked so hard in her capacity as press secretary.

Khara stood beaming by Riddick's side when the Immigration Ministry awarded him Lytuan citizenship. It humbled her, that this man loved her so much he'd become a citizen of her homeland. He'd excelled in all that was required of him—testing, training, civic service in the Ministry of Ecology.

He pressed a light kiss to the back of her hand when he saw her teetering on tears. "Committed, remember? I'm all in."

"You didn't have to. It means the world that you did, but you so didn't have to." She sniffed and dabbed at her eyes.

"I know. And that's exactly why I wanted to."

On the back end, Riddick had to adapt to having security, and Khara empathized with the initial awkwardness. His new assistant was keeping his schedule in order and guarding his time like a lioness. Between her and Lena, Riddick couldn't have been luckier on that front.

Implanting the subcutaneous tracker was a painless, straightforward procedure. Khara hadn't balked about it after the kidnapping, but she wouldn't even consider it without stringent privacy requirements. Riddick was in and out with no fuss.

Melanie Goodnight had implemented brilliant tech upgrades for the jewelry trackers that included built-in protocols for a two-word voice command and remote activation as a last-resort failsafe. Not having physical access would never be an impediment again.

Chapter Seventy-One

Trina Krove ambushed Khara the day after the press conference, catching her in the hallway en route to her office. Dispensing with any pleasantries, she leveled her accusation. "You said you don't date. And now you're marrying an American?"

Surprised at the vitriol in her words, Khara turned to face the woman, signaling her escort not to intervene. "At the time, I didn't. Not that it's any of your business."

"Do you not care that you've broken my son's heart?"

"Deputy Chief Krove." Khara was weary of this foolishness. "This is the last time I will have this conversation with you or your husband. As I've stated many times before, I am flattered that Cyrus is interested in me, but I am not, nor have I ever been, interested in him romantically. The fact that his parents keep asking for dates on his behalf is...." She managed to stop herself before uttering the word *pathetic*. "I'm not interested."

Trina's face contorted as though she were in pain. "You're just intolerant. You won't accept him because he has a disability. Is that it?"

"Of course not." Both she and Richardson had accused her of this in the past, and it was still absurd. She would love Riddick just as much if he had a speech impediment.

She didn't like the gleam in Trina's eye. Rumors abounded that she had a cruel streak and a short temper. Khara had no desire to antagonize her.

"Well, what's so special about *him*?"

Everything, Khara thought, but didn't say. "This conversation is over."

Trina looked like she was well on her way to blowing a gasket, but she took a deep breath, turned on her heel, and marched out of the hallway. It sounded like she might be sobbing. She didn't even say goodbye.

"Should we ban her from your office suite, *Avlah*?" a concerned Guard asked.

Khara shook her head, squinting as a tension headache threatened to form behind her eyes. "No, she's just upset. She's still a citizen and I still represent her.

"I don't like how she speaks to you."

"Nor do I. But I do still represent her."

Trina always gave Khara a sense of vague unease, and not just because of her spouse, though she could never put her finger on any specific thing to explain why.

Khara gathered herself and went about her day.

Chapter Seventy-Two

T RINA'S SECRETARY CALLING HIM came as an unwelcome surprise. Corey Richardson knew Fabiola, of course, but not well. She'd called on his private cell phone number, her voice anxious as she blurted, "I'm worried about the Deputy Chief, Senator."

Corey was about to head home from work. Instead, he retreated to his office and closed the door.

He listened without interrupting as Fabiola detailed Trina's strange behavior. She didn't know who else to turn to with her suspicions. Trina had grown more and more impatient these past weeks, and was missing appointments, disappearing for unexplained stretches of time, making bizarre requests.

"Like what?" Sweat popped out on Corey's forehead, and he dabbed at it with the back of his wrist.

"She asked me to look for dirt on the Queen's fiancé. She wanted me to get information for her. I—I think she may be trying to hurt the Queen. I know she doesn't care for her, but— She left in a hurry today and her computer was unlocked. So I snooped, because she never leaves it unlocked. I know I shouldn't have."

That alone was cause enough for concern. Trina had hacker roots and never left any device unlocked. Had this been a test of some sort?

"What did you find?" Richardson interrupted, his heart racing.

"Can we talk about this in person? I'm worried. The Deputy Chief has been acting out of character of late. She's been so volatile."

"Tell me what you found, dammit."

"She's... been accessing *Avlah's* official schedule, the one no one is supposed to have outside the Elite Guard. Like tracking the Queen's movements. I did some digging and cross-checking. The Deputy Chief went to Washington, DC, when the Queen was there, right around the time of the kidnapping." She lowered her voice to a frantic whisper. "I think she may be involved somehow."

Richardson coughed a little. Fear was a boulder sitting on his chest, making it difficult for him to breathe. "That's absurd. She was on a shopping trip with her sister."

"That's what I thought, too, but.... I don't want her to know I'm talking to you. Her temper has been explosive recently. And this could be nothing, right? Logical explanation and all?"

"Of course it's nothing." He couldn't keep the snap out of his voice.

"Should I go to Zildrei Everly? There's also—"

"No. Can you prove this?"

"Yes."

"Gather whatever evidence you can. Then we'll talk in person."

They arranged to meet at her house the next week, after he returned from scheduled travel.

Richardson went about his evening, discomforted by how Fabiola's concerns about Trina's behavior mirrored his own. She'd been irrational, venomous, even. Trina did not care for the Queen any more than he did, but that didn't equate to involvement in a kidnapping. No, Fabiola must be overreacting or misinterpreting. He'd sort this out and get to the bottom of this later. He wouldn't have Trina's good name sullied with unfounded accusations. No, that wouldn't do at all.

Chapter Seventy-Three

TRINA WAS SO ENGROSSED in her plans to supply Corey with the embezzlement evidence against the Queen she failed to notice how her son was deteriorating until it was almost too late.

She and Cyrus were watching *Lytua Tonight* in the family room, as they often did. Trina left the room for something inconsequential when the sound of Cyrus wailing and smashing about brought her at a run.

The television lay in sparking ruins, hanging at a precarious angle from its mounting bracket on the wall.

Trina leaped back to avoid her rampaging son. It took an hour to get him calmed down enough to pry the story out of him. Lillianna and that horrid American had done a live segment on the show announcing their wedding date.

This precipice was where Trina had to choose between her son's well-being and satisfying her own thirst for vengeance. There was no question. Once she'd assured Cyrus she'd prevent Lillianna from marrying someone else, she retrieved her untraceable laptop and hit "execute" on the endgame tracing program attached to the falsified evidence.

And now Trina had a final hand to play. It was a gamble she'd hoped to never need to take, but the situation was desperate.

Corey sensed the discord in the air the moment he entered his home. He found his wife and son in the garage, packing her car with tools.

"What's going on?"

Trina instructed Cyrus to keep going and drew Corey into the kitchen so they could speak in private.

"That was the last straw. I'm done putting up with this disrespect, and I'm shutting this whole thing down as soon as I can."

"What are we talking about? What was the last straw?"

"Lillianna announced her wedding date on *Lytua Tonight*."

"Oh. I see. How is he taking it?"

"Not well, but I've got a plan. Lillianna will marry Cyrus. She will choose him, you'll see."

"I've seen those two together. They are very much in love. How will you—"

"For once, Corey, could you please have a little faith in me? Just a little? I've got this, really, I do. We're finally going to get Cyrus what he deserves. I just need to get the American out of the way and he'll be home free." She kissed his cheek. "Don't wait up."

A sense of foreboding settled in Corey's stomach as he watched them leave.

Chapter Seventy-Four

GUILT WAS NOT AN emotion Corey Richardson was accustomed to feeling, but it twisted in his gut as he looked down into the dead eyes of his wife's secretary. He'd dismissed the girl's concerns about her safety. Now, it seemed, he was at least partially responsible for her death.

When Trina and Cyrus had not come home last night, he'd asked Fabiola if they could meet later. He had to get to the bottom of whatever was going on with Trina and Cyrus.

When he arrived at Fabiola's apartment, no one answered as he called. Richardson frowned and checked his watch. He was a few minutes early. But her house seemed quite deserted. The door was ajar. He called out again. Had she stepped out? That didn't make any sense, though. She'd sounded frightened and paranoid over the phone. Richardson felt a sense of dread as he entered the tiny apartment.

He found her lying at the foot of the stairs, her neck at an impossible angle. Richardson stumbled back from the sight of her body, horrified. He gathered himself and kneeled next to her to check her pulse. She was gone.

There were clear signs of a struggle—items scattered on the counter, a lamp knocked over. He dug for his phone, then stopped once he had it in his hand. He could be standing in the middle of a murder scene, he realized with some panic. The police would suspect him right away. He was supposed to meet her here, after all. He'd even left her a voicemail saying he was on his way. Had anyone been around when she called?

What should he do? He cast a frantic glance around the living room. There was no evidence he'd been here. No one had known he was coming. He should call the police, emergency services. But a nagging thought wouldn't go away.

She wanted to talk to him about Trina. About something that scared her enough to hide at home. Something she needed to show him. He knew in his heart Trina was involved in this somehow. With her erratic behavior and then the episode the night before, Richardson was positive something bad was happening.

And now, here he was, looking at a dead body and wondering what the hell he should do.

Calling the police was out of the question. They were all in Trina's chain of command. He needed to be discreet. Otherwise, he might ruin both his and Trina's careers. He'd have to figure out a way to report this without bringing himself under suspicion. Trina hadn't answered his calls all day. Did she know her secretary was dead?

Richardson got in his car and drove out of the neighborhood. With it being the middle of a weekday, it was unlikely anyone would have seen or recognized him, but you never knew. He needed to put some distance between himself and Fabiola's place fast.

He needed to speak with the Queen.

Chapter Seventy-Five

THE WORLD WENT TO hell on an unseasonably chilly weekday.

Jaden received a frantic call from Brixton, one of the Guards on afternoon duty with Riddick. An older woman t-boned their SUV in a downtown intersection, totaling it. The woman was uninjured but had been beside herself with worry, uncalmable. She'd insisted on taking Riddick to the hospital herself to be checked out. Brixton already called emergency services and would stay behind with the damaged car. The hospital was just a few blocks away. The other Guard on duty, Stanford, went with them. Or would have if the lady hadn't floored it before he could get the passenger side door open. Riddick was already in the car.

The Queen's fiancé had been abducted in broad daylight.

Brixton had gotten the license plate number. A horrendous electronic screeching emitted from the phone when he attempted to dial for help. It was the same result with his partner's phone and the radio. None of his clearance codes worked to access any of the other encrypted, secure lines in the Elite Guard network on phones borrowed from bystanders. Once the first responders arrived, Brix tried to explain, but they cut him off, advising him he'd been reported to the police as compromised.

He convinced an officer to drive him to the Hub, where it took another half hour to get sorted and authenticated. By then, almost a full hour had passed before Brix could report what had happened.

Jaden slammed his hand on the console to activate remote access to all the GPS devices assigned to Riddick. They'd worked in redundancies after Khara's kidnapping, tested and refined the devices. A handful showed as stationary in Khara's building—those would be the other tie pins and watches he wasn't wearing. But no others. Not even the subcutaneous one.

"What the hell?" This shouldn't have been possible.

Brix verified the devices had been operational that morning.

Stanford bounced off the woman's car at the scene and fallen into an awkward heap; the ambulance transported him to the hospital. Brixton protested when Jaden gave him the same order.

"You were just in a car accident. The hospital. Not negotiable."

He strode down the hall toward Khara's office, where she plowed right into him, running full tilt. She bounced off his chest and would have fallen if he hadn't steadied her with a quick hand under her elbow. "Whoa. *Avlah*, what—?"

"Trina Krove, Riddick—" Khara gulped in a breath, eyes wild. "Has—Riddick is—have to—no time—"

"Breathe, *Avlah*. You're going to hyperventilate." Jaden had never seen level-headed Khara so panicked. He let out a sharp whistle, summoning the rest of the team. Khara was so rattled she couldn't breathe or think straight.

Jaden caught both her elbows and didn't let go until her breathing was under control. "Now tell me what's going on." The rest of the Elites crowded into the hallway with weapons drawn, confused but on alert. They took up protective stances around their Queen, already deciding which route to best evacuate her.

"Trina Krove has Riddick," Khara cried, shaking all over. "She's going to kill him!"

Khara spilled the entire story, wringing her hands, her eyes wide and terrified.

Until that point, Jaden had hoped against hope that someone was just playing a cruel trick.

"Make sure Mr. Riddick's mother is safe," Cenn ordered one of the hovering Guards. "Keep her home, but don't alarm her." The young woman set off.

They retrieved Khara's phone, where Trina had sent proof that she did, indeed, have Riddick as her captive. A close-up picture of Riddick showed him gagged, his eyes closed. The background appeared to be a car.

As the team secured the distraught Queen in her conference room, Cenn ordered the building to lock down.

Trina was supposed to text in two and a half hours with the location of where Khara should meet her and "settle this."

Khara paced, chewing on her thumbnail.

"She didn't ask for money or anything else? Just you? What does she mean 'settle this'?" Alene's voice was calm.

"I don't know!"

Riddick's cell phone was not broadcasting a location. It was eventually found broken on the side of the road, as though tossed from the vehicle.

The license plate came back as belonging to Trina's sister, Bella.

Jaden buzzed the Guard secretary on the intercom. "Get Corey Richardson in here."

"He actually just came in, sir, demanding to see the Queen."

"'Demanding?'" Wyn echoed. "That asshole doesn't get to *demand*—"

Cenn cut his tirade off. "Bring him up."

Khara launched herself at Richardson upon his entering the conference room. No one expected it of her, least of all Richardson. The perfect sweep she executed took him down to the ground with a thud and she followed, just as she'd learned. When he was flat on his back and pinned, she yelled in his face, "Where is he?" Everyone stared, stunned. No one knew how to react right away.

Then there was a flurry of activity. It took both Jonnis and Link to haul a struggling Khara off Richardson. She grabbed the lapels of his suit jacket and smashed his face with her elbow. It was a powerful blow; a sickening crunch sounded. Richardson howled as blood gushed from his face. Khara kicked him in the side. Wyn and Jaden helped the senator to his feet. When Khara tried to lunge again, Link held her back.

"Easy, *Avlah*. You already handed him his ass."

"You bloodthirsty bitch," Richardson whined. "My nose. You broke my nose!"

"I'll kill you if she hurts him." The threat came out in a snarl.

Richardson flinched away from her harsh words. "Keep her away from me. I'll press charges! You all saw how she attacked me, didn't you? And threatened me!"

The stone-faced Guards around him looked on. "Nobody saw any such thing, Senator," Jonnis deadpanned.

"You should be more careful about walking into those doors." Link handed him a wad of paper towels for his nose.

Richardson made a noise of disgust, realizing the Guards would never say a word against the *Avlah* and gave it up. "I don't know where they are."

"Who's 'they'?" The Elites asked in unison.

"My wife and Cyrus, my son. I think my wife snapped or had some sort of mental break and may have done something terrible. I can't get ahold of her."

Jaden resisted the urge to yoke him up, forced calm into his voice instead. "Explain."

"She said she was done with the disrespect and she and Cyrus didn't come home last night. This was after the interview."

"What are you on about?"

"The interview. The one on *Lytua Tonight*."

"Make sense, man. Which fucking interview?"

"The one where *Avlah* and Mr. Riddick announced their wedding date?" Alene interjected. She had been with them at the studio.

"Yes. I didn't think much of it, but she and Cyrus packed the car with tools. She wouldn't answer me when I asked what she was doing. There's more,"

Richardson admitted, then told them about the phone call from Trina's secretary and finding her body. "That's why I'm here."

Jonnis asked what they were all thinking, "Why didn't you go to the police? Why come to *Avlah*?"

"They would have asked too many questions. And I wanted you to know that I have nothing to hide, that I was cooperating."

"Ever the politician," Wyn sneered.

Richardson's phone rang. "It's my sister-in-law. Hello? Slow down, Bella. You and Trina did *what*?"

Chapter Seventy-Six

RIDDICK CAME TO LASHED to a chair and with a man he didn't recognize screaming at him to wake up. As his eyes opened, a meaty fist slammed into the side of his face. The screaming continued, as did the blows. The beating was vicious and emotional, but haphazard in its application. Riddick had been captured and interrogated once as a Ranger. He knew how to take a beating.

A woman he thought he recognized interceded, tugging the man's arm and telling him it was enough. Then he remembered. The woman was Trina, the Deputy Police Chief and Senator Richardson's wife. That would make the man their son. The one they'd been after Khara to date. *Cyrus.*

The man loomed over him, his eyes filled with hatred. "You can't have her. She's mine. You'll see."

Riddick scoffed. Cyrus could hang that up right now. He'd be a dead man walking if he laid a finger on Khara. His eyes skimmed over his surroundings slowly. This was a cave furnished as an apartment. The air had that cool feeling you only got when you were deep underground. The bright light of a standing floodlight revealed a large area rug, a dining table, and chairs. It was bizarre.

He couldn't feel his watch; they'd taken it.

The watch wasn't his only tracker; another remained hidden in his tiepin, but he couldn't get to it with his hands bound and tape over his mouth. No way to activate it with the verbal cue. The Elites would do it via remote—they'd set that procedure up as a failsafe, but GPS wouldn't penetrate down here. Wherever "here" was.

Cyrus and Trina retreated to where Riddick couldn't make out their words. He flexed his hands to test his bonds. They'd secured him to a heavy chair, his arms bound behind him, each leg tied to the front legs. Not handcuffed. Good. Careful to keep his movements inconspicuous, Riddick went to work to loosen the bindings.

He'd been foolish at the accident site, allowing himself to be separated from his escort. He'd just wanted to make the upset driver feel better, so she'd stop freaking out.

The accident hadn't been that bad. She seemed harmless. While he knew better than to trust appearances, worry for Brix and Stanford distracted him. Were they injured? He'd given her his hand when she'd asked for it. The prick came so fast he almost wasn't sure it happened, but the immediate wooziness was very real. Then he'd been thrown against the back seat as the car sped off. The last thing he remembered was fumbling with the seat belt, trying and failing to get the activation words out.

Chapter Seventy-Seven

BELLA KROVE STARTED GETTING cold feet when the talk of killing Riddick had started. She'd high-tailed it to the Richardson-Krove home, hoping her brother-in-law would help figure the situation out. Not finding Richardson at home, she'd reached him on his cell.

She'd come to the Hub as instructed with no fuss. By the time she arrived, the Elites had run out of patience with Richardson. They hustled him out before Khara tore him limb from limb and sent him home with instructions to stay there. He'd have to make statements and such, but he'd finished for the time being. He promised to cooperate with the investigations.

Municipal police confirmed Richardson's story after they were dispatched to Fabiola Sinclair's home. The scene was just as described—Fabiola was dead, her neck appeared to be broken.

A waif of a woman, Trina Krove's much younger sister shook when a Guard led her into the conference room. Most of the team remained assembled there. After the whooping she'd laid on Richardson, the Elites escorted Khara back to her office, away from the meeting. Bella couldn't even speak right away. She'd never been in any sort of trouble in her life and was now neck-deep in it. The men and women around her wore hard expressions.

Bella calmed down some after gulping down a glass of water. Enough to tell them what had happened. It sounded absurd when she recounted the events leading up to that moment. Trina asked for her help with a training exercise, one designed to highlight flaws in the Elite Guards' security. Although Trina was not a fan of the Queen's, Bella admired her sister's commitment to her job. She was happy to help. Trina assured her everyone involved knew about the exercise. Bella would be playing a vital role in national security.

It was the most exciting thing she'd ever done. Bella stayed in character and played her part. She remembered thinking at the time that everyone's acting was quite good. Believing she was *helping* the Elite Guard, she'd followed the instructions Trina gave to the letter. She'd waited in the spot Trina chose, rammed the SUV with her car, activated the jamming device Trina issued her, and then spirited Mr. Riddick away, just as planned.

She'd arrived at the rendezvous point right on time and presented Mr. Riddick with a flourish. Two things concerned her right away: her nephew's presence and the lack of police or Guard personnel. Cyrus was not law enforcement at all. When Bella asked about it, Trina snapped at her to hurry, that they had little time.

"It all sounded so logical and harmless when she was describing it," Bella continued. "But then she started saying all kinds of nonsensical things. She hasn't been herself in recent months and I think she's going to hurt that man. Somehow, she's convinced he's in the way of Corey being king. She said once Riddick is dead, *Avlah* will marry Cyrus."

"As if," Cenn spat.

The Elites looked at one another in confounded silence.

Wyn looked Bella Krove over. She was five-four at most and on the thin side. No match at all for a man of Riddick's size and strength. "How did you subdue Mr. Riddick? He's a big guy."

Bella looked down at her shaking hands in her lap. "I, ah, tranqued him. I asked to see his hand and jabbed him. He was just about out before we got down the street. The three of us got him out of the car and into... we tied him up."

"No tranq is that fast-acting. Try again," Link said.

Bella wanted to hide. "We're working on a fast-acting, short-term sedative in my lab, for use with aggressive psychiatric patients in emergencies."

They all stared at her in disbelief. Jaden was the first to recover. "You used... an *experimental* drug on the man who will be the Queen's Consort?"

"I titrated it for his height and weight. It's safe. I thought I was helping!"

"Where are they?"

She hesitated, worrying at her lower lip.

Cenn put a reassuring hand on Bella's shoulder and spoke in a gentle voice. "Your sister duped you, Ms. Krove. You did the right thing talking to us, but you need to tell us the rest right now and hope nothing irreversible has been done."

"Is my sister going to get in trouble? Is my nephew?"

"They're already in a great deal of trouble and, frankly, it will be much worse if they hurt Mr. Riddick."

"She has a history of mental health concerns. They both do. Does that make a difference?"

Alene wanted to shake some sense into the woman. The clock was ticking. "It might. I promise we'll take it into consideration. I know you want to protect your family. The best way you can help them is by telling us where they are, so we can end this before anyone gets hurt."

Fat tears slid down Bella's cheeks. She shook her head. "I'm sorry, I can't."

"Then we have no choice but to arrest you." Cenn signaled the Guards. "Get her out of here."

Bella broke down into piteous sobs as Guard personnel led her out. The team took a collective breath.

Cenn folded her arms in disgust. "That's not how I thought that interview would end. I feel sorry for that woman."

"Well, I don't," Wyn snapped. "Her sister didn't give a shit about getting her mixed up in all this shadiness. She should have just told us. It's not like they can hide forever."

"Family is complicated," Khara said from the doorway. She appeared much calmer, though her brow remained furrowed. "What do we do now?"

Another picture came two hours and thirty minutes after the initial threatening phone call. This time, Riddick's face was bloodied, his eyes blazing. Khara choked out a distressed sound and fell back hard in her chair. When the phone rang, she put it on speaker.

"I assume the Elites are listening in," Trina said. "So, I'll make this brief."

"Don't hurt him. I'll do exactly as you say."

They listened with rapt attention to the instructions Trina gave. They seemed unnecessarily elaborate, but she held all the cards.

"Get here or he dies. And I won't make it quick."

Khara jumped to her feet after the call finished. There was no time to waste. "I'm going."

"No, *Avlah*. Jonnis will double for you. We'll take care of this."

Adamant, Khara shook her head. "No. She'll know it's not me and kill him. *I'm* going. "

An uproar ensued. Each of the Elites shouted protests.

"There's no time to debate. Would you hesitate if she had Aimee? Or any of the others? Help me figure this out," Khara pleaded.

The timeline Trina had given was short, probably to avoid them having time to strategize a counterattack. As it was, they scrambled to coordinate even nominal defenses.

Cenn expressed uneasiness about the cave chosen for this showdown; the location must hold a tactical advantage for Trina. It was remote, so she'd hear vehicles approaching and no one was likely to stumble upon them. Trina threatened Khara to come alone, though she must have known there was no chance of that.

Trina didn't seem concerned at all about how she was going to get out of this, nor about keeping the Elites out of it—both of which caused concern. Did it mean she had no intention of getting out of it and would kill them all? How did she think this would play out?

Khara refused weapons and body armor, not wanting to do anything that might antagonize Trina. She would not risk harm to Riddick. Her job was to stall. There was only time for minimal instruction before she started the long drive to the far side of the island. They had to assume Trina had her service weapon with her. Khara was to watch for other weapons. They were all talking and planning up to the moment she put the SUV in gear.

The team stood clustered in the garage after Khara drove off.

"Well," Cenn sighed, after Khara'd turned out of sight. "It's been nice knowing you. Mr. Riddick's going to kill every one of us."

"He knows how headstrong she is," Jaden pointed out.

"It won't matter to him."

"Wouldn't matter to me, either, if it was Aimee."

The rest of the team agreed, then finished suiting up in their protective gear. None of them had confidence in the current plan, but they'd run out of time and would have to improvise. Their Queen was counting on them.

Chapter Seventy-Eight

S TAY CALM. KEEP THEIR *attention. Keep as much distance between you as possible.*

Khara repeated the Elites' instructions like a mantra to steady her nerves. Despite shaking hands, she squared her shoulders and strode into the cave with her head held high. This ended tonight. The Elites wouldn't let anything happen to her or Riddick. They'd find a way to get in here undetected.

Her stomach pitched when she spotted Riddick bound to a chair. She looked away from his bloody, swollen face before the upset got the best of her. "I'm here."

"Finally," Cyrus cawed, all but skipping over to Khara and pulling her deeper into the cave. She tried not to recoil at his touch. Why did it look like an apartment here?

"She came for him, just like you said she would."

Trina looked as disheveled as Khara had seen her. Dirt smudged her face, her clothes were rumpled, hair unkempt. That worried Khara almost as much as the wide grin that lit her face. Trina always looked polished and pulled together. Now, she appeared... unhinged. But the hand on the gun pointing at her was steady. "I told you, honey. Bring her over here."

Cyrus tugged Khara over to his mother.

"How are you proposing we settle this?" Khara resisted the urge to pull away.

Before she could continue, Cyrus hissed, "You whore!" and backhanded her across the face. The crack echoed through the cave. It was so fast, so violent.

Khara staggered but managed to remain upright. She tasted blood from where she'd bitten into her cheek.

Riddick made an outraged sound against the tape, as he strained against his bonds.

"That's for spreading your legs for the American, love. And for taking so long to submit to me."

Submit to him? A chill skipped down Khara's spine at the malice in his eyes. This wasn't the awkward misfit who'd given her the creeps when they were in school together. His entire demeanor hardened, from his voice to his body language. He was cold, with an unnatural stillness. Like a serpent lying in wait.

Hulking over her, Cyrus wiped the trickle of blood from her split lip, giving her a menacing smile that promised more pain. Everything clicked into place a half-second too late. They weren't settling anything. Taking Riddick was just to lure her here. She was in real trouble now.

"Let her go for now, Cyrus. The three of us have to talk, remember? She won't be able to do her part if we don't and we don't have much time." Trina had come close and placed a hand on his shoulder. "We must stick to the plan."

Cyrus released Khara's arm, and she stumbled. He'd fooled her into believing he was harmless, and he was anything but. She was dealing with a different adversary now. The plan to tell them what they wanted to hear wasn't going to work. Her heart thudded so loud she could scarcely think. The laugh Cyrus let out had a maniacal edge to it. "Tell her."

Trina hovered nearby, a frown creasing her forehead. "First, you're going to call off your engagement with this horrible American. You'll marry Cyrus. You'll tell everyone you were secretly in love with him, but thought he was too good for you. Then you're going to abdicate, and Corey will be king. You'll stay home so you can raise all the children you'll have."

Words failed her. What could she say in the face of such ill intent? *Stall, Khara.* "Sounds like you've put a lot of thought into this."

Cyrus brushed the back of his hand over her throbbing cheek. Her skin crawled. She didn't dare react. His eyes were cold. Devoid of decency or compassion. It was like staring into a yawning void.

He leaned close. "I'm going to have so much fun punishing you. Just like the others." He hit her again, his open palm connecting with the same spot. "Don't get any ideas about trying to placate me. None of that phony shit. You're going to learn your place."

"Cyrus, honey—"

Cyrus had always been sweet to her. This dark side of him terrified her. *Just play along*. Help was coming. She hoped Riddick understood she was stalling, not considering any of this madness. Looking at him was out of the question; she'd burst into tears if she did. What if the Elites didn't get here in time?

Cyrus ignored his mother's pleas. "Just give me a few minutes." He took a step toward Khara–sauntering–and it was only through sheer determination that she remained where she was. "You've been very naughty, Khara. I know just how to punish you, and I can't wait. I practiced." He grabbed a handful of her hair and used it to turn her body around. She let out an involuntary hiss. He pointed to a wrought-iron bed against the far side of the cave. Handcuffs attached to the head and footboard and leather straps. The bedspread had stains on it she didn't want to think about. Revulsion and panic fought for primacy in her roiling belly.

Tears pricked the backs of Khara's eyes. *Keep them talking*. It was the second time he mentioned others. *He wants to brag*. She glanced at Trina, who looked troubled. A fierce frown furrowed her brows.

Khara tried to keep her wits about her in the face of these threats. That's all this was—threats. Cyrus wouldn't be doing anything to her. The Elites wouldn't allow it. But what if they didn't get here in time? "Who else did you practice on?"

"You don't need to worry about them."

Them. Plural. *Oh, mercy*.

Cyrus tightened his already painful grip on her hair to shake her upper body. Khara suppressed the cry of pain.

"Cyrus...," Trina's voice was small, bewildered. "You—swore you wouldn't do that again."

Khara tried not to wince when he shoved her.

"I really tried not to this time."

Disturbing images crowded Khara's imagination. Cyrus withdrew a knife from somewhere and began twirling it through his fingers like she'd seen Cenn do so many times. He handled it like he knew what he was doing.

His mother sounded bereft. "But you've worked so hard, Cyrus. You were doing so well." Her voice quavered. A schism had opened between the two of them. Khara could use that.

"Fooled you, didn't I?" His laugh still had that deranged edge. "The doctor, too. Saying what they want to hear. Too easy. So little expected of Cyrus."

"I don't–I need a moment. I need to think!" Trina was fidgety and agitated.

"Hmm. I have a better idea." Cyrus stalked over to Riddick, the knife dancing in and out of his grip. He scraped the blade down his cheek. If he pressed any harder, he'd draw blood. Riddick didn't flinch. "Let's not overcomplicate things. Just take our chances and kill him."

"No!" Khara shouted, surprised when Trina said it at the same time.

"We can always say the gun went off by accident."

"It—it would look bad for a woman whose fiancé just died to get married right away. Even if she has been in love with someone else the whole time." It made Khara sick to her stomach to say it.

"She's right. He's our ticket out of here. We need him. They love this American." Trina looked unhappy, like this was an unexpected turn of events. Apprehension laced her voice.

"They love him *now*," Cyrus said, the knife point hovering over Riddick's throat. "But if she tells everyone he was cheating on her, they'll turn on him."

"That's true. And we need the public on our side, so they'll accept Corey as king."

When Trina turned the gun toward Riddick, Khara maneuvered herself between them. "Why don't we sit down and figure out our next move before we do anything hasty?" Khara did her best to draw Trina's focus. Cyrus and that knife worried her. The sick feeling intensified.

Cyrus swung back to her, moving behind Riddick's chair, playing with the knife. "We're going to play a game."

"We don't have time for any games. Cyrus! We have a plan to stick to!"

"We'll make time for this. I've waited a long time." Cyrus looped an arm around Riddick's neck and addressed Khara with a bone-chilling tranquility. "You're going to take your clothes off. I want to see what's mine."

"Cyrus!" Alarm tinged Trina's voice.

"This has been a long—"

Riddick threw his head back in a vicious head butt that caught Cyrus off guard. He stumbled back with a curse, his face bloody. He lashed out with a kick to Riddick's thigh. The meaty thud was excruciating.

"Stop!" Khara cried out. Panic clawed at her insides. Where were the Elites?

Cyrus regained his composure, struck Riddick on the side of the head with the knife in his hand. A cut opened on his temple, blood flowing down the side of his face. "You—I know what you're doing. Trying to make me angry enough to forget about *her* and hurt you instead. No, no. That won't do. I'll never forget about Khara." He continued tossing the knife back and forth from one hand to the other. With a flick of his wrist, he flipped it up, snatched it out of the air, and jammed the blade hilt-deep into Riddick's upper thigh. Riddick made no sound, but hatred blazed in his dark eyes. Khara cried out, tears spilling down her cheeks.

To Khara, Cyrus shouted, "Start taking your clothes off! I'll cut his fingers off one at a time if you hesitate." He yanked the knife from Riddick's thigh and pointed it at her. Blood dripped from the blade's tip.

Khara blinked back tears and reached for the top button of her blouse. She willed her hands to stop shaking. The Elites would get here. They would stop this. They would—

"Trina? Cyrus? What are you doing?"

Relief flooded Khara when Richardson stepped out of the shadows. He was the last person she thought she'd be happy to see, but maybe he could get through to his family. His face was pale and drawn, a bandage over his nose.

Trina deflated a little. "What the hell are you doing here, Corey? *Shit.*"

From the corner of her eye, Khara spotted Cyrus affecting his simpering, non-threatening demeanor. That affable persona that had convinced everyone he was innocuous.

"I didn't want to believe it. The police and Guard are going to be here any minute. I want to end this peacefully. Stop this and come home. Bella's worried about you and so am I."

"Dammit, Corey, I told you I have a plan. You're messing everything up!"

"And Fabiola—what happened there?"

Trina thumped her chest with the pistol. "You think I got to where I am by not knowing everything that's happening around me? We tried to reason with her. But she just wouldn't cooperate."

"I didn't mean to hurt her," Cyrus said. "That was an accident, promise." Abandoning pretense, Cyrus straightened and faced his father head-on. "I would much rather have toyed with her, but time was short. She wouldn't go with me, and we struggled. She put up a good fight."

"Jesus, Cyrus." Richardson curled his lip in disgust. "I told you he should have stayed in that facility, but you wouldn't listen to reason. They could have helped him there, Trina."

"Don't talk about me like I'm not here!"

The first punch snapped Richardson's head back. He stumbled and fell as Cyrus kept hitting him. Sitting on his father's chest to pin his arms, he rained down blow after powerful blow.

Khara wasn't sure what to do when Trina leaped onto Cyrus' back, screaming at him to stop.

The trio stood between her and Riddick. There was no way to get to him unnoticed.

Trina hung from Cyrus's arm. "We'll go to prison if we don't get her to agree to this before the Elite Guards arrive!"

Cyrus stood and whirled on his mother. The rage drained away, and reason returned. It was horrifying how easily he turned it on and off at will.

Richardson was either dead or out cold. His battered face resembled a tenderized steak.

"We'll discuss your lapses later. Let's finish our business here. You," Trina motioned at Khara's middle with the gun. "Sit down."

Khara complied, her mind racing.

Breathing like a bull, Cyrus clenched and unclenched his bloodied hands. "You were going to leave me in that place?"

Trina smoothed his shirtfront down, cupped his face in one hand. "No, honey, never. We were just scared for you."

Cyrus snatched up his fallen knife and started toward Riddick again, but Trina was ready for him with soothing words. "Let's see this done. We must hurry." She was searching for a way out now, trying to regain control of the situation. "Cyrus!"

His disposition transformed at the urgency in his mother's voice. Cyrus nodded, blinking hard.

"Lillianna, you have two choices. Either you refuse Cyrus and the American dies."

"And I'll carve him up like a pumpkin, love." Cyrus' casual pronouncement made the hair stand up on the back of Khara's neck.

"O-or you accept Cyrus, and we'll release the American after you're married."

"Only after we have our wedding night, though." Cyrus put in. "I don't trust he won't come after me if I haven't made you mine yet."

"Cyrus, honey, we're almost there. I'm sure the Elite Guards will be here any minute. Stay with me." Trina was straight-up pleading with her son. "When they get here, Lillianna will call them off, get them to stand down. To interpret what this means for the American, if the Queen orders them, they'll face treason charges if they disobey. We all walk out of here, pardoned, and the four of us go right to the High Court. I've made sure one of the Justices is there late."

"You mean get married *now*? No big, royal wedding?"

"You're stalling now. What's it going to be?" Trina's voice was shrill and wreathed in panic.

Cyrus turned his attention to Riddick once again and began toward him. "Wait, I want him to get a good look at this."

Trina was starting to say something to Khara when there was an outraged bellow of pain. They both looked up to see Riddick and Cyrus grappling. When Trina tried to run to her son's aid, Khara didn't even think. She put her foot out and tripped her. The older woman went down heavily, losing her grip on the pistol. It clattered to the floor a few feet away.

Khara was upon her in a heartbeat, wrestling to get to the gun. Trina may have been a trained police officer, but she'd been out of the field for a while. Khara, in contrast, trained almost every day with Special Forces. She knew how to fight.

And this bitch would not hurt her man, not while she still had breath in her body.

Chapter Seventy-Nine

RIDDICK FOUGHT SAVAGELY AND without remorse. Every blow was full of precision and power.

As soon as everyone's attention turned toward Richardson, Riddick risked reaching down to work on the knots securing his legs to the chair. He'd only just worked his hands free of the bonds. Trina and Cyrus were spiraling, and this shit was getting out of hand. With no idea how close the Elites were, he needed to act.

He wasn't concerned with his own safety, but Khara's life might depend on him neutralizing this threat. He'd caught Cyrus by surprise when he smashed him on the side of the head with a rock he'd scrabbled to pick up, but he was a beefy guy, strong as an ox.

Riddick detached from the anger that would make him sloppy and focused instead on being faster than this brute. He tore the duct tape from over his mouth, paying no heed to the pain.

Cyrus was on his feet, that damn knife still in play. But Riddick had placed himself between Cyrus and the women. If he wanted Khara, Cyrus would have to get through him. The only way that was happening was if Cyrus killed him. Riddick would defend his Khara to his dying breath.

This motherfucker wouldn't lay another finger on his Khara.

An uncontrolled slash came at him; he reared back out of range, hoping to get at an exposed flank, but Cyrus was smarter than that. Crashing and furious grunts from behind him meant Khara was still in the fight. He had to trust she could handle Trina while he took care of Cyrus.

A yelp sounded; he couldn't tell which woman made it. A fantastic crash echoed in the cave.

Riddick let Cyrus think he was gassing out to draw him in closer. He feinted with a hook and delivered a crippling blow to the man's solar plexus. As it connected, Riddick rushed forward and took him down to the ground. With colossal effort, Riddick succeeded in getting Cyrus in a headlock. He rolled onto his back to muscle the struggling man into his lap.

Going for a rear naked choke, Riddick wrapped his legs around his waist and squeezed to hold him. Cyrus managed a few swats and stabs as he bucked and fought; it was like wrestling a giant eel. Riddick ducked the knife as best he could, not daring to let go with even one hand to deflect. A frenzied swipe narrowly missed his eye and caught his bare forearm instead. Riddick ignored the slice of pain.

The bastard's flailing kept Riddick from attaining the proper position. Redoubling his efforts, determined to either snap his neck or choke him out, Riddick grunted when Cyrus jammed an elbow into the burning knife wound in his thigh. He refused to let go.

Now the anger returned, flooding Riddick with just a bit more strength, more reach. The thought of Khara having to live with this fucker still around enraged him. Looking over her shoulder. The very thought of him could hurt her. He wouldn't have it.

Cenn and Link appeared in his periphery.

"Your... knife," he ground out, hoping she'd understand. "Ends—now."

"Mr. Riddick, think of Khara." Cenn got a firm grip on one of his ankles where he'd pinned Cyrus' legs.

"I... am," Riddick yelled, but it came out an agonized whisper. The struggles were weakening. Riddick increased the pressure, even though his own body was trying to shut down. *No.* If it was the last thing he did, Cyrus died.

"It's not what she'd want for you." Riddick could barely hear Cenn over the blood thundering in his ears. "We'll take care of him."

Link's hand was on his forearm, squeezing, but not enough to stop the desperate hold.

Cyrus didn't deserve a swift, merciful death. Riddick wanted him to *suffer*. For every time he'd threatened Khara. Each moment he'd frightened her. Made her worry.

"She won't understand, Riddick." Those words got through his bloodlust. Riddick lifted his head a fraction to make eye contact with Link, who was now kneeling next to him with both hands on his arm.

"I've been on that side," Link said. "Right where you are. With an asshole's life in your hands who doesn't deserve to keep breathing for one more second. Because he took something precious from the woman you love."

"Not... live." *He doesn't get to live,* was what he was trying to say. It sounded more like a gurgle.

"He won't." Link's low voice held steel. "I swear it. He'll be taken care of. You don't want Khara to look at you with anything less than complete trust. Let me take him, Riddick."

The anguish in Link's eyes promised he'd keep his word.

The choice was his. Neither Cenn nor Link would prevent him from finishing Cyrus.

Khara *wouldn't* understand, wouldn't think it was worth it for him to become a killer. And that's just what he'd be. A cold-blooded killer.

She wouldn't want this for you.

Cursing, Riddick released the pressure on Cyrus' thick neck. A deliberate choice. The big man was just losing consciousness. Link and Cenn got him restrained and led off, gasping for air and coughing.

Riddick sagged backward, a multitude of hurts making themselves known. One eye was swollen shut. His ribs hurt like hell; cracked maybe. His limbs were uncooperative when he tried to rise. He barked out an expletive when someone slapped a hand over the stab wound and squeezed. He gritted his teeth to keep from passing out.

Once Alene hauled a limp, moaning Trina from her, Khara rolled over, panting and exhausted from fighting for her life. She winced as she scrambled to all fours on the cave floor before getting to her feet. The adrenaline in her system had kept her from feeling the knocks and scrapes she collected, even when they crashed through a freestanding mirror. Khara tried to run to Riddick, but nausea and a spear of pain in her side slowed her steps. Breathing hurt. She pushed Alene's assisting hands away, couldn't hear what she was telling her. Riddick lay on the cave floor, unmoving, and she limped toward him, calling out his name.

Everywhere she looked, blood covered him. "Medic," Khara shouted, her voice raw and broken. She dropped to Riddick's side with a muffled grunt. "*Medic*!"

In her moment of panic, Khara forgot that each of the Elites was a trained medic. She didn't see Wyn already there, securing a field dressing on Riddick's thigh. *It shouldn't hurt to breathe. Why did it hurt to breathe?*

"I'm here, *Avlah*." Link, their most proficient medic, appeared, his med kit in hand. Jonnis was there, too. Khara shoved their hands away from her.

"Help Riddick," she croaked. The jagged pain in her side worsened, and her vision doubled. She shook her head to try to clear it. Another wave of nausea hit her. *Concussion.* Khara swayed and blinked hard, her vision graying out at the edges. She was reaching out for Riddick when her strength gave out.

"*Whoa!*" Jonnis grabbed at the Queen and caught her arm an instant before she face-planted in the dirt. Then they all saw the blood.

Chapter Eighty

H E REALLY DIDN'T WANT to get stabbed anymore.

Riddick remembered little of the ambulance ride, only anxious voices surrounding him as he faded into unconsciousness.

His mother was sitting next to him when he awoke in the hospital. "Khara–?"

"Take it easy, Joshie." Parie's stern voice halted him.

Riddick tensed. Lord, *everything* hurt. "Where is she?"

Parie Riddick touched her son's cheek, then pressed the call button for the nurse. "She needed surgery, but she's in recovery now," she said, softening her tone.

He'd utterly lost his shit after Khara passed out in the cave. His throat was raw from all the screaming he'd done at everyone. He'd tried to lunge for her, but Wyn and someone else held him down. He struggled against them until Jonnis got in his face and snapped, "We can't help her if we're fighting with you!"

Jaden arrived with the nurse, a doctor right behind them. Once the medical personnel declared Riddick stable for the moment, Jaden turned to Parie.

After giving her the traditional Lytuan greeting, he asked, "Dr. Riddick, will you excuse us for a few moments?"

Parie swatted Jaden's arm. "I keep telling you I'm retired. You don't have to keep calling me that."

"It's a mark of respect, Ma. He's not being cheeky."

"You may be retired, but you are also an honored elder and our future Consort's mother. You command the utmost respect, and we are duty-bound to give it."

Riddick winced.

"My goodness, if I were twenty years younger and your wife wasn't so adorable—"

"Ma."

"Okay, okay, thirty years younger."

"*Ma!*"

But Jaden was already ushering Parie across the room, where he put her into the care of the Guards stationed at the door. "We'll just be a few minutes. You don't mind, do you? Thank you so, so much."

"Stop buttering my mom up," Riddick muttered crossly once they were alone. His throat felt like he'd gargled with glass. "But smooth move getting her to leave."

"My God, that woman is protective of you. There was no way I'd get a private word with you otherwise."

"That means we probably don't have long, then. Give it to me straight. Khara first."

"Right. Trina jammed a small, concealed knife into Khara's side. Tactical knife, like the one Cyrus had."

"That bitch stabbed her?"

"She did. The blade glanced off one of her ribs, but then they'd rolled back and forth over it before it got shaken loose. And that was before they crashed through a mirror. Khara was airlifted, then rushed into emergency surgery for a collapsed lung, but it's the concussion that's concerning everyone the most right now. We won't know how bad it is until she wakes up."

Riddick sustained two cracked ribs from vicious elbow strikes and a fractured wrist in the struggle with Cyrus. The stab wound to the thigh hadn't hit anything vital; Cyrus must have been going for his femoral artery. Various cuts and bruises had been cleaned and bandaged, the worst ones stitched or glued. As it was, the doctors expected Riddick to make a full recovery. Because of the unknown substance Bella Krove had dosed him with, the doctors couldn't give him anything for pain until they were sure they'd flushed the drug from his system.

Jaden kept the after-action brief but included that the two of them had beaten the shit out of Trina and Cyrus. Both had required medical attention before being taken to jail.

Corey Richardson had survived his son's brutal attack and received treatment at the hospital. He remained under house arrest. Jaden recounted a blow-by-blow of Khara's epic ass-whooping of Richardson. "You should have seen her. She was *ferocious*. Couldn't be prouder. We didn't exactly rush to break it up."

Riddick laughed, but grimaced when it made his cracked ribs hurt. "That's my girl."

"She beat Trina half to death. Like cage-match level of beatdown. Seriously, we could have sold tickets. I'll never have to worry again about if her training is sinking in. I'm sorry we let it go as long as we did. We wanted ironclad evidence. We would never have let him hurt her. But then, it looked like the two of you didn't need us at all. It was too risky to use a flashbang. We didn't know what we were walking into, if there were other people in there. Or how this drug would affect you."

"And Cyrus?"

Jaden gave a minuscule shake of his head, his eyes narrowing. *Dead*, he mouthed.

Riddick nodded, satisfied that Link hadn't been bullshitting him.

"Was Trina telling the truth about disobeying Khara's orders being treasonous?"

"Yes. But when faced with imminent threat, we can—"

"*Override her wishes and instructions*. I remembered."

"And that's where her plan fell apart. Next thing we knew, you two were handing everybody their asses."

"Where is that woman now?"

"In jail. Guards outside her command structure are securing her. She'll go to house arrest too until trial, since she's a prominent member of society and all."

The door to the hospital room whooshed open and Parie Riddick stomped inside, jutting an accusatory finger at Jaden. "You pawned me off!"

Jaden looked chagrined. The jig was up. "I wouldn't go so far as to say pawned."

Another laugh made Riddick hiss.

"Joshie."

Riddick didn't want to wake up. He tried to turn over, but sucked in a breath when he jostled all the hurting bits.

Cracked ribs. Right. *Ow.*

"Joshie, they're bringing Khara in."

Alert at once, Riddick watched as the orderlies wheeled Khara's hospital bed in and parked it next to his. He reached for her hand, gritting his teeth against the agony that ripped through his midsection. Her eyelids fluttered open and soul-numbing relief flooded him. His heartbeat stuttered. It took a moment for her to focus on his face. Hers was bruised and swollen.

"Hello," she whispered, her brow wrinkling. "Who are you?"

His stomach dropped. Riddick roared for the nurse and jabbed the call button, then groaned as both actions jarred his ribs again. "Ma, get the goddamn doctor!"

Khara let out a soft laugh. "I'm teasing you, *schwe*. I know precisely who you are."

She fretted until Riddick assured her he'd suffered worse injuries. He only experienced a throbbing headache and jittery feeling as side effects.

Doctors kept them overnight at the hospital for observation before discharging them to bed rest.

Chapter Eighty-One

COREY RICHARDSON HIRED ONE of the best attorneys for his wife and son, then resigned from Parliament in disgrace. How ironic that someone who wanted to manufacture a scandal found himself at the heart of his own.

Years of abuse and codependence came to light. Trina was the power behind the Senator and the push for the throne. The relationship was the epitome of toxic, although they'd done a decent job hiding it.

Hurt people hurt people.

Trina refused his help; he wouldn't hear of it. She'd battled depression and anxiety for years. That didn't absolve her actions. The High Court found her competent to stand trial. Upon learning her son was dead, she grew disconsolate. She hadn't cried, just seemed to accept the news and was hollow.

She'd wanted power. Even more than she already wielded as the Deputy Chief. She believed with Khara's protection and her husband on the throne, she would be untouchable. There was no reasoning with her.

Despite her counsel's advice, she confessed everything, as though waiting for an opportunity to brag. There was no remorse when she spoke of hiring those goons to snatch Khara. She'd wanted to plant evidence to make it appear as though Khara arranged her own kidnapping to embezzle the ransom money Lytua would have paid for her safe return.

Fabiola tried to do the right thing when she grew suspicious. Cyrus shoved the secretary when she'd tried to leave, and she fell down the stairs to her death. Fabiola had been clever enough to take screenshots of the incriminating evidence she'd found and email them to herself.

Joanne was heartbroken when she learned Trina used her work to spy on the Queen. Khara refused her resignation, assuring Joanne that she'd done nothing other than be her usual efficient self, keeping meticulous records. The fault lay squarely with Trina.

Both teams of Elites conducted extensive after-actions. They would be over-hauling the security procedures.

Khara shuddered in Riddick's arms once she'd heard and read everything. She took a few moments to gather herself before whispering, "Does it make me a bad person that I still can't stand Richardson?"

Riddick kissed her temple, rubbed his cheek against the top of her head. "No. It makes you human. He caused you a lot of heartache."

It was time to move on without that shadow over them.

Chapter Eighty-Two

With resignation and no hint of surprise, Trina stared at the Glock Demisha pointed at her. The moment she stepped around the island in her kitchen, Trina spotted her protruding belly.

"Ah. I see. His?"

"He's CIA."

A pause, then a sigh. "Deep cover? Of course. You would have done better to just turn me in."

"Who says I didn't?"

At seven months into her pregnancy, Demisha was careful to keep her distance from the wily Trina. Trina made no move to defend herself, though. Her time had come. There would be no escape. She might have been able to wield her authority to manage things in Lytua, even from a jail cell, but with the Americans and Interpol, it was a different story.

"Keep your hands where I can see them. You don't seem surprised to see me."

"Figured this was coming at some point. For what it's worth, I'm sorry."

"This is the only way to keep my son safe."

"I...." Trina couldn't continue. The reminder twisted her expression into one of agony and loss. Whatever else she was, Trina was a mother who'd loved her child. "I do understand that. Demisha—"

Double tap, high center mass, and Trina was gone. Demisha felt nothing but relief firing the suppressed shots. She would not give the horrible woman absolution; she needed this up close and personal. The house arrest put a wrinkle in her plans. Trina's husband was a worm, but Demisha had no quarrel with him. He was at a doctor's appointment.

Demisha would be long gone by the time Trina's body was discovered, disappeared for good. Her final act before shedding her assassin identity would be sending the remaining files to the Inspector, as promised.

Then she was off to build a stable life for her son.

She was free.

Chapter Eighty-Three

J ADEN AND CENN SAT dumbfounded in the Chief of Police's office after they reviewed the materials Inspector Chinard at Interpol had brought with her. The Chief had already been reeling after the hostage situation and fallout and Trina's murder. Fatigue lined her face, like she hadn't slept in days.

"I hate that this happened on my watch and I didn't see the signs. And poor Fabiola. I'll handle this, Zildrei, Lieutenant. I just wanted you in the loop."

The whole sordid tale was told in Demisha Murray's own words, backed up with a mountain of evidence.

Her story was heartbreaking.

At twenty-four, the Army-trained sniper took a fateful, impromptu trip abroad while on leave. She'd been sexually assaulted and then victimized again when it turned out that one of her attackers had been a local police officer. No one would listen to her. The police made the records of her complaint, the evidence disappear. Demisha was left with a contentious *they said/she said* situation. She persisted, believing that with the truth on her side, she'd get justice. The defense attorney ripped her apart, trashed her reputation, and humiliated her in court. Made it out that *she* was the one in the wrong. The judge dismissed the case, devastating Demisha.

With no family or close friends to turn to for support, she floundered. She received a dishonorable discharge from the Army on drummed up charges of desertion. Now she had no home, no income, no purpose. That was what she had needed most from the Army and she thrived before her life changed. Those men had taken that from her, too. It wasn't a far fall to rock bottom. She had no job skills other than expert marksman accuracy with several variations of sniper rifles. What little money she had left, she spent on her only friend: alcohol.

When Trina came to her with an opportunity for justice that the courts had denied her, Demisha was mad at the world and bloodthirsty.

She speculated Trina had arranged for the attack to recruit and groom her into an assassin. Demisha lived in Lytua for a while, training with Trina. After meting out punishment to her attackers, Demisha attempted to get on with her life. But Trina had her hooks in deep. Demisha was trapped. All she could do was keep records and bring Trina down with them.

She was in the wind. They'd never find her or see her again unless she wanted to be found.

This woman could have killed Khara. Instead, she chose to confess. And it was almost certain she'd killed Trina. It didn't wash away her wrongdoing, but it put it into perspective.

Khara was safe. They wouldn't have to worry forever. It felt like a burden lifted off her shoulders. Trina would never hurt her again.

Chapter Eighty-Four

KHARA WAS EAGER TO make love as soon as their injuries healed enough for them to try. She wanted the painful memories wiped out and replaced with loving ones.

But Riddick caught her wandering hands and brought her fingertips to his lips. She was still having the occasional nightmare. "Let's wait a little longer."

"He didn't hurt me."

"Physically."

"He doesn't get to take the joy and pleasure I have with you!"

"No, he doesn't. Let's ease into it, just the same. Those shadows in your eyes concern me."

They both held back, concern for each other's physical and emotional wounds at the forefront of their minds. It wasn't until they were wrapped in each other that the initial caution yielded. Those first tentative moments gave way to affection until they were a laughing, exhausted, satisfied, and relieved mess of sweaty limbs.

A special dinner at their favorite restaurant was on deck. No official function, just the two of them on a date. Watching Khara turn this way and that to check herself in the mirror ignited something in Riddick. Her engagement ring sparkled as she smoothed her dress down at her sides, soon to be replaced with a wedding band. That knowledge filled him with warmth. When she whispered his name, their eyes met in the mirror. The next moment saw them clutching at each other. They made hot, fast love against the closet door, standing and almost fully clothed, giving into primal, voracious need.

Out of breath and slumped against his chest, Khara murmured, "We're definitely staying in tonight."

Chuckling, Riddick kissed the top of her head, then took his frisky fiancée to bed.

Chapter Eighty-Five

LYTUA HAD NEVER EXPERIENCED a royal wedding, so there was no way out of a huge celebration. Under different circumstances, Khara would have opted for an intimate affair with close friends and family only.

"The closest we've ever gotten is when Wyn married the previous Queen's granddaughter. That was a big-ass wedding."

"Seems to me there aren't many Black royal weddings."

"There is that."

"Will I get to wear a sash? Will you wear your crown?"

"To be honest, I have no idea. Joanne will know."

Joanne looked ready to swoon when Riddick and Khara asked if she would be interested in planning the royal wedding.

Score, Riddick thought. He'd made an ally for life.

Khara was impatient with the entire wedding process—the planning and endless tasks exhausted her. She wanted very much to be finished with the whole wedding business and get on with being married to Riddick. Her half-joking suggestion that they elope was met with horror. Riddick and Joanne reminded her how important it was to Black children worldwide to witness a Black Queen's wedding. It was bigger than the two of them. Since Riddick was enjoying the spectacle, Khara relented and turned it over to him and Joanne.

They worked with Maxine the stylist, who'd nearly fainted at the opportunity to dress Riddick. Something about his proportions. Maxine was in rare form.

Khara stopped listening, though, when she started musing about them having complementary ensembles for the New Year's Eve and Carnivale festivities.

Khara was game for most things, but drew the line at any dress that looked like extravagant curtains in favor of something more subdued. She declined dress shopping, maintaining that she would just ruin everyone else's fun. She relented some and tried on several styles Maxine brought her. "Silhouette check only," Maxine had promised and, true to her word, was in and out.

The public embraced Riddick as their own. Even more so when they learned how Riddick had gone to great lengths to surprise Khara. Being injured while trying to keep her safe, too? He had the press and citizens eating out of the palm of his hand.

Khara played along with the surprises and allowed herself to be blindfolded during her dress fittings. It ended up being quite fun. She and Riddick made a game of her trying to guess details about the wedding.

In no time, the momentous day arrived and when the first big reveal came, it took Khara's breath away.

Khara didn't look in the mirror until everything was done—hair, makeup, shoes, jewelry. She could tell by the sniffs and sighs around her when the gown floated into place that Maxine had outdone herself.

Khara stared back at a majestic Queen Lillianna in the mirrors for a long time, trying to take in all the details.

She'd never looked or felt more beautiful.

The gown was gorgeous. It was perfect—her style, with just a touch of whimsy. No extravagant curtains in sight.

"Oh," she breathed. "It's beautiful. Riddick will love this."

"He helped design it," Maxine enthused, crying happy tears.

Joanne was crying as well. "Your parents would be thrilled to see you like this."

Khara had to flutter her hands at her face to ward off the gathering tears. She didn't want to ruin her makeup.

"Okay, as I've heard Dorian say, let's kick this pig."

When she stepped into the doorway, Khara's eyes found Riddick's and the love shining there made her feel like the luckiest woman in the world. Riddick was devastatingly handsome in his Lytuan-styled tuxedo with his locs braided and adorned with flowers, fabric, and gold cord that matched her dress.

In Lytuan tradition, a bride wasn't given away. She walked to the altar within a circle of her closest friends and family, who called and sang of her attributes. Her intended waited at the altar within their own circle, doing the same. The two circles combined into one larger one as the couple greeted each other in the center.

The ceremony itself was small and intimate. They'd allowed only one photographer into the room and she was unobtrusive as she worked, not taking attention away from the ceremony. The entire island watched their Queen marry via live web-cast and streaming.

Khara's hand trembled when Riddick took it in his. He gave it a reassuring squeeze, his broad smile crinkling the skin around his eyes. Riddick speaking his vows in Lytuan surprised Khara and moved her nearly to tears.

"So. Here we are, beautiful Khara. In the place I didn't know I was working toward my whole life. I never could have imagined you, but I started falling for you the moment you gave me the business for hanging up on you. It took a while for my brain to catch up to what my heart already knew. What my soul already knew. You are the sun in my sky, the moon, and all the stars.

"There's no place else in this world for me other than with you. You're my complement and counterpart in every way. My partner, an anchor, a mirror and I love you so much.

"I hope to be even half the man you believe I can be and I'm a better man just from being in your orbit. I will always be the man whose heart you hold in your hand.

"I'm humbly offering everything I have within me to give. I'll spend the rest of my life cherishing you and giving you the best of me.

"From this day forward until the moment I draw my last breath, you, my love, my beautiful Khara, will always be the Queen of my Heart."

He bent to kiss her knuckles, then pressed his forehead to them. Khara cupped his chin and tilted his face up to hers. She curved a hand around his cheek, brushed the wetness glistening there with her thumb.

"Oh, Riddick, my love." Khara smiled, fighting her own tears. "I knew I should have gone first."

The laughter of their loved ones echoed throughout the room.

Once he'd straightened and she'd composed herself, Khara took a deep breath so she could speak without bawling. "Riddick, I knew my life would never be the same the moment I met you. But I could not have anticipated just how marvelously it would turn out. I stand before you not as a queen, but as the luckiest woman in the world. Your love is my true crown, the treasure my soul has searched for. You see me and love me exactly as I am. I have never felt so loved, so uplifted.

"I am thankful every day for the gift of you, for the love that binds us and makes us whole.

"Today I put my trust and my heart into the hands of the most extra-ordinary man I've ever known. You make me think and consider and strive to be the best version of myself. When I'm with you, you make me feel like the most beautiful, most adored and engaging woman there ever was."

"You are."

"Hey, you had your mic drop moment!"

"Sorry, you're right, go ahead."

"And you make me laugh. Yours is the face I most want to see, whose smile fills me with light and warmth.

"In your eyes and in your arms, I have found my home, my sanctuary, my everything. I vow to love and honor you every day of my life and to stand by your side always."

Then she kissed his hands the way he'd kissed hers.

In no time, they were sharing their first kiss as a married couple. House Riddick-Therin was official.

She wore a crown, of course. He wore a sash.

Khara's heart overflowed with happiness at the festivities, sharing this event with their loved ones. Riddick learned so much about Lytuan traditions and executed them with enthusiasm. When they made an appearance from the palace's second-story balcony, cheering citizens filled the streets, throwing flowers and confetti. The scene touched Khara profoundly.

"I needed you," Riddick whispered into her ear. "The world needed this. Somewhere, at least one little Black child is going *wow*."

Khara had to admit she was glad she'd let him talk her into this. As she looked around at the wonderland he and Joanne had created, she realized this must have taken endless hours of planning and effort. "This is quite the to-do you and Joanne whipped up. Everything is gorgeous. Magical. Thank you."

"This is the restrained version, if you can believe it. Dion wanted to release doves. I figured that'd be pushing it."

The Palace declared the rest of the day as one of celebration, with feasting and dancing and laughing and merriment for all. Riddick and Joanne made sure to include plenty of American customs and traditions, too. Khara fell against her new husband, trying to jump the broom in all that dress, shrieking with laughter. He caught her to him and steadied her, then told her how beautiful she was.

With his hand out of view, he brushed his knuckles against her thigh while retrieving the garter. His nostrils flared when he realized she was wearing a garter belt with her stockings. His favorite.

She winked at him.

Riddick gave serious consideration to taking his new wife somewhere for a quickie. No one would blame him.

Riddick looked over at his wife as she performed the ceremonial married women's dance and felt an explosion of joy within his breast.

His *wife*.

She'd almost stopped his damn heart when he'd first seen her. She was luminous, radiant as the sun.

He was so busy admiring his new wife, he was paying no attention to the person talking to him.

A stolen moment while slow dancing saw him promising her in a low voice, "I'm going to make love to you in this dress as well as out of it tonight."

"How soon can we get out of here?" was her cheeky response.

Riddick laughed and gave her a chaste kiss on the cheek. "You did warn me you were greedy. Good thing we only need to go upstairs to the official residence, then."

Later, once he'd swept her into his arms and carried her across the residence's threshold, Khara gasped as she took in her surroundings. Lush tropical flowers bedecked every surface, awash with the golden glow of candlelight.

"This is beautiful," Khara breathed.

"*You're* beautiful."

They fell laughing into the artfully arranged rose petals covering the canopied four-poster bed.

"I propose a toast." Riddick retrieved the magnum from the ice bucket on the nightstand, where it waited next to a tray of chocolate-covered fruit.

He'd scarcely torn the foil off the bottle when Khara called his name. He did a double-take when he saw how she'd rolled onto her stomach and drawn up her dress to expose the back seam on her stockings and her strappy high heels. Heat arrowed straight to his groin.

Riddick took one look at the mischievous smile his gorgeous new wife wore and decided the champagne would have to wait.

Chapter Eighty-Six

THEY SPENT A MONTH on honeymoon, as was tradition for Lytuan new-lyweds. Bali made for a perfect location—exotic and romantic, with lots to do beyond each other. Or not. Khara worried they'd get bored with *just* a bungalow over the water, so they chose some place with options to suit every mood and sensibility.

Because it was such a long time to ask them to be away from home, Khara invited the Elites' families to come along for the working vacation. She also invited Dion, Parie, and the Sloanes. They wouldn't all be able to stay the entire time, but they were thrilled to join the party. Seventeen adults and ten children made for a raucous once-in-a-lifetime trip.

A month in a tropical paradise with plenty of downtime worked its magic.

Riddick took to island life and continued to work uninterrupted. In short order, he'd opened the Augustus branch of Riddick & Sloane. Riddick and Khara agreed to stay in her home, but Khara wouldn't hear of him just squeezing his life into it, so she ordered everything removed so they could start over as a couple with furnishings and decor chosen together.

When it came time to choose a meaningful ceremonial name, Riddick de-clared that "Riddick" was the most powerful name he knew. Parie bawled when he told her so. His honorific after the wedding was *Ondli*, which translated to "beloved Consort."

Khara often smiled to herself, more content than she ever dreamed possible. She loved her life. Her work fulfilled her, her family and friends grounded her.

Her interests and the passions she pursued sustained her. But Riddick added an extra dimension to it all. With a husband she adored at her side, her world was brighter, in full bloom.

When Riddick looked at Khara, his heart soared. Hell, his spirits lifted whenever he thought of her. For someone who'd believed they weren't capable of love, Riddick had only a hazy recollection of what his life was like before Khara entered into it. Loving her transformed his outlook on what mattered and what was possible. He took nothing for granted. He knew he was the luckiest, and he vowed to make sure the Queen of his heart knew it every day.

C OFFEE ROUSED RIDDICK'S SUSPICIONS.

Khara wrinkled her nose at her usual morning cup and left it on the counter untouched. When that happened several days in a row, Riddick paid closer attention. Besides being off her favorite beverage, she seemed more tired and hungry all the time. When Riddick put the pieces together, it was a rare Saturday afternoon off spent relaxing and being lazy. He gazed at her with a bemused expression.

"What?" Khara asked from her prone position on the sofa. She kept dozing off throughout the morning and waking to him watching her with a peculiar intensity. "Do I have something on me?"

Riddick rubbed his chin with the tips of his fingers, a slow grin spreading over his face. "I think you're pregnant," he said.

She sat up so fast she got lightheaded for a moment. "I'm not even late!"

Riddick steadied her, then leaned over to press a light kiss to her lips and brush his nose against hers. "Your energy is... different."

Khara chortled and poked a playful finger at his side. "Well, that's not exactly scientific. You're dreaming."

"You don't think I'm tuned into you by now?"

"We'll see."

Riddick dropped a small paper bag into her lap the next evening as she sat at her laptop, fine-tuning a commencement speech.

Khara stifled a yawn and glanced at the wall clock, wondering how she could be ready for bed when it hadn't even hit nine yet. Must be the recent heat wave sapping her energy. "What's this?" He piqued her curiosity when he only sat down beside her and smiled. Khara closed her laptop and set it aside. Her stomach grumbled. Hadn't she just eaten dinner? She opened the bag and peered into it, then gave her husband the side-eye. "Are you serious?"

His grin widening, he offered a saucy wink and made a shooing motion. "Humor me."

"Fine," she huffed and took the bag to the bathroom.

Five minutes later, Khara looked up from the two pink lines on the positive pregnancy test, her expression gob-smacked.

Riddick hooted and swept her into his arms, kissing her face all over. "I knew it!"

"How did you—?"

"Told you—your energy's different. Plus, you've been jumping me damn near every day the past few weeks."

"Is that a pregnancy side effect? I thought it was just February."

Her deadpan made him chuckle as he placed her back on her feet. "I've heard it can be. Not complaining."

Awestruck, tears glistening in her eyes, Khara squeezed his hands in hers. "Riddick, we're... we're having a baby."

Riddick gathered her up into his arms and pressed a soft kiss to her temple. "We are having a baby, beautiful Khara. Beautiful *mama*." Her tears overflowed.

He kissed them from her cheeks. Excitement flickered through him like electricity. Pride, too. Some nervousness. He was going to be a father. His gut tightened with the myriad of emotions rocking him. "I love you so much."

Before she could respond, her stomach let out a distinct rumble. His knowing gaze upon her, Riddick led his wife to the kitchen, where he pulled out fixings for grilled cheese sandwiches, her favorite comfort food.

Khara sat at the kitchen island to watch, her chin propped in her hand. While waiting for the griddle pan to heat, Riddick poured her a tall glass of water. He'd been reading. She'd need to stay hydrated. The Lytuan heat was no joke. "How quiet do you want to keep this?"

"I love how you've adjusted to life in the public spotlight so well. Just us for now. Then close friends and family? Let's hold off on an official announcement as long as possible."

"It'll be a circus. Lytua's beloved *Avlah* having my baby? That's big news. You'll tell the Guard, though. Now?"

"Yes. They'll need to know. And Joanne. And Parie and Dion, too."

"Of course. They'll all be thrilled."

The sigh she let out after polishing off her sandwich and an apple was one of pure satisfaction.

Noticing how much she'd perked up with a little sustenance, Riddick filed the info away. He'd remember that. The love of his life was having his baby. That knowledge evoked a fierce, protective determination within him. He would stay tuned in to her needs. His woman would want for *nothing* on his watch. "How do you feel?"

"Overjoyed. Terrified. I've been tired lately."

"Growing a human is hard work. Ha, I knocked up a sitting Queen. How many men can say that?"

"How many indeed?"

"How shall we celebrate?"

"Well, I have a few ideas." Her tone turned flirtatious as her features settled into the *come hither* expression that never failed to rev him up. "Almost all of them are encore performances of how I got pregnant in the first place."

"'*Almost* all'? Good thing it's February." Riddick laughed, then stood and carried his Queen—and the little prince or princess she now carried—to their bedroom.

THE END

**Before *International Incident* and *Queen of His Heart*,
Sparks flew with Jaden and Aimee....**

In the Queen's Service (Crown & Heart Book 3) transports readers to the turbulent early days of Khara Therin's reign. Before Jaden Everly was the devoted husband and father we know and love, he was a grumpy, inflexible know-it-all too used to being in charge.

He's juggling national security and a royal transition, with zero time—or interest—for romance.

Until Dr. Aimee Sebastien dances into his life at his brother's wedding and makes it very clear she isn't here to be impressed.

Challenge accepted.

Coming soon—join my newsletter so you don't miss the release.

Join here.

In the Queen's Service

Need more Riddick and Khara?

Unlock an exclusive bonus epilogue when you join my newsletter.

More swoon. More secrets. More love.

You'll also receive:

• Sneak peeks

• Behind-the-scenes extras

• Early access to new releases

Plus a top-secret short story as a thank-you.

Queen of His Heart Bonus Epilogue

If this story made you smile, swoon, or stay up too late, I'd be so grateful if you shared your thoughts in a review.

Reviews help more than you know and only take a minute.

Leave a review here.

Queen of His Heart Reviews

NIKKI DAVENPORT IS A contemporary romance and romantic suspense author and the creator of the Crown & Heart/Destination: Lytua series—where Wakanda meets *Bridgerton* in a lush, all-Black world of royal romance and unapologetic joy. Her stories reimagine royalty through high-stakes emotion, deep friendships, and characters who fight for love and legacy.

Her debut novel, *International Incident*, became an Amazon bestseller, ranking in the Top 15 of Romantic Suspense and Top 55 of Contemporary Romance, and was selected as a 2023 finalist for the Audio in Color Award. Book two in the series went on to hit #1 in Black & African American Women's Fiction, launching a royal universe readers can't wait to return to.

A lifelong lover of love stories, Nikki holds a BA in History and a Master's in Social Work. She is also the founder of Granite Clover Publishing, LLC, and Granite Clover Author Services, a boutique author-services company offering culturally responsive manuscript support for fiction and nonfiction writers. She works in education by day, paddles with a dragon boat team of fellow breast cancer survivors in her off time, and belongs to a fabulous book club. She lives in Northern Virginia with her husband, a snarky teen, and two spoiled feline overlords—and is rarely without an audiobook or podcast.

Nikki is passionately committed to centering Black love on the page—and isn't stopping anytime soon.

Follow her on Goodreads (37165373.Nikki_Davenport), Book Bub (@nikkidavenportauthor), and Facebook (AuthorNikkiDavenport)!

Also by Nikki Davenport

The Crown & Heart Series

International Incident — Crown & Heart Book 1

A Matter of Taste — A Crown & Heart Novella (Book 1.5)

Queen of His Heart — Crown & Heart Book 2

Season of the Heart — A Crown & Heart Prequel (Book 3)

In the Queen's Service — Crown & Heart Book 3

Worth the Risk — A Crown & Heart Prequel (Book 4)

Healing Reign — Crown & Heart Book 4

Fool Me Once — A Crown & Heart Novella

Also Appearing in Anthologies

Courage: An Anthology to Kick Cancer's Ass — "A Matter of Taste"

Holly & Heartstrings Holiday Anthology — "Season of the Heart"

Crown & Heart Series Guide

Acknowledgements

Creativity doesn't happen in a vacuum.
An artist can't create their best work without having understanding people around them. Understanding comes in many forms, such as inspiration, encouragement, late-night plot masterminding, frilly coffee
drinks, tacos, patience, and even margaritas.
A few of the unsung heroes who made this book possible:

- F, G, & Q: for not only tolerating my wild-eyed intensity, but for giving me space, silence, and snacks (and snuggles in Maya & Mosley's case) to facilitate it.

- LaToya & Christie: keepers of the details and identifiers of plot holes and character inconsistencies. When you raise questions, my story gets better.

- Rebeka Alvie: I got so lucky connecting with such a fantastic editor. She's a writer, too!

- Trish: *gracias por esto y por todo lo demás. Te debo el almuerzo (y cena tambien!).*

- The Fictionary Community, Elaine, Willi, Nichole, GoPink, The Babes, my FERR and FSP fams, the Life With Cancer crew, and everyone else – thank you!